TREASURE
COAST
Homecoming

EMERALD BAY
BOOK 1

LEIGH DUNCAN

Treasure Coast Homecoming
Emerald Bay, Book #1

Copyright ©2023 by Leigh D. Duncan

This book is a work of fiction. The characters, events, and places portrayed in this book are products of the author's imagination and are either fictitious or are used fictitiously. Any similarity to real person, living or dead, is purely coincidental and not intended by the author.

Digital ISBN: 978-1-944258-34-4
Print ISBN: 978-1-944258-35-1
Gardenia Street Publishing

Published in the United States of America

Welcome to Emerald Bay!

After a lifetime of running the finest inn in Emerald Bay, Margaret Clayton has to make a decision...sell the Dane Crown Inn to a stranger or put her hopes for the future in her family's hands. For most people, the choice would be simple. But nothing about her family is simple...especially not with her daughter and four nieces whose help Margaret needs now more than ever.

The five cousins know the inn as well as Margaret does. As young girls and teenagers, they spent every summer keeping the cottages and suites spotless, and enjoying the gorgeous beach as a tight knit family. Thirty years later, though, these five women have complicated, important, distant, and utterly packed lives. The last thing any of them can do is drop everything and save the inn. But, when it comes to family, the last thing is sometimes the *only* thing.

As the once-close cousins come together on the glorious shores of Florida's Treasure Coast, they learn that some things never change, but others can never be the same. And the only thing that matters is family which, like the Dane Crown Inn, is forever.

One

Amy

"Oh. My. Stars!"

Amy Sommer Peterson's breath whistled softly through her lips even though the situation didn't exactly call for hushed tones. After all, it wasn't like the flock of parakeets flitting between the tall palms would take flight the moment they heard her voice. If the rumble of the delivery van's engine or the sound of tires on the crushed coquina driveway hadn't startled the birds, a few whispers weren't going to do the trick. "I wonder if Aunt Margaret has seen them yet."

She doubted it. Though the sun had barely risen above the distant point where the ocean met the sky, her eighty-year-old aunt was, in all likelihood, dressed for the day and already

1

tackling one of the many chores required each and every morning at the Dane Crown Inn. Amy was most apt to find the elderly woman bustling around in the kitchen, a cane looped uselessly over one arm, while she filled a tall pitcher with juice from oranges grown right here on the sprawling estate. Or, having finished that task, Aunt Margaret might have moved on to the front porch, where she made a point of plumping every pillow on the white rattan furniture each morning. Sitting on the back deck with her feet propped up while she watched the birds flit from frond to frond was the one place Amy almost certainly wouldn't find Margaret. In fact, she couldn't remember the last time she'd seen her aunt relax. Or take a moment for herself.

Which really was a shame. If Gramma and Grampa Dane had had their way, that's exactly what their daughter would be doing right now. Amy's grandparents had dreamed that all four of their children would live nearby and work at the inn they'd built in the heart of Florida's Treasure Coast. They'd looked forward to having generations of Danes continue the tradition of providing tourists with nothing but the best accommodations north of Miami.

But things hadn't exactly gone according to her grandparents' plan. Uncle Edward, the oldest of the Dane children, had thrown the first monkey wrench. Not at all interested in catering to the needs of the inn's well-heeled guests, he'd moved to Houston after college, where he'd spent an all-too-brief career working for NASA. Aunt Shirley, the baby of the family, had followed suit.

Um, not exactly, Amy corrected. Shirley hadn't shown the least bit of interest in furthering her education, but she sure had been attracted to the space program's engineers and astronauts. She'd gotten involved with one of them and ran off when she was still in her teens. Which had left Aunt Margaret and Amy's mom, Liz, to shoulder the responsibility for the family business. A task they'd done and done well for the better part of fifty years. But since Amy's mom had passed five years ago, Aunt Margaret had been running the inn on her own. Which didn't seem fair. Didn't she deserve to relax and enjoy her twilight years?

Amy couldn't solve that problem entirely, but she made sure her aging aunt took a break now and then. She checked her watch and quickly ran through the list of deliveries she needed to make before she headed across Emerald Bay to open the doors to Sweet Cakes. Dawdling was definitely not on her agenda for

3

today, but she could spare ten minutes for a cup of coffee with her aunt. It would do them both good to relax on the wide deck out back. They'd watch the bright green parakeets dart among the palms. Enjoy listening to their squeaks and chirps.

Doing her best not to annoy the birds, Amy held her breath as she opened the van's door and slid to the ground. With one eye on the flock, she walked past the Sweet Cakes logo emblazoned on the side of the vehicle and withdrew a single tray of assorted breakfast rolls and Danish from the built-in rack in the back. As she did, her lips compressed into a tight, thin line. It hadn't been that long ago that she'd have hauled three or four trays of breakfast treats, plus several loaves of bread, into the airy kitchen on the west side of the two-story inn her grandparents had built.

But that had been before. Before she and her cousins had developed dreams of their own and scattered to the four winds. Before the accident that had taken her mother and robbed the inn of its cook. Certainly before weeds had grown between the pavers that led to the entrance or the paint on the back door had begun to peel or a thousand other little problems had tarnished the luster of the Dane Crown Inn. As a result, the rambling hotel travel agents had once touted as "the jewel of Florida's Treasure Coast" now rarely hosted more than a handful of guests.

Hefting the tray, Amy sighed. The place couldn't be still turning a profit, could it? Maybe her brother Scott was right and Aunt Margaret should cut her losses. Sell the property to one of the many developers who were waiting in the wings, eager to make an offer. With the money she'd get, Aunt Margaret could afford to move into the best retirement home on the Treasure Coast and start reaping the benefits of all the years she'd spent catering to the needs of others from sunup to sundown.

Yeah, like that was going to happen.

Amy shook her head. Much as she loved her aunt, she had to admit the woman was a stubborn old goat. Aunt Margaret had sworn on more than one occasion that she would never—under any circumstances—sell the property that had been in the Dane family for more than half a century. She meant it, too.

So what *would* happen to the estate once Aunt Margaret joined her parents, her sisters and her brother in the Great Beyond? Was the next generation supposed to abandon the lives they'd built, rush back to Emerald Bay and take up the reins of the family business? Amy smothered a laugh. No one in their right mind would expect

Belle to walk away from all her fame and fortune. Or Scott to give up his law practice. Kimberly and Diane surely wouldn't discard their careers. And what about her? Would she close Sweet Cakes, lay off the employees who counted on her to provide their livelihoods and spend the rest of her life running the inn's kitchen? That idea was simply too ludicrous for words. She was a baker, not a cook.

Careful not to trip over an uneven paver, Amy slowly made her way around to the side entrance. From beyond the house came the muted roar of the Atlantic. The comforting sound of the waves rolling onto the inlet's sandy beach provided an interesting counterpoint for the noisy birds that had decided to linger near the main house and the six small cottages surrounding it. Legend had it the flock had gotten its start decades ago when a pair of monk parakeets had escaped their cage in Miami. They'd quickly adapted to their newfound freedom, and now large colonies of the bright green birds ranged the lower part of Florida. They rarely ventured north of Stuart, though. Their appearance in Emerald Bay, located on a thin barrier island between Vero Beach and Sebastian, was almost unheard of. Amy hoped they'd stay. She wanted them to build nests in the trees on the grounds of the Dane Crown Inn, to lay eggs and raise their young. Most of all, she hoped they'd draw tourists and would-be guests to the once-popular inn.

She picked her way past three cars with out-of-state plates that sat in a parking area large enough to hold another forty vehicles. Where the path branched, she took the fork that led toward the employees' entrance. She used her key to let herself inside. After brushing her feet on the mat, she stepped into a good-sized laundry room. The lingering smell of detergent and bleach struck her and instantly sent a trickle of sweat down her back. She and Scott and Diane and their cousins had spent their summers and every school holiday working at the inn. How many hot, muggy days had they worked in this very room—washing, drying and folding the inn's linens? Far too many to count, for sure. Back then, they'd had to run the washers and dryers constantly to keep up with the need for clean sheets and towels. By midafternoon each day, the room had grown as hot as a sauna. Though the machines mostly sat empty and quiet now, memories kept her feet in motion. Eyeing the short hallway that led to the kitchen, she raised her voice loud enough to be heard by someone who refused to admit she was hard of hearing.

"Aunt Margaret? It's me, Amy. I'm here with your bakery order." Not that her aunt should be surprised by her arrival. After all, Amy delivered Sweet Cakes' rolls and breads to the inn every morning at just about this time. "Aunt Margaret?" she called again when no one answered. "Do you have time to sit and chat for a bit?"

She sniffed, frowning when she didn't catch the scent of freshly brewed coffee. Had her aunt slept in? Was she sick? Or worse?

That last thought propelled her quickly past the roomy pantry her mom had kept under lock and key when the inn was in its heyday. But the boxed lunches and casual suppers the inn provided for its guests had ended when her mom died. As a result, the pantry door now opened onto mostly bare shelves.

Amy's sturdy bakers' clogs scuffed against the red Mexican tiles as she hurried into the kitchen where, at first glance, everything appeared fine. The off-white counters and stainless appliances that ran along one wall glinted in the early morning light. The countless built-ins and the Shaker-style cabinets remained undisturbed. A large fruit bowl stood in its usual spot on the spacious island, where it tempted guests and staff alike to help themselves to an apple, an orange, or a banana on their way out the door.

As much as Amy told herself that everything looked normal, she couldn't shake the feeling that something was amiss. Holding her breath, she swept the kitchen again, this time searching for even the smallest sign of trouble. She breathed a tiny sigh of relief when no water ran in the empty farm sink. Another when she noted that no broken glass littered the granite counters. When flames didn't flicker unattended on the gas stove, she nearly chalked her unease up to her earlier, maudlin thoughts. But when her focus landed on the coffee station, her pulse jumped.

A single red light glowed from the front of the three-burner machine. A metal canister lay on its side nearby. Grounds spilled from the open top. They fanned across the creamy granite like a large brown stain. The filter basket sat upside down on the counter as if someone had dropped it. Only one person would do that.

"Aunt Margaret?"

Amy's heart fluttered when a low moan came from the space between the island and the counter. Her fingers lost their grip on the tray of baked goods, which landed with a loud clatter on the closest table. She rushed forward, one hand instinctively patting the pockets of her chef's pants, searching for a way to call for help.

"I'm here. I'm here," she called.

Imagining the worst, she darted around the corner of the island and nearly tripped over her aunt's feet. Struggling to keep herself upright so they both didn't end up in a heap, Amy grabbed the counter with both hands. When she did, she lost her grip on the cell phone she'd pulled from her pocket. The device skittered across the glossy granite before finally coming to a stop a couple of inches from the far edge.

"Amy? Oh, I'm so glad you've finally come."

At the sound of her aunt's thin, wavering voice, tears sprang to Amy's eyes. She eased back a step or two as the figure on the floor stirred. Amy immediately dropped to her knees. She reached out, her fingers landing on her aunt's thin shoulder.

"Lie still, Aunt Margaret," she coaxed. "Don't try to get up. I'll call an ambulance." She blinked rapidly, grateful beyond measure that her aunt was alive and yet fearful that the elderly woman had sustained a bad injury. Had she broken a hip? Hit her head? Amy searched for blood. She swallowed dryly when she didn't spot any.

"An ambulance?" White curls bobbed when her aunt, who by this time had propped herself up on one elbow, shook her head. "No need for that," Margaret protested. Her voice grew firmer by the second. "I'm all right. Be a good girl now and help me up."

Despite the awfulness of the situation, Amy bit back a laugh. No one called a woman who was pushing fifty a girl anymore. Not even the cashier at the Winn-Dixie, and she had pet names for everyone.

Beneath her, Aunt Margaret struggled to sit up.

"Now, Aunt Margaret. Just lie still a minute. We don't know how badly you're hurt. Did you pass out? Can you tell if anything's broken?"

"Good grief, child. I'm fine. I just took a little spill. Do you have any idea how hard it is for an old lady with a bum leg to get herself up off the floor? I figured, as long as I was laying here, I might as well take a nap. I knew you'd be along soon enough. Now help me."

"You took a nap?" Amy's mouth worked. Was her aunt all right, then? She didn't act like someone who was in pain. If anything, she sounded more and more like her fiercely independent self with each passing minute. Still...

"At least let me check you over before we try something we both might regret."

Not that Amy had the slightest idea what she should be looking for. Would she even recognize a broken bone if she saw one? Or a serious head injury? She hadn't actually had any medical training. At least, not beyond the first aid classes she'd been required to take when she opened the bakery. But she'd watched enough medical dramas on TV while she whiled away the hours of countless lonely nights. She'd seen how the pretend doctors assessed a patient. They made it look easy. She'd follow their example. How hard could it be?

Starting at her aunt's feet, Amy slowly felt upward. While she poked and prodded, she studied her aunt's lined face for any sign of a grimace and listened for an involuntary gasp. Relief coursed through her when Aunt Margaret only giggled as if she thought the whole idea was some kind of joke. Nevertheless, Amy repeated the process with her aunt's hands and arms. "You're sure you didn't hit your head?" she asked when she'd finished without hearing her aunt cry out.

Impatience flashed in a pair of blue eyes that hid a wicked sharp intelligence despite their age. "I would have told you if I had. Are you ready to help me up yet?"

"I suppose." Doubt swirled in Amy's chest as she eyed her aunt's prone figure. Trying to lift the woman on her own had disaster written all over it. Margaret might be skinny as a rail, but at five feet ten, she had to weigh more than two of the fifty-pound bags of flour Amy routinely hefted at the bakery. Deciding the last thing she wanted was to get her aunt halfway to her feet and then drop her, Amy hesitated. "I, uh, I'm not exactly sure…"

"Be a dear and bring one of the kitchen chairs over here, won't you?"

That surprised her. "A chair?"

"Yes. I just need a little help getting to my knees. Then I can use the chair to pull myself the rest of the way up."

Her aunt sounded so confident and self-assured that Amy had no choice but to comply. Following Aunt Margaret's directions, she moved the sturdy, wooden chair into position, helped her aunt roll to one side and gently but firmly held onto her as the older woman slowly regained her feet.

"Do you feel steady? You're not dizzy? You don't feel like you're going to pass out?" she asked once her aunt was upright again.

"Oh, for heaven's sake. I'm fine," Aunt Margaret snapped. She paused before her shoulders slumped the tiniest bit. "But I wouldn't mind if you made the coffee while I just sit a spell. The Bradys—George and Jenelle—are here for the week. They'll probably be out soon. They like to do a little beachcombing before the tide comes in. They'll want their coffee." Relying heavily on her cane, Aunt Margaret slowly crossed to the kitchen table, where she plopped onto another of the wooden chairs. "Did you bring the chocolate croissants like I asked? They're George's favorite."

"I did." Nodding, Amy glanced at the tray of baked goods, which, thank goodness, had landed on the table instead of the floor. "Why don't you sit and rest for a minute and let me take care of things. You've had an upsetting morning."

Truth be told, they both had. Amy turned toward the coffee maker while tears she didn't want her aunt to see escaped her eyes and dripped down her cheeks. How often had Aunt Margaret fallen? One thing was certain: This wasn't the first time. The older woman had known exactly how to get herself up off the floor. That kind of knowledge came from experience. The kind Amy didn't want to think about. When she thought of what could have happened, she…

She shuddered. Get a grip, she told herself. Her aunt might want to brush this accident aside with a wave of her hand, but Amy couldn't pretend it had never happened. She and her aunt needed to talk about it, and losing control right now wasn't going to help either of them.

Grabbing a napkin, she blotted her eyes.

"What about Helen?" she asked without turning to face her aunt. One of the cars in the parking lot belonged to an author who turned one of the inn's six beachfront cottages into a temporary home whenever she was on deadline.

"Oh, we won't see her before noon," her aunt insisted. "She's a loner, that one. Dedicated, though. Up and hard at work before dawn most days. Sometimes, when the wind is right, I can hear her pecking away on her laptop into the wee hours."

"Working on the next Great American Novel, is she?" Though the bookstore in town featured Helen March's books in a prominent display, Amy had never read any of them. One of these days, she promised, she'd duck into the small library off the main parlor, borrow one of the copies the author had signed for her aunt and see for herself what the fuss was all about. For now, though, she had bigger concerns.

"Who knows?" Aunt Margaret smiled softly. "She likes it here, and I enjoy our chats. She usually wanders over for a quick hello around lunchtime. She doesn't stay long. Just pops her head in before she goes back to her writing."

While the coffee brewed, Amy took care of arranging the breakfast items on the buffet in the dining room. As she worked, she placed a quick phone call to the bakery and brought her helper up to speed.

"You're sure she's all right?" Deborah fretted.

Once she'd reassured her assistant, Amy moved on to the reason for her call. "I'll make today's deliveries, but I need you to open the shop this morning. Can you start on the decorations for the Porcher cake?" Today was little Sarah's fifth birthday, and her mother had requested a Chatty Chipmunk-themed cake. "She'll be in this afternoon to pick it up."

"Got it. I'll make marzipan figures and decorate the sides with all of Chatty's friends. Becky Bluejay. Rachel Rabbit. Ollie Orangutan. It'll be adorable."

"I'm sure it will." Amy nodded, not at all surprised the woman knew all about the popular cartoon series. Deborah's young son kept her informed on the current stars of kiddie TV. She, on the other hand, had been forced to scour the internet for information about the cheeky chipmunk. Satisfied that the bakery was in good hands, she ended the call and finished up in the dining room. When everything was all set for the inn's guests, she poured two cups of coffee and carried them to the kitchen table, where her aunt sat staring out the window.

A new awareness of the woman's fragility stirred in Amy's chest. Despite a healthy tan, Aunt Margaret looked pale and drawn. Her long, thin fingers trembled slightly until she wrapped them around her coffee cup. She gazed into the distance with unfocused eyes.

Amy thought back to the last time she'd taken a tumble. She'd been out for her usual pre-dawn jog when she splashed through a puddle on the sidewalk. The next thing she knew, she was airborne. She was lucky enough to get her hands out in front of her. They broke her fall, and she ended up with nothing more than a couple of scraped palms. She brushed herself off and continued her run, but she'd replayed that moment a thousand times, trying to figure out what she could have done differently.

Was Aunt Margaret doing that now? Or had she been hurt more than she cared to admit? Either way, Amy felt it was her duty to get to the bottom of the accident. Sliding onto the chair beside her aunt, she cleared her throat.

"So you want to tell me what happened this morning? How'd you end up on the floor?" She braced herself, half expecting to hear her aunt tell her in no uncertain terms that she should mind her own business. Instead, the tall, angular woman merely sipped her coffee.

"Stupid rug," Margaret grumbled at last. She angled her head toward the coffee station, where a cushioned floor mat lay atop the terra cotta tiles. "Dang thing's more trouble than it's worth. Your mom swore the rug made things easier on her back, but the edges have curled up a bit. I'm usually very careful about them. My cane must have caught one end this morning. The next thing I knew, I was flat on my back."

Amy swore the temperature in the room dropped ten degrees as she pictured her aunt striking the unforgiving floor. "You're so lucky you weren't hurt worse," she whispered.

"Guess the fall knocked the wind out of me, 'cause I just lay there for a bit. Then you came in, and, well, you know the rest."

Amy doubted that was the whole story. "But…" she began.

"But nothing." Her aunt eyed her with the same stern look she'd used whenever she caught Amy and her cousins lounging on the inn's front porch when they knew full well that area was reserved for guests. "Now don't you go off half-cocked and make more out of this than it was. I had an accident, pure and simple. People have them all the time. I'll get rid of that infernal rug, and that'll be the end of it."

"That's a step in the right direction, but…"

The rug wasn't the only problem. On the first floor alone, the inn boasted three separate sitting areas, a massive kitchen and dining room, and two spacious bedrooms, each with their own private bath, plus the family's living quarters. Upstairs, a long hall led to another dozen suites. In a place this size, how many dangers waited to trip her aunt? Thirty? Forty? Even one was too many. This time Aunt Margaret hadn't been seriously injured, but what about the next time? Or the time after that?

Margaret thumped her cane on the tiled floor. "I am perfectly capable of managing on my own. And I'll thank you kindly for letting me get to it." She pushed her coffee aside. "Don't you have somewhere else to be this morning? Deliveries to make? Cakes to bake?"

When it came to dealing with her aunt, Amy had long since learned to choose her battles carefully. She'd been thrown into this one off guard. Unprepared as she was, she couldn't win. At least not right now. Right now, pushing for changes would only cause the older woman to dig in her heels. Later—after she'd marshaled more information and had come up with specific suggestions for ensuring her aunt's safety— she'd raise the subject again. For now, though, it was time for a distraction, and as luck would have it, she just happened to have one.

"Did you know there's a flock of monk parakeets in the backyard?" She gestured toward the window that overlooked a broad deck and the acres of prime real estate that stretched out on either side of the house. Bordered on one end by the ocean and on the other by the Indian River Lagoon, the land sloped upward from the sandy beach to a series of dunes dotted with sea grapes and tall grasses. Native plants thrived on the rest of the property. The birds had flown past a cluster of orange and lemon trees in one corner of the estate to settle in the swaying palms closer to the main house and the cottages arrayed beside it. "I saw them on my way in this morning."

"Really?" Her aunt's eyes sparkled with the first real sign of interest Amy had seen in them all morning. "Are there many of them?"

Amy shrugged. "It's hard to get a good count with them flying about so, but I'd guess there's thirty or forty, maybe."

"I'll have to tell the Bradys." Margaret cocked her head as a floorboard creaked from somewhere beyond the kitchen. "Speaking of which, I think my guests are about to put in an appearance. I'd best wish them a good morning."

If Aunt Margaret was smarting from her fall,

she did a good job of hiding it while she rose from her chair with what looked like very little effort. Recognizing her cue to leave, Amy sprang to her feet as well. She drew her aunt in for a fierce hug. "I love you," she whispered.

"Love you too, girl," came the reply. Clutching one of Amy's hands in her own bony fingers, Aunt Margaret added, "Thanks for your help this morning. Now don't you worry about me."

"As if," Amy muttered as she battled down a fresh wave of concern. "You'll call me if you get to feeling bad later, won't you? Promise?"

Aunt Margaret folded her long fingers over the top of her cane. "Only if you promise to keep what happened here to yourself," she said sternly. "There's no need to get anyone else riled up over nothing. I'm fine."

Amy's jaw clenched. Calling Margaret's daughter Belle had been at the top of her list of things to do once she was safely out of her aunt's earshot. "You know I only want what's best for you, don't you?" she asked, ignoring the demand.

"I do. But you know as well as I do how dramatic Belle can be. If you tell her I fell, she'll blow it out of proportion and drop everything to fly down here and check on me. Tell me I'm not right about that," Aunt Margaret dared.

"She always did have a tendency to make a mountain out of a molehill," Amy admitted. "Like the time that black-and-white cat got into the shed out back. Belle swore it was a skunk. She pitched such a hissy fit over it that Dad had to go in after it."

"Oh, I'd almost forgotten that." Aunt Margaret smiled at the memory. "We kept the storm shutters in that shed. Belle wouldn't rest until your father had hauled every one of them out and found the cat hiding in the corner."

"Poor thing was so scared it was shaking," Amy recalled. Belle had been, too, but once she realized their uninvited guest wasn't a skunk, she'd fallen in love with the half-wild kitten.

Amy eyed her aunt. She couldn't deny that the woman was right about one thing—Belle wouldn't react well to the news of her mother's most recent fall. But whether or not her famous cousin could break free long enough to personally check on her mom, that was a different question entirely. Unlike Aunt Margaret, Amy wasn't sure she knew the answer. One thing she did know, though—she couldn't keep this information to herself forever.

"Look," Aunt Margaret said after a beat, "you know she calls me every Sunday. I'll tell her then. I promise." Slowly, she crossed her heart.

"There's no need to bother her with this right now. Especially not when I'm fine."

As compromises went, Amy recognized a good one when she heard it. "I'll still check in with you this evening. And I'll be back tomorrow, the same as always," she said.

"All right. Now scoot. Let me tend to my guests."

As she retraced her steps to the delivery van a few moments later, Amy weighed the consequences of honoring her aunt's request. She inhaled deeply. What if Aunt Margaret fell again? What if, the next time, she sustained more than a bump or a bruise? How could Amy explain then that she'd known about the earlier falls but kept quiet? No, this news was too important not to share with at least one other person in the family.

For the time being, though, she had deliveries to make, and thanks to the extra time she'd spent with her aunt, she'd fallen behind schedule. The next hour and a half she drove the length and breadth of the small town of Emerald Bay. She made five stops at various shops and mom-and-pop hotels. At each one, she doled out cheery greetings along with cakes, pies and other baked goods. She'd nearly emptied the contents of the racks in the back of the van when, shortly before

LEIGH DUNCAN

nine, she pulled into the small parking area
behind the Pirate's Gold Diner and turned off the
engine. She made quick work of delivering the
diner's standing order for two carrot cakes, a
chocolate fudge layer cake and one coconut cake,
as well as an assortment of pies. After checking
in with Deborah to see that her assistant had
things in hand at the bakery, Amy moved the
van to a spot beneath a shade tree just beyond
the town limits. There, she punched a button on
her phone.

"Call Diane, mobile," she ordered as she
mentally crossed her fingers. Calls to her sister
frequently went straight to voice mail. Her heart
sank a little when this one did, too. She'd been
counting on taking advantage of Diane's solid,
common-sense approach to life. Rather than
leave a message, though, she placed a call to her
brother.

"Hey, Scott," she said when he picked up on
the first ring. "Are you at home?"

"No. Big case this week. I'm already in the
office." Scott was a founding partner of Sommer
& Associates, a law firm in nearby Vero Beach.
"What's wrong?" he asked, his voice sharp and
to the point.

Leave it to her brother to imagine the worst,
Amy thought. She shouldn't be surprised. "Be

24

prepared" had been his motto for as long as she'd known him. Which, considering he was two years older than her, had been, like, forever.

"Aunt Margaret is fine." She offered reassurance before she delivered the rest of her news. "But she fell this morning. As near as I could tell, she didn't break anything. No cuts, either. She could probably win a blue ribbon for bruises, but she was lucky." This time, she added silently.

"You didn't take her to the emergency room? Didn't call her doctor?" Scott asked.

Hearing accusation in her brother's tone and not liking it one bit, Amy shot back, "I tried. She absolutely refused. But I gave her a thorough once-over. I really think she's okay."

The voice coming through the speaker softened. "I'm sure you did, Amy. She's lucky you stopped by when you did and were able to help. I shouldn't have said anything. I just, um, I worry about her."

"Me, too," Amy agreed. She didn't have to deliver the inn's bakery order herself each morning. She did it because it gave her a chance to check in on her aunt. Just like Scott did his part by handling Aunt Margaret's legal affairs. And they weren't alone; the others pitched in, too. Belle called her mom at least once a week and insisted on helping out financially whenever there was a need. Each month, Diane used one of her vacation days to balance the inn's accounts. Kim flew down from Atlanta twice a year to visit with their aunt. With the exception of Jen, who was—as usual—off being Jen, everyone in the family helped care for Aunt Margaret.

"At the risk of sounding like a broken record, I'll say it again: She shouldn't be running that place by herself," Scott grumbled. "It was different when Mama was alive. The two of them watched out for each other. But when she died, things changed."

Amy sucked in a breath. The night of the car accident had been one of the worst nights of her life. Expecting a pizza delivery, she'd opened her front door and come face-to-face with a police officer so wet behind the ears his voice had hitched when he delivered the news. She'd blindly followed the flashing lights and siren of his patrol car all the way to the hospital. But it was already too late when her car slewed to a stop beneath the awning of the emergency room. By the time a kindly nurse led her into one of the curtained cubicles, her mom was gone, her aunt in surgery.

The rest of the night had passed in a blur of endless waiting. Of making phone calls she'd never dreamed she'd have to make. Of seeing the grief-stunned faces of her brother and sister, of her cousins and friends and neighbors as they trickled into the waiting area. That had been five years ago, and just mentioning that night still had the ability to send her world spinning.

"It's too much for one person. It'd be too much for me, and I'm thirty years younger than she is. It's time we had the talk."

Suddenly aware that her brother had rambled on while she relived the past, Amy snapped back to the present. "I'm sorry. What did you say?"

Scott's voice grew impatient. "I said, 'It's time we had *the talk.*'"

"She's not going to take that well." Amy didn't need her brother to explain what he meant. Scott had launched a campaign to sell the family homestead during Aunt Margaret's six-week stint in rehab following the accident. Since then, watching their aunt struggle to keep the place going on her own had only reinforced his position.

"I'm sure she won't," he acknowledged.

"You know she wants the inn to stay in the family," Amy pointed out.

"I want to win the lottery, but you don't see me living the life of a millionaire, do you? In this case, it's up to us to do what's best for her."

"What did you have in mind?" Amy had a pretty good idea what his answer would be, but she needed to hear him say it.

"Emerald Oaks is a top-notch assisted living facility right there in Emerald Bay. They have all the amenities—a pool and recreation room, tons of activities. There's even a car service to take her to church on Sundays. She'd be close to her friends. We could visit just as often as we do now."

"Someone's done his research." Amy lifted one eyebrow. Scott had obviously been planning for this day, and he was right about one thing— Emerald Oaks was the best retirement home in the area by a wide margin. She'd delivered cakes and doughnuts to the others often enough to know that much. But she still couldn't see Aunt Margaret giving up the home she'd lived in for most of her life. "You know, she could just as easily fall there as she could at the house."

"Yeah, but at least at Emerald Oaks, someone would be on hand to help her up. She wouldn't be lying there for who knows how long."

"I don't know, Scott," Amy hedged. "She's dead set against the idea."

For a long moment, her brother didn't say anything. Amy had almost decided he'd hung up on her when she heard him nearly whisper, "She gave me power of attorney some time ago. It might be time to exercise it."

Amy's chest tightened to the point where her breathing grew difficult. "You can't do that! It would destroy her." Not only that, her brother's plan would pit cousin versus cousin as, one by one, the entire family took sides.

"You think it's better to just stand by and watch until something really bad happens? What if she hits her head next time? Or, God forbid, she breaks a hip? At her age, she'd never recover. Do you want that on your conscience?"

"No," she admitted softly. She really couldn't blame her brother for wanting what was best for their aunt. She did, too. It's just that, well, they went about getting what they wanted differently. "Look," she said, trying to come up with a better plan and failing miserably. "Let's not rush into this, okay? We need to consider all the angles. Maybe…"

"Emerald Oaks has a waiting list. I'm going to put Aunt Margaret on it," Scott said as if the decision was his alone to make. "After that, well…We just can't ignore this problem and hope it will resolve on its own." Somewhere in his office, a persistent alarm buzzed. "I have to go. That case I mentioned—I'm due in court. We'll talk later."

Staring at the blank screen on her phone a few seconds later, Amy blew out her frustrations in a long exhale. *Men!* What was it about them that made them see each situation as something they needed to fix? She hadn't wanted—or needed—her brother to "solve the problem" of their Aunt Margaret. She'd simply wanted to keep him informed. Okay, if she had to be completely honest, she'd wanted to spread the blame around in case their aunt got hurt the next time she took a tumble. Now, though, Scott was determined to "fix things." Only his solution would make the situation worse.

Amy flexed her fingers. Her aunt hadn't wanted anyone else to know about the fall. She'd practically begged Amy not to tell the others. Now there was no way around it. She'd have to involve Belle, Diane, and Kim. Maybe even Jen, if anyone knew how to reach her. Otherwise, Scott would bulldoze his way through Aunt Margaret's life, uprooting her and destroying the entire Dane family in the process.

Reluctantly, she reached for her phone again.

Two

Kim

Kimberly Ann Dane's car crept forward two feet before the taillights on the box truck in front of her glowed bright red. With a resigned sigh she mashed the brake pedal, bringing the ten-year-old Honda Accord to a wheezing stop. Behind her, a driver laid on his horn as if the added noise would magically part the sea of cars in downtown Atlanta's morning rush hour and allow him to pass. Kim shook her head at the figure in her rearview mirror. The man kept right on honking.

"Do you honestly think that's going to work for you?" she asked.

If something as simple as tapping on the horn would kick-start the line of stalled vehicles ahead, she'd have long ago added her own beeps to the symphony of squealing tires. To the rev of motorcycle and truck engines that rose above the shouts of street vendors. To the complaints of motorists like the guy behind her. She gasped as a messenger in skin-tight attire whizzed past her window. The cyclist threaded his way through the stalled traffic at a speed that made Kim wish she could still afford spin classes at the gym.

Fat drops of rain pelted her windshield, harbingers of the deluge that, according to the weather station, would soak the city throughout the day. Kim rubbed her forehead where a headache threatened. In the wake of the passing storm front, temperatures were predicted to fall, delivering an early taste of winter to the city.

Not that shop owners were waiting for a particular date to kick off the lucrative Christmas season. Halloween hadn't even arrived, and already garlands and wreaths decorated the doorways of shops along the busy street. She eyed a pair of women who emerged from a cafe carrying cups of some exotic concoction of beans and nut milk. Dressed in power suits and red-bottomed stilettos, they slid onto the back seat of a car that was double-parked, its motor running. She fought down a twinge of jealous envy. Once she'd been one of those women. But no more. Today, her morning coffee came from a machine she'd picked up at Goodwill along with a secondhand set of dishes. No driver had waited patiently while she shopped, either. She'd had to lug her purchases up three flights to her apartment by herself.

It hadn't always been like this. For the better part of their marriage, she'd totally believed Frank when he promised that one day their ship would come in. That when one of his many business ventures succeeded, he'd buy her the big house in Buckhead. That they'd live the life of Riley. Until then, he'd promised, living from paycheck to paycheck on her salary was only a temporary measure.

Oh, there'd been some good times. Times when, like those women in the black sedan now edging into traffic, she hadn't thought twice about forking over ten bucks for a jolt of caffeine. When the stones in her earrings had been real diamonds. When she'd lingered over two-martini lunches with her friends at Durham Lakes while the kids played golf or swam in the Olympic-size pool. When Frank occasionally surprised them all by whisking Joshua and Natalie off to a popular Florida theme park.

Over the years, though, the lean times had outweighed the good. One after another, Frank's business ventures had crashed and burned while she'd struggled to provide her family with the kind of stable home life she'd never had as a kid. She'd moved mountains to give her children every advantage. Hadn't she brown-bagged it for an entire month so Joshua could go to science camp? Or skipped lunch entirely to pay for Natalie's tennis lessons?

But that was before. Before Frank had squandered the last of their savings on yet another harebrained investment gimmick. Before he'd involved their friends in his latest doomed, get-rich-quick scheme. Before he'd run off with his twentysomething assistant. And before Josh and Natalie had defended their fun-loving father in the divorce.

A sudden dampness stung Kim's eyes. She blinked to clear them. Of all the rotten cards she'd been dealt, her children's betrayal had hurt the worst. But it wasn't their fault. That blame fell squarely on her own shoulders. She'd done too good a job of shielding the kids from the mess Frank had made of their lives. Now that Josh and Natalie were adults, though, it was no longer her job to protect them from the truth. Sooner or later, they'd see through their father's false promises and realize how much she'd sacrificed for them.

Wouldn't they?

Her phone trilled. She checked the cars ahead before she glanced at the device she'd propped in the cup holder. One glimpse of Natalie's name on the display sent her pulse into overdrive. Was this it? The moment she'd been waiting for? Her fingers trembling, she accepted the call and put it on speaker.

"Hey, sweetie." She held her breath.

"Mom." On the other end of the line, Natalie yawned.

No one started an apology with a yawn, Kim reasoned. But why else would Natalie call? The image of her beautiful daughter lying on a hospital gurney set every nerve in her body on edge. "Is everything all right? You're not sick or hurt, are you?"

"Why would you even go there?" Natalie shot back in the exasperated tone Kim had grown used to hearing. "Why can't I just call because I want to hear your voice?"

Rather than point out it had been two months since the last time she'd heard more than her daughter's voice on an answering machine, Kim clamped her mouth shut. She slowly counted to five before, giving herself points for staying cool, calm and collected under pressure, she said, "Of course, dear. But you don't usually call this early in the morning."

"Tell me about it. It's not even six o'clock out here."

"Oh? Where are you?" Planning to embark on a career in social media, Natalie had moved to the Big Apple last year.

"Aspen. Geez, Mom. You really ought to follow me on Insta and TikTok."

"I'll get right on that the next time I upgrade my phone." This time Kim didn't hold back the note of sarcasm in her tone. An expensive data plan was so not a luxury she could afford. Not after losing her job when Connors Industrial restructured the entire company. Which, Kim had quickly learned, was a polite term for replacing loyal, long-term employees like herself with recent college grads who'd do the same work for half the salary. Confident she'd land on her feet, she'd brushed up her resume and plunged into the hunt for a new job. That had been a year ago. As it turned out, the corporate world wasn't exactly a middle-aged woman's oyster. Things had gotten so bad lately that she now relied on a series of temp jobs to cover her rent and necessities. "But it's going well? Your…what do you call it?"

"I'm an influencer, Mom." Self-importance framed Natalie's words. "Over six thousand people already rely on me to tell them what's hot on the fashion scene, which restaurants are the bomb, and the best hair and makeup products to use. It won't be long before companies are knocking on my door, begging me to wear their clothes, review their restaurants or oh-so-casually mention how much I love their new lipstick."

"Hmmm." Kim deliberately refrained from commenting. She might not know a lot about the latest media platforms, but she'd been involved in several of Connors' promotional campaigns. She'd heard the advertising execs talking about ads with millions of views, not thousands. Despite her determined efforts to be supportive, she couldn't help but ask, "And you're making a living from this?"

"No." Natalie sighed dramatically. "I do enough graphics work to pay my rent, but success is right around the corner. Once I build up my following a little bit more, I'll get name recognition. That's when the real money will pour in. Other influencers, like Mandy and Gorg, charge a hundred thou for a single post."

Kim shook her head. Her daughter's words were straight out of her father's playbook. And, like her father, she thought Natalie might be deceiving herself. The truck in front of her rolled another ten feet forward. She cleared her throat.

"Listen, Natalie. This traffic could free up any moment. Why don't I call you back when I get off work."

"Nat, Mom. I go by Nat now." Her daughter followed the reminder with another dramatic sigh.

"Nat," Kim dutifully repeated, although the nickname never failed to remind her of an annoying insect. "We'll talk later?"

"I'm busy tonight. Besides, this can't wait. I need you to do something for me."

Of course she did. Natalie only called when she wanted something. What was it this time? Not the Gucci purse Frank had given Kim during one of his rare, flush times, or the little black dress she'd picked out on a whirlwind shopping trip. Her daughter already had those.

Kim swallowed dryly. If Natalie asked for the pair of diamond studs Frank had given her on their tenth wedding anniversary, her daughter would be sorely disappointed. Kim had long since pawned those in order to pay for car repairs. But she was getting ahead of herself. Maybe this time, Natalie only wanted something simple. Like a box of her mother's homemade cookies. Holding her breath, Kim asked, "What?"

Natalie's voice dropped to a whisper. "I need you to wire me five thousand dollars."

"Five th—?" The request was so ridiculous, Kim laughed out loud.

"Mo-om, stop. You have to send it. I need to get out of here. Like, today."

The pleading note in Natalie's voice was so uncharacteristic that Kim sobered while her brain practically tripped over a picture of her little girl sitting in a jail cell. "Are you in trouble? Have you been arrested?"

"Uhn," Natalie huffed. "No."

Okay. Take a breath. She's not in the hospital. She hasn't been arrested.

Kim summoned patience and waited for an explanation.

"If you must know," Natalie said, making it perfectly clear she shouldn't have to explain, "as an influencer, I have to be seen in all the best places. There's a party I need to go to in New York next week. Sasha and Dayglo will be there," she said, dropping the names of America's latest celebrity sweethearts. "If I can post a pic with them, it'll send my ratings through the roof. All I need is a plane ticket and a new outfit. Maybe something from that little boutique on Greene we like. You know the one."

Kim did. As a girl, she'd dreamed of going on a shopping spree in New York City à la Julia Roberts. For Natalie's eighteenth birthday, she'd

39

made that dream come true for both of them. They'd made a day of it—jetting into the city, grabbing lunch in a café overlooking Times Square, and shopping till they dropped before catching the red-eye back to Atlanta. She'd ended up working ten hours of overtime a week for three months to pay for the dresses they'd bought on that trip. At the time, she'd deemed it worth every penny. Now, though, Natalie had both the frilly pink concoction she'd chosen and Kim's LBD. Idly, Kim wondered why Natalie—Nat, she corrected—couldn't wear one of those to her oh-so-important party.

"Well? How soon can you send the money?" Natalie's voice broke through her memories.

"Sorry, hon." The words burned her tongue like the mashed potatoes in last night's TV dinner, but she had to say them. "I would if I could, but I just don't have that kind of cash lying around." Her checking account barely held enough to pay for this month's groceries and the electric bill. As for savings, that was for absolute emergencies. A party didn't make the cut.

"Mom, you know I wouldn't ask if I didn't *need* this," Natalie pleaded. "My whole *career* depends on it. You can't let me down."

For a second, Kim felt her resolve waiver. She could give Natalie the money she'd saved up for first and last month's rent on a new place, she supposed. But then what? The word around the mailbox was that the owners had decided to renovate her apartment building and turn the units into condos. If that happened, what would become of her when her lease ran out at the end of the month? Would she end up living in her car? No matter how much she loved her daughter, that was a risk she couldn't take. She squared her shoulders, forced herself to admit the truth. "I simply don't have it to give to you." Much as she hated to do it, she suggested, "Why don't you ask your dad?"

"I already have."

Natalie's defeated tone told Kim all she needed to know. She could practically hear her ex-husband spinning one of his usual yarns about how this wasn't a good time. That all his money was tied up in some new business venture, one that was sure to succeed. That when he hit it big, he'd be glad to give Natalie everything she asked for and more. Just, you know, not right now.

Yeah, right.

"Can you take on more freelance work?" After leaving a position with a well-known graphics design company, Natalie had grudgingly taken on enough freelance customers to meet her basic needs.

"No. I'm late on several projects already. Besides, I need the money now."

Knowing she was venturing into dangerous territory, Kim gave her daughter the only thing she could spare—a piece of advice. "Sounds like you could use a job."

"A what?" Natalie's voice rose.

"A job. There's nothing wrong with getting a regular paycheck and benefits. And it doesn't have to last forever. Think of it as something to tide you over while you build up your, what was it? Your following?"

"I have a job. I'm an influencer."

To combat her daughter's shocked indignation, Kim took a steadying breath. "Yes, but it doesn't sound like that's putting food on the table just yet." Natalie had big dreams, and maybe one day she'd make them all come true. Kim sure hoped so. In the meantime, though, her daughter needed to take off the rose-colored glasses and get a reality check. Kim's own childhood, followed by twenty years as Frank's wife, had taught her that much.

"The holidays are just around the corner, and everyone is hiring." Kim packed as much enthusiasm into her voice as possible. "I bet you could work at one of those big department stores. With your knowledge of fashion and style, you'd make a great sales clerk. Or maybe you could waitress. In the right restaurant and with the right attitude, you'd make enough in tips to save up what you need in no time."

"Honestly, Mom, you're impossible. Dad warned me you'd be like this. I don't know why I even tried."

The Call Ended banner flashed on Kim's phone just as the cacophony of horns grew louder. She tore her gaze from the blank screen. Traffic had finally started moving again. Fighting tears, she shifted her foot from the brake to the gas pedal. She sure could use a shoulder to lean on, but who could she turn to? Certainly not her sister. Jen had never liked Frank or approved of Kim's parenting methods. Not her mom—she'd passed so long ago, all Kim had of her were faded memories. Few of those were pleasant. That left Aunt Margaret or one of her cousins.

Kim inhaled deeply, lost for a moment in memories of the summers she'd spent working at her Aunt Margaret's beachside inn. How the crisp, clean sheets snapped and crackled when she and her cousins changed the linens in the guest rooms each morning. The hot afternoons when she dreamed of finding a gold doubloon or an emerald among the sea shells the last high tide had washed ashore. Listening to her aunts' chatter while they sipped iced tea on the front porch at the end of each day. Her future had seemed so limitless back then, so full of possibilities.

Yet here she was, divorced, at odds with her children and struggling to make ends meet with a series of dead-end jobs. How had that happened?

Kim straightened her shoulders. Dwelling on the past wasn't going to help. Neither would fretting over the things she couldn't change, including her own daughter. She'd be better off focusing on the future and the things she could do something about. And, at fifty-one, she needed to figure out how to turn her life around, like, yesterday.

Following the lead of the driver in front of her, Kim gave the Honda a little more gas. As she did, her phone chimed. Was it Natalie? Did she want to apologize for her attitude? Ever hopeful, Kim accepted the call without glancing down at the screen.

"Hey Kim. Am I catching you at a bad time?" As sweet as the cakes and pastries she sold in her bakery, her cousin's voice drifted up from the speaker.

"Oh, man, it's good to hear your voice! I was just thinking of you." Kim couldn't help but smile. The summers she'd spent in Emerald Bay with Amy and the others had been the only bright spots in an otherwise bleak childhood. "But to answer your question, I'm driving. Have to be at work in fifteen minutes. What's up?"

"I won't keep you long then, but we need to talk. How about this evening?"

"I'll be home by seven. Any time after that is good." Her smile deepened. She was already looking forward to the call. Until now, the most exciting thing on tonight's agenda had been choosing which TV dinner to pop in the microwave.

"Seven it is. I'll let you know if anything changes after I speak with Belle and Diane."

"The whole gang?" A faint worry drew Kim's eyebrows together. She'd been looking forward to a chance to reminisce and catch up. But there might be more involved if Amy was reaching out to the rest of the family. "Anything I need to know?"

"I, uh, I'd rather go over everything once, instead of with each of you. But it's nothing that can't wait till tonight."

Hmmm. That only sounded slightly ominous. "You want me to call Jen?"

"Do you even know where she is these days?"

"Now, now." A wave of protectiveness rushed through Kim.

45

"Oh, geez!" Amy swore softly. "That came out wrong. I didn't mean…"

"Relax. It's a fair question." Kim rushed to reassure her cousin. Most sisters probably knew the whereabouts of their only sibling. Then again, most people didn't have a sister who packed up and moved on a whim. Jen rarely spent more than six months in one place. In that way, her footloose sister was a lot like their mom. "Last I heard, she was in Biloxi. But I have her cell phone number."

"Um…" Amy hesitated before saying, "It's probably a good idea to include her. I'd hate for her to feel left out."

"No one wants that." Kim swallowed. Her sister might still be figuring out her place in the world, but Jen was one of the family. She was glad Amy recognized that.

"I'll call Belle and Diane and send you all the details later today."

"Yeah." Kim nodded. She glanced at the thick clouds beyond her windshield. "Let's make it seven thirty, okay?" she asked. The way her day was going, the predicted storm would stall out over Atlanta and turn her evening commute into an even worse nightmare than this morning's rocky start.

Three

Belle

*B*elle Dane paused just beyond the entrance to the spacious living room of her apartment in The Eldorado, an exclusive co-op overlooking Central Park's beautiful reservoir. She checked her image in a strategically hung mirror one last time because appearances were important, even in the privacy of her own home. The artfully applied eye shadow and the hair she'd spent over an hour wrangling into a casual topknot that was "just messy enough" earned a nod of approval. The moisturizer she'd added to her beauty routine last year had done a great job of minimizing the crows' feet around her eyes. The worry lines ever-so-slightly bracketing her mouth, though? Not so much. She gave her cheeks a resigned pat. Thank goodness for plastic surgeons. A little nip and tuck—already on her pre-tour schedule—was sure to take years off her face.

As for the rest, no one looking at her would ever guess she'd spent fifty-two years on this earth. She cupped her hands beneath the girls she'd snugged into a spangled halter top and gave them a little bounce before she smoothed her fingers down the outside seams of her skin-tight jeans. Her personal trainer was a harsh taskmaster, but he'd earned her grudging respect along with his hefty paycheck. The hours they spent in the gym each day worked wonders at keeping her tummy flat, her hips and thighs well-toned. Both were absolute necessities if she expected to sing and dance her way across the stage in front of sold-out crowds next spring.

She bared her teeth, making sure no trace of that vile kale smoothie her nutritionist had called "breakfast" lingered in her mouth. As if on cue, her tummy gurgled a protest.

"Now, now," she chided. Starvation was just part of the price she paid for fame and fortune. Not that she wouldn't absolutely die for a plate of pancakes like the ones Aunt Liz used to fix for her before school each morning. But like her aunt, the days when she could afford to eat carbs, much less drown them in butter and syrup, were gone forever.

She closed her eyes for a moment, letting a rush of memories flood over her. The sound of beaters scraping against a bowl while her Aunt Liz whipped up something fabulous for family and guests alike in the kitchen. The warm welcome her mom gave to every new arrival at the Dane Crown Inn. The uneven *ka-thunk, ka-thunk* suitcases made when her dad or her cousin Scott hauled guests' bags up the wide staircase. The songs she and her cousins sang each night as they washed and dried the dinner dishes.

The old inn was quieter now, she supposed, now that her cousins had scattered and Aunt Liz was gone. Did her mom miss those chaotic summer days when she and her cousins hired on as the inn's maids and bellhops? Or the retreats at the beginning of each summer, when the entire Dane family would descend on Florida's Treasure Coast for two weeks of fun and family time in the tiny town of Emerald Bay? Thinking of how lonely her mom must be, she wondered if she could sneak a quick trip home onto her schedule this fall. Anticipating the look of surprise on her mom's face when she opened the front door and saw her only child standing on the inn's front porch, Belle smiled. They'd make a whole weekend of it, just the two of them.

Deciding to add the getaway to the things she'd mention during their meeting, Belle squared her shoulders, ready to face Lisa Connolly and the bevy of personal assistants and attorneys who traveled with the agent.

Why had Lisa asked to see her anyway?

Belle dismissed the question with a flick of perfectly groomed acrylic nails. The why of it didn't matter. It had been Lisa, after all, who'd discovered Belle busking on street corners back when she was a green and inexperienced nobody. The talent agent had taken her under her wing, introduced her to the right people and gotten her the right gigs. She'd been at her side when Belle had signed on with Noble Records, the number one label in the country. With Noble's backing, Belle's first pop single had shot to the top of the charts. Thirty years later, a row of platinum albums lined one wall of her office.

So when Lisa asked to meet—even if it was at the ungodly hour of eight in the morning—Belle cleared her schedule. Taking a breath, she smiled through lips she'd given her signature pouty outline.

"Lisa, darling," she gushed, striding into the room on four-inch heels as if she were performing for an audience. Which, considering the size of the agent's entourage, wasn't far from the truth.

"Belle." Lisa set her cup on the white, ultra-modern coffee table and rose from the white settee that had been precisely arranged for viewing a piece of oversize artwork. "You're looking fabulous, as always."

"I hope I haven't kept you waiting long," she said, knowing full well she had timed her arrival perfectly. She clasped the woman's hands as they exchanged air kisses while Belle did her best to ignore the oddest scent of sweat that clung to her agent.

"No. Not at all, love." Lisa glanced at the massive canvas, where colorful lines swirled across a surface that had been painted to resemble a blackboard. "It gave me a chance to study the Twombly. I find something new in it each time I see it."

Belle spared the pricey artwork a single glance. She'd never understood what Lisa and the others saw in the painting. As far as she was concerned, her nieces and nephews had created better scribbles when they were in kindergarten. But the artist was all the rage, and her decorator had insisted the piece would stand out against the otherwise deliberately sterile decor. And so she'd splurged—extravagantly—on the artwork.

"I'm so glad you enjoy it." Belle turned to greet Lisa's usual crowd of assistants and lackeys but stopped herself when she realized the chairs scattered about the room remained empty. The tiniest bit of unease fluttered in her chest. The last time the agent had shown up alone, she'd brought an advance copy of a scathing review of Belle's latest album.

Well, that couldn't happen this time, could it? She hadn't had a new song out in ages. She would soon, though. Thanks to a popular sitcom that had chosen her number one hit as its theme song, her star was on the rise again. After months of practice, she and the band were heading into the recording studio next week to lay down tracks for her next album. This one, unlike her last couple, was sure to top all the charts and replenish her ever-shrinking coffers.

Bolstered by that happy thought, Belle smiled brightly. "What a treat to have you all to myself this morning. Can I get you anything? More coffee? A smoothie?" She eyed the tray of fruit and beverages Gretchen, her personal assistant, had thoughtfully left on the table.

"A little more coffee would be nice."

Belle graciously poured from the carafe and tried not to notice when Lisa added a rather large dollop of cream to her cup. Wary of the added calories, as well as milk's tendency to muffle her vocal chords, she'd given up all dairy products decades earlier.

"How are things with you and Greg? Did you try that new restaurant in the West Village I recommended?" Greg was the latest of Lisa's husbands. Was he number four? Or five? Not that it mattered. Lisa discarded men nearly as often as she changed outfits. She'd soon be on to her next conquest.

Lisa licked her lips. "Greg is yummy. He spends a lot of time lifting weights, for which I am most grateful."

"Good to hear it." Belle felt heat rise in her cheeks and fanned herself dramatically, all the while pretending the topic—not another hot flash—made her skin glow. Angled so Lisa couldn't see her face, she filled a crystal tumbler with ice water.

Lisa's demeanor sobered. "You don't, um, have company of your own, do you?"

"No." Belle suppressed a wry grin. Everyone thought someone as rich and famous as she was lived the high life. Parties every night. Surrounded by sexy men who'd jump at the chance to share her bed. The truth was, one-night-stands had never been her thing. She'd set her sights on something better—a love that would last forever, like the love her parents had shared. Unfortunately, the men who could handle being in a relationship with someone more famous, more successful than themselves were scarce as hen's teeth.

"Good," Lisa declared. Abandoning her coffee, she stared through the floor-to-ceiling windows as if unable to wrench her focus from the stunning view of the park.

The bead of sweat Belle spotted trickling down Lisa's temple sent another nervous flutter through her chest. Setting her glass aside, she cleared her throat. "What's going on, Lisa? You didn't like the demo?"

Maybe she should have waited a bit longer before recording her latest practice session with the band, but Lisa had been hounding her for weeks for a rough cut of her new material. Still, Belle told herself she might have jumped the gun. After all, her lead guitarist had had the audacity to go and give himself a heart attack just days after they'd finalized the arrangements. The new guy was still learning all the licks and riffs that made up her band's signature sound. He was brilliant, though, and he was working hard. By the time they started laying down tracks for the new album next week, she had no doubt he'd smooth out all the kinks.

"It's not the demo. I mean, that's part of it, but it's not the main reason I'm here."

"Oh-kay." Belle drew out the word while she sank onto one of the sleek side chairs designed by someone whose name she hadn't bothered to memorize. "What's up?"

"It's the tour. Noble hasn't exactly been able to line up the venues we'd hoped to book."

Not the songs, then. That was a relief. She needed a hit to replenish the accounts that had all but been depleted by years of paying the members of her band, the dance instructors, and the fitness gurus and the many assistants who worked with her. She was counting on this album to be the one that sent her name soaring to the top of the charts again. She'd spent months working with songwriters and musicians to create the numbers for it. Starting over at square one would be an expensive, time-consuming proposition.

A tiny niggling doubt creased her brow. None of the new songs rose to the level of *Jimmy, Jimmy Oh*, the one that had skyrocketed to the top of all the billboards and made her a household name. The one that, thanks to a hugely popular sitcom, had everyone humming along to her music again. It was also responsible for Noble Records' sudden interest in launching her come-back album and tour. Deliberately relaxing her facial muscles, Belle reassured herself that every one of the new cuts had rhythm, a sweet melody and a catchy chorus—all the things her fans expected from the artist *Variety* had once touted as the Queen of Pop.

"So there's a problem with the schedule?" she asked. "That should be easy enough to fix." A dozen years ago, she'd performed to sellout crowds at some of the largest sites in the world. Kicking things off at the Hollywood Bowl, she'd worked her way back east, where she'd finished up strong in front of twenty thousand screaming fans at Madison Square Garden before taking her act across the Atlantic. Noble had been planning a repeat of that tour, but she could be flexible. "If the dates don't line up, I'd be okay with switching things around. I can play the Garden first and wind up in LA."

"It's...not that simple." The normally unflappable Lisa seemed to struggle for words. "Look," she said at last, "I wanted to break all this to you first before you heard it through the grapevine. Or worse. The truth is, we can't guarantee enough ticket sales to book the bigger venues. In order to preserve the tour, you're going to need to lower your expectations a bit."

Belle smoothed the bridge of her nose with two fingers. Using second-tier venues like Red

Rocks or Wolf Trap took the same amount of time and energy as, say, the Merriweather Post Pavilion but generated half as much in revenue. That, in turn, meant half as much money to pay the band, the dancers, the pyro techs, and the hundreds of other people required to take a first-class show on the road. To say nothing of replenishing her nearly empty bank accounts. "Just exactly how low are we talking?" she asked cautiously.

"Actually, the label is thinking more along the lines of the Tower Theater or Brooklyn Steel. Maybe Stubbs in Austin."

So much for a big, splashy comeback tour.

Belle sucked in a harsh breath. "Those barely hold two thousand," she protested. "We can't hope to break even in places that small."

Lisa's head tilted to one side. "They're going to send you out with a stripped-down crew. One tour bus. A truck or two to haul the equipment."

"What?" No smoke machines? No elaborate staging? No backup singers? Belle stared at her agent while a righteous indignation soured her stomach. This couldn't be happening. She swallowed. Hard. "That's my only option?"

"Unless you want to open for Sizzler or BTK."

Her? Open for a boy band?

"Wait." Belle struggled to catch her breath.

"Wait just a minute." She sprang from her chair and paced the room while she tried to wrap her head around this unexpected turn of events. She was Belle Dane, after all. A legendary pop star. She had so many platinum albums, awards and Grammys in her office, she'd lost count of them all. Yet here Lisa was, suggesting she open for a boy band. What was Noble thinking?

She snapped her fingers. They weren't thinking. They were just reacting. Okay, so a few of her most recent albums hadn't made platinum and, if she was going to be honest, the last one had been a dismal failure. But this new album was going to be different. She'd invested every dime she had to make sure of it. This album was the one that, by all that was holy, would send her popularity soaring and put her on the top of the charts again. She'd make sure of it. She'd go over every note, every word of those songs again herself. She just needed to tweak a couple of them—that was all. Punch them up. Maybe make them a little more up-tempo. That'd do the trick. She'd choose the best of the lot and ask Noble to release it as an EP. Once her voice filled the airwaves again, the label would have no choice but to throw its considerable weight behind her tour.

Certain she'd found the answer, she perched

on the edge of her chair. "Lisa. Darling. I think all this talk of venues is premature. You heard the demo for this new album. Now I'll be the first to admit it still needs work, but by the time I finish with it, it'll top the charts. When it does, the fans will fill those stadiums. You'll see."

But the approval Belle expected to dawn in Lisa's eyes never formed. Instead, the agent's expression only drooped.

"Yeah, about that," she said on a sigh. "More bad news, I'm afraid."

Belle's head whipped up so fast, a few tendrils of the hair she'd so carefully tucked and teased worked loose. "What?" she demanded.

"You didn't send the demo to Jason, did you?"

"Of course not," she scoffed. She wasn't stupid. She'd never hand a sample over to her record label until each and every song on it was as perfect as she could make it. And especially not to Jason Dennis. It'd be different if Ronald Keys was still in charge. Like Lisa, Ron had been with her from the beginning. They shared a vision for her career, her continued success. Jason, a relative newcomer, was only filling in until Ronald came back from an extended leave.

Another one of those pesky doubts swirled through her head. This one sent her stomach on a downward spiral. Just how long had Ron been on vacation anyway? Hating the tentative note she heard in her voice, she asked, "Jason hasn't taken over permanently, has he?"

"There's been no official announcement, but it certainly looks that way."

Belle groaned. Jason didn't care that she'd earned millions for Noble over the course of her career. He was one of those "what have you done for me lately" guys. What other explanation was there for the way he'd left her cooling her heels in the waiting area the last time she'd dropped by the office for a friendly chat? Plus, word on the street was that Noble had brought him on board to make sweeping changes.

Was *she* one of those changes?

"Somehow, Jason got hold of a copy of your demo." Lisa continued to stare through the plate-glass windows while a torrent of hateful words fell from her lips. "At best, he said it's derivative and not the best use of your talents. He canceled your studio sessions and put the whole project on hold."

Squeezing her eyes shut, Belle shook her head. The whole point of the tour was to promote the new album. But without time in the recording studio, there'd be no new album to promote. And without an album, how was she supposed to recoup her money?

Lisa continued. "He's asked us to meet with him at Noble next week to discuss 'your future' with the label."

"They're canceling my contract?" The world spun around her. She fought to breathe.

"No. Not yet, at least." Lisa's attention shifted to Belle. "For now, he's merely suggesting you take your music in another direction."

Say what now?

She'd cut her teeth on pop. On songs about the love between a teenage boy and a teenage girl. That music had been her bread and butter for going on thirty years, and now, just because some executive without a lick of respect for all she'd accomplished thought it was a good idea, her label wanted her to change course?

"Did Jason happen to mention which direction he'd like me to go?" Her voice dripped bitterness like one of her Aunt Liz's biscuits dripped honey. She pinned Lisa with a deadly stare.

Lisa held up a hand. "Don't shoot the messenger, Belle. None of this was my idea."

Belle felt a pang of instant remorse. "I'm sorry. I didn't mean to take it out on you. It's just that, well, this is all such a shock."

"I know, and I'm sorry, too. Believe me, I tried to make him see things your way, but his mind is made up."

"What exactly does he want me to try next? Rap?" She shook her head at the idea of walking out on stage in dreadlocks and black leather.

Lisa chortled. "Certainly not."

"Folk? Can you see me perched on a stool singing ballads about flowers, magic dragons and clear, blue mountain streams?" Puh-leez. The only body of water she liked was the ocean. She waved a dismissive hand.

"Not folk."

She was running out of ideas. "What does he expect me to do, then? Pretend I suddenly got religion and promised God I'd use my music to spread the Good Word?" No one who knew her would buy that. Why, she'd accepted Jesus Christ as her savior when she was ten and hadn't missed a Sunday service since.

"Country," Lisa said as if simply saying the word was painful.

The air in Belle's chest whooshed out. "Geez, Lisa. I didn't see that coming," she whispered. She shot a rare pleading glance at her agent. "You and I have worked together for thirty years, right? In all that time have you ever known me to willingly spin the dial to a country station? To hum a few bars of 'Honky Tonk Angels'? To wax poetic about Patsy Cline?"

"No, but there's always a first time."

Signaling the end of their meeting, Lisa stood. She cast a sidelong look at the Twombly and sighed. "I really do see something new in it every single time."

"This isn't going to work, you know," Belle said, her voice barely audible.

"Like it or not, Jason is the boss now. It's either his way or…"

"Retire?"

At the mere thought of never walking onto a stage again, Belle's eyes filled. Retirement was for aging rock stars. For guitarists whose arthritic fingers could no longer find the chords. For people like Ron, who'd achieved all they'd set out to do in life. Not for her. She was far too young to quit. She still had songs to sing, fans who'd pay top dollar for a ticket to one of her concerts, who'd buy her CDs.

But without Noble's support, there'd be no concerts, no CDs.

And Noble wanted her to "go country."

She had no idea how long she sat in stunned silence after Lisa saw herself out. Protests whirled through her mind. She was Belle Dane, for crying out loud. Radio announcers across the country called her "legendary." Some still called her the Queen of Pop. Teenagers danced to her music at their proms. Aspiring young talents grew up singing her songs, wanting to be her. And yet...and yet her label expected her to switch gears. To embark on a whole new career and start over.

Did she have a choice?

At last, she stirred. Her fingers closed around the coffee carafe. She hefted it. She wanted—no, needed—she needed to throw something. To hear glass shatter. To ruin something like that new upstart at Noble was ruining her career.

She eyed the Twombly. For several long seconds she weighed the option of actually dousing the painting with the bitter brew.

"Ahem. Ms. Dane?"

Startled, Belle scanned the room. Her focus landed on the slim form of her personal assistant. The sedately dressed young woman lingered near the entrance to the living room. Deliberately, Belle resettled the carafe on the table. Unwilling to let anyone, not even her closest employees, see her cry, she averted her eyes while she blotted them with the tips of her fingers. She didn't look up until she'd reassured herself that mascara wasn't running down her cheeks. Raising her head, she asked, "Yes, Gretchen?"

"I hate to bother you, but Amy is on your personal line. Are you available?"

Her cousin. Emerald Bay. Mama.

"Please, Lord, don't let this be more bad news." Bracing for the worst, Belle took a breath. "Did she—did she say why she was calling?"

"No, ma'am."

Belle forced herself to take a breath. Her personal staff came and went with such regularity that she'd made sure everyone in the family knew how to reach her in case of an emergency. If her mom had been rushed to the hospital, Amy would have led with the news rather than risk having to leave a message.

"I'll take it in my office." Her fears melting, Belle stood. With a regal air befitting someone of her stature, she strode down the hall. Once her office door clicked shut behind her, she collapsed into the plush leather chair behind her desk and grabbed the phone.

"Amy, you're just what the doctor ordered," she gushed. "I've had the most awful morning. I absolutely, positively can't take one more piece of bad news. Tell me something good!"

Amy giggled as if Belle had just told the funniest joke. "Would it help if I tell you Kim and Diane and I are getting together to chat tonight? I really hope you can join us."

"Why, that sounds wonderful," Belle said. Without reaching for the computer glasses that lay on the desk, she squinted at her calendar.

Other than her usual workout sessions and a dance class this afternoon, she had nothing on her schedule. "I'd love to. It's been ages since we all got together." And after the day she'd had, she wouldn't think of passing up the chance to talk with her cousins.

Not that she'd ever dream of mentioning her current troubles—financial or otherwise—to anyone in her family. She was their success story, the one they all looked up to, the one who'd "made it." She couldn't expect her cousins or her mom to understand what Lisa's news meant to her finances. Or what having to start over in a brand-new style of music would mean. How hard she'd have to study. The endless weeks it would take to develop her own sound. To say nothing of her look. Why, she'd have to remake herself, from how she wore her hair all the way down to her footwear. She closed her eyes as she tried to imagine herself decked out in sequins, satin piping and cowboy boots. It wasn't a pretty picture. But what good would it do to complain?

She sighed. Oh, how she wished there was someone she could confide in. But the only place lonelier than the top was on the long, slow slide to the bottom.

Four

Jen

The pounding beat of classic rock nearly drowned out the clamor of bells, whistles and spinning wheels that drifted from the casino floor into the employee dressing area. Jennifer Dane Miller Passel ignored the sounds designed to entice everyone from senior citizens on limited budgets to whales with fat wallets into sliding more money into a slot machine. She fought an urge to pinch herself as she studied her image in the full-length mirror. Was she really wearing the coveted uniform of a hostess in The Deluxe Room? She was, but after six weeks in her new position, she could still hardly believe it. Her gaze traced shimmering stockings from a pair of strappy heels north over slim legs without spotting a single snag or, worse, a run. The nylons disappeared under the slight flounce of a skirt a mere three inches below her cheeks, but at least here at the River Delta, her rear was fully covered.

That was something to be thankful for. The list of jobs she'd held where even more of her had been on display was longer than she cared to admit. She hadn't minded so much when she was in her twenties and thirties. Back when everything was firm and tight, she'd loved flirting with the guys and raking in the tips when they got all worked up. Not that she'd ever let things go too far. "You want it? Put a ring on it," had been her standard response whenever a guy showed more than a passing fancy. Two had actually taken her up on her challenge, but neither had fulfilled her dreams of a white picket fence. Which was why she was still serving drinks, albeit at much nicer places than dive bars and honky tonks these days.

She continued her examination, her focus shifting to the waspish waist she maintained through intermittent fasting and daily workouts despite a metabolism that slowed with every passing year. Bending, she nodded her approval when, thanks to strategically placed strips of double-backed tape, her uniform's plunging neckline offered no more than a tantalizing glimpse of the best breasts money could buy. Frequent trips to the beauty salon kept the hair cascading onto her shoulders dark and glossy. Her skin glowed with a youthful sheen that, these days, came straight out of a bottle. Expertly applied makeup accentuated the bone structure that was holding up well for a woman pushing fifty.

"You'll do," she pronounced with satisfaction.

At the last possible minute, she slipped her feet into a pair of stilettos that guaranteed two things—first, her toes would ache like a son of a gun by the end of her shift, and second, the tips she'd earn by wearing the high heels would more than make up for the pain. Summoning the bright smile expected of all the casino hosts, she headed for the high roller section.

"Evening, Kurt," she said, giving her usual greeting to the former pro wrestler who manned the red velvet rope at the entrance to The Deluxe Room. Kurt's expensively tailored suit camouflaged a solid frame, but there was more to the man than mere muscle. In that way, he was much like the plastic sifter she'd used to remove shells and bits of sea glass from beach sand when she was a child. Like the toy, Kurt possessed an uncanny ability to separate the well-heeled patrons who could afford to drop $500 on a spin of the roulette wheel from those whose bank balance had worn a little thin. Plus, he never forgot a name or a face.

"Anything special I need to know tonight?" she asked.

"Mr. Peterman's grandson is here for his bachelor party." Kurt nodded in the direction of the roulette table, where six men in matching polo shirts were busy placing bets and commiserating with their scantily clad dates. "Carlson's the tall one."

"Carlson." She repeated his name in an effort to etch it into her memory. "What's Carlson drinking? Old-fashioneds like his grandfather?" The older Peterman preferred his made with Michter's and had a tendency to over-tip that had earned him a place on her list of personal favorites.

"So far the group's been sticking to martinis—dirty—but they've asked for a couple of bottles of Dom for a midnight toast."

She nodded. She'd make sure the corks popped and the bubbly poured on the stroke of twelve.

"Mr. Borman texted that he'd be stopping by later with a couple of whales."

"Good for him," she murmured. Whenever

celebrities came to town, managers of the casinos that lined Biloxi's shore practically tripped over themselves in their efforts to lure the rich or famous to their tables. Borman must have won the jackpot this time. "Who'd he snag?"

Excitement danced in Kurt's eyes. "The developers of *Preservation.*"

"Whoa!" No wonder the bouncer was impressed. The guard had a passion for video games. He especially loved *Preservation* and bragged about his high scores whenever he had the chance.

As for their whales, word on the street had it that *Preservation* had recently been sold for sixty-five million, a tidy sum for the two college dropouts who'd reportedly developed the popular video game at their parents' dining room table.

"Do we know anything else about them?" The more she knew about the pair's likes and dislikes, the more she could make sure they never wanted to leave the River Delta or its tables.

"Not much. Borman said they're in a celebratory mood."

Which probably meant they'd want all the pomp and special attention she and the rest of the staff could muster. No problem there. She'd do her part to make sure the two men enjoyed their stay. "I'll keep an eye out for them," she promised as she moved past the velvet rope.

For the next few hours, she made the rounds of the exclusive section, smiling at the winners and sympathizing with the losers while she and the other hostess served drinks made with top-shelf liquors to people who were used to getting what they wanted, when they wanted it. Knowing word of how they were treated would eventually make its way to his grandfather, Jen paid special attention to Carlson Peterman and his friends. She was glad when the young men enjoyed a run of good luck at the roulette table. Their celebrations were infectious, and when people were happy, they tipped more.

"Can I get you another Jameson and ginger, Matt?" she asked, whisking an empty glass from in front of one of the party.

The young man's head whipped around. "How do you know who I am?"

"It's part of my job to know who I'm serving and what they like to drink." Jen, who'd heard the others congratulate Matt earlier when he'd placed a winning bet, upped the wattage on her smile.

The young man shook his head. He gestured toward the crowded tables. "You know every person here?"

"Pretty much," she conceded. "The ones in my section, at least. People like it when I call them by name. It lets them know I care about them. It makes them feel special." She brushed her fingers under her name tag.

"Good to know. I'll have that Jameson and ginger ale, if you don't mind," he said, flipping a chip onto her tray. He paused for a second before he grinned and added, "Jen."

"Thanks, Matt." She showed her own appreciation by giving her hem a practiced flounce as she strode off to place his order.

Flirting with the customers was part of the job. A dip here or there to give the boys a glimpse of cleavage. A slight hike of her skirt when the tips were extra good. Nothing more, though. She had her standards, after all, and worked hard to maintain her self-respect in a business where that commodity was often in short supply.

Which meant none of those so-called "friendly" pinches. No wandering hands, either. Over the years, she'd gotten pretty good at enforcing those boundaries. It was easier now that she worked behind the velvet ropes. Beyond them, on the main floor, men—and women—had been apt to get handsy. Not so much here among the high rollers.

At the bar, Jen paused beneath the mirrored glass where the names of the top distilleries in the world were on display. Her favorite bartender, Sammy, hustled over when she approached. "Good crowd tonight," she murmured, discreetly adding Matt's generous tip to the stash of chips and cash she kept in a hidden pocket of her uniform.

"Sweet," Sammy replied, knowing he'd reap the benefits when Jen divvied up her tips with him and the busboys at the end of their shift. He began fixing Matt's drink and replenishing the three other orders she handed him.

With her back to the room, Jen took a moment. Letting her mouth relax, she gently massaged her lower back, which had stiffened after four hours on the floor.

"Tired?" Sammy asked, placing the new drinks on her tray.

"No more than usual," she answered, though she felt her age more every night. Wearing a bright smile and towering heels was a young woman's game. No doubt about it. Not that she'd let anyone ever catch her complaining. There were tougher ways to make a living. Much tougher. She should know. She'd tried her hand at more than a few of them. She scooped up her tray, refreshed her smile and wiggled her fingers at Sammy. "See you in a few," she said as she returned to tending to their well-heeled guests.

It was nearly eleven before a stir at the velvet ropes signaled the arrival of Mr. Borman. The bevy of stunningly beautiful women who accompanied him clustered around a pair of men so new at being rich, the geek hadn't entirely worn off. Though the pair had obviously gone on a buying spree, Jen hid a smile as she imagined them pointing to an image in a catalogue and telling some random personal shopper, "Make me look like that." As if mere clothes could remake the man. These two—with their scuffed shoes and messy hair—were still rumpled around the edges, like two guys who'd be far more comfortable in board shorts and T-shirts.

She watched closely as Mr. Borman introduced his guests to Kurt. Ralph, the taller of the two men, seemed to revel in all the attention. Linking arms with two of the women in their party, he headed for the blackjack tables as if he'd been waiting for success since the day he was born. The rest of the women followed in his wake. Meanwhile, his partner—Garrison, Jen noted—lingered at the entrance, apparently waiting for Ralph to realize he'd left his friend behind. After a long moment, Garrison's lips compressed until his doughy face took on a sour expression. Thrusting his hands deep into the pockets of a pair of ill-fitting Armani slacks, he finally trudged toward a bank of slots at the opposite end of the room.

Jen felt a twinge of compassion when Garrison hoisted his considerable bulk onto a well-padded barstool and slid a shiny silver card into one of the machines. She knew what it was like when someone you'd worked side by side with suddenly took off in a different direction. Hadn't the same thing happened to her when she and Chris split? He'd been the first to take her up on her offer to "put a ring on it," and she'd been sure she'd found her Mr. Right. They'd planned on spending their whole lives together, just the two of them. Which had boiled down to precisely three years and two months before Chris had announced it was time to start a family. Like her opinion didn't matter. Like he'd forgotten she'd said from the get-go she didn't want children. After that, one argument led to another until, almost before she knew what was happening, the divorce papers had been signed, sealed and delivered. Six months later, he'd married a woman who'd given him that family he'd wanted more than he wanted her.

So, yeah. Garrison and Ralph might be multimillionaires, but it looked like all their newfound wealth had created a rift between the two partners. One she could clearly relate to. She aimed her feet toward the machines and the lonely millionaire.

"Garrison, my name's Jen, and I'll be happy to serve you this evening. What's your pleasure?"

Ignoring the Spin button on the front of the machine, Garrison tugged on the metal handle. Cheerful music played as numbers and images of fruit spun through the windows. The turn ended with two sevens and a clump of red cherries on display. Lights flashed, encouraging him to try again.

"Just my luck," he muttered before turning a baleful eye on her. "What are you, my consolation prize?"

"No, sir." Jen summoned her sweetest smile. Movies and television shows often gave people the wrong impression of women in her profession. She hurried to correct Garrison's. "I'm here to bring you whatever you'd like to drink. What'll it be? Hennessy? Glenlivet? Chivas? Maker's Mark?" She rattled off several of the more popular choices.

"Why don't you come right over here and help me with my next pull." Garrison patted a knee with one hand while he gripped the lever with the sausage-like fingers of his other hand. "Bring me some luck."

"Sorry, no can do," Jen replied firmly. "I'll stand here while you play, though, if you want." Casino policy strictly forbade employees from interfering with another person's bet. Breaking that rule, whether the customer begged her to or not, would get her fired quicker than she could snap her fingers. As for climbing onto Garrison's lap, a move like that violated her personal rules.

With a shrug, the big man gave the lever another tug. This time when the images came to rest, sevens lined up across the screen. Bells rang, and the sound of a waterfall of coins filled the air.

"Hey!" Eyes that had been at half-mast cast a more appreciative glance in her direction. Garrison's lips erupted into a wolfish smile. "Looks like it's gonna be my lucky night after all."

Jen tried not to flinch when the man flung a sweaty arm across her shoulders. "Whoa, cowboy," she said, stepping out of his grasp. "I just serve drinks. I'm not part of the entertainment."

"Is that so?" Garrison's cheeks flamed red. Reaching into his pocket, he withdrew a handful of ones and tossed them on her tray. At the same time, he leaned close enough for her to smell his boozy breath. "Mr. Borman said I could have anything I wanted." His eyes gleamed.

Ones? Really? What was this guy thinking?

Though her smile remained firmly in place, Jen gritted her teeth while she sized up the man in front of her. She'd been wrong about Garrison—he didn't deserve her sympathy. The man was trouble with a capitol *T*. Sidestepping his next grasp, she sent an imploring look in Kurt's direction.

Disappointment shot through her when the bouncer gave a barely perceptible shake of his head. Jen sighed. The message was clear. She needed to keep Garrison happy if she wanted to remain employed at the River Delta...and she was on her own. She should have guessed. Cocktail waitresses, even ones with her talent at making their guests feel at home, could be replaced a lot easier than whales of Garrison's magnitude.

Holding her ground despite instincts that told her to run, not walk, to the nearest exit, she summoned all her hard-earned skills. Okay, she told herself, you can do this. Her knack for dealing with difficult customers was one of the reasons she'd been promoted to casino hostess in the exclusive VIP area, wasn't it?

Edging marginally closer to Garrison, she

pulled one of her favorite tricks from her sleeveless uniform. "Everybody loves a winner," she cooed. "Especially those pretty ladies over there." She gestured to the women who crowded around the man's partner. "All you have to do is hit the jackpot a time or two, and they'll come running. You'll see." She nodded pointedly to the slot machine. "Why don't you try your luck while I get you that drink?"

"I don't need another drink," Garrison grumbled. "You're my lucky charm. I need you to stay right here beside me."

This time when he lunged for her, she was ready for him and neatly avoided his grasping fingers. "Tell you what," she said, responding with a lighthearted giggle tempered with the hands-off attitude she'd perfected over the years. "Our bartender, Sammy, owes me a favor. I'll have him whip up something special just for you." Without giving Garrison a chance to argue, much less make another grab for her, she high-stepped it to the bar.

There, she slid her tray onto the polished surface and sighed.

"Trouble?" Sammy asked.

"This guy Garrison is a first-class peach," she whispered to Sammy. "Nothing I can't handle, but he's handsy. I needed to get away from him for a minute. Promised him you'd make him something 'special.'" She framed the word in air quotes. "What do you think? One of your towering Bloody Marys?" Not only was Sammy's spicy blend of vodka and tomato juice refreshing, the olives and pearl onions he skewered between loops of crispy bacon made an impressive display.

Sammy gave Garrison the once-over. "Nah. He doesn't look like a man who loves his veggies. A King's Mule is more his speed."

Jen licked her lips. She'd only tasted the concoction once, but once had been enough for her to decide she'd make it her beverage of choice if she ever had money to burn. As it was, seventy bucks a pop was a wee bit too rich for her blood. Not Garrison's though. She imagined the way his eyes would light up when she presented him with the drink. Dusted with edible gold flakes and garnished with pickled ginger, the mix of flavored vodka and other ingredients was a work of art fit for a man of his newly achieved station. Plus, it packed a powerful punch that just might take the edge off Garrison's libido.

"Sounds like we've got a winner," she said. A discreet glance at the clock hidden behind the bar told her it was nearly midnight. "Tell you what. While you fix the mule, I'll take the Dom to the

Peterman party." No matter how important Mr. Borman considered Garrison, she couldn't neglect her other customers.

"Make it quick," Sammy warned. He grabbed two bottles of the expensive champagne from the cooler and handed them to her.

Jen noted the location of the younger party. Hoisting a tray laden with flutes and champagne above her head, she sashayed across the room to the craps table, where Carlson and his entourage were in high spirits. After popping the bubbly on the promised stroke of midnight, she faded into the background while the men clapped their host on the back and raised their glasses in a series of good-natured toasts. By the time she returned to the bar, Sammy had arranged Garrison's drink along with a box of gold-dusted popcorn on a gold edged tray. The display was spectacular, and she smiled her thanks to the bartender, who was busy filling another order. Then she headed toward the troublesome newcomer.

"Garrison," she said softly, not wanting to interrupt if he was on a winning spree.

Garrison yanked the lever on the slot machine. Without bothering to see if he'd won or not, he swung toward her. "What took you so long? You kept me waiting forever," he said, sounding like a petulant child.

Jen knew she'd been gone less than ten minutes, but she refrained from pointing that out to the man. In most businesses, the customer was always right. That went double for the high rollers at the River Delta. "I'm sorry you had to wait. A King's Mule takes a little extra effort, but it's worth it. Believe me." She held the tray out, giving him the chance to admire the gold inlays on the handle and rim of the traditional copper mug. In the light of the flashing neon lights, gold dust gleamed from the beverage's surface. A gingery fragrance wafted from the cup.

Garrison's nose wrinkled. "What is that?" he demanded.

"A King's Mule," she repeated evenly. "Made of the finest ginger-infused vodka, with our own specially crafted ginger beer and Tahitian lime juice." Smiling, she motioned for him to take a sip.

For a big man, Garrison moved at a blinding speed. His fist struck the edge of the tray, ripping it from her fingers. Jen stood in stunned silence as the mug and snacks went flying. Her mouth gaped open when the whole mess rained down, drenching both her and her VIP customer in a gingery brew.

"What, what'd you do that for?" she asked. Liquid dripped from her hair onto her face. She grabbed the linen napkin that had landed on the next machine over.

"Me? You did that on purpose," Garrison bellowed. Before Jen could react, he was on his feet, shouting. "Look what you've done!"

The sudden outburst drew the immediate attention of Mr. Borman, who'd been schmoozing with some customers on the other side of the room. The casino manager hustled over.

"Oh, good gracious. Garrison, what on earth happened?" he asked in a tone that oozed sympathy for his newest guest. Without sparing so much as a glance at Jen, who'd taken the brunt of Garrison's assault, he said, "Let's get you cleaned up." Snapping his fingers for emphasis, Borman barked, "Sammy! Towels!"

"Look at my clothes!" Garrison pulled his damp shirt away from his chest. "Look at this mess she made!"

Jen reeled back a step as Garrison shot her a look filled with smug satisfaction. "That's not…" she started to explain. When her protest drew a harsh glare from Mr. Borman, she swallowed the rest. The manager clearly had no interest in anything she had to say.

Sammy appeared with a handful of fluffy white bar towels, but Garrison only shoved the employee aside when the bartender tried to hand one to him. "Get away from me. You'll only make it worse."

As Garrison continued to fuss, Ralph hurried to his partner's side. "Garrison! What in the world?" he asked, his face a mask of concern.

"She did it."

Jen wondered if Garrison intended to get her fired when he pointed a finger at her. Unable to believe what she was hearing, she listened as the man she'd shown nothing but kindness continued his tirade.

"This place needs to hire a better class of waitress," he said somehow managing to look both pitiful and indignant at the same time. "She was all over me. Gah! She's old enough to be my mother. When I wouldn't play ball, she said she was gonna get me a drink. She did that all right. She threw it right in my face." Adding insult to injury, Garrison flicked a slice of ginger off his shoulder. With a wet plop, it landed on the toe of Jen's shoe.

In comparison to his partner's whine, Ralph's voice was a steel-edged sword. His chest puffed out, he crowded the casino manager. "This is the way you let your staff treat important customers? I expect better of any establishment that wants my business."

"As you should," Mr. Borman hurried to

agree. "Garrison, Ralph, on behalf of the River Delta, let me offer my sincerest of apologies. We'll make this up to you, I promise. We'll comp your entire stay. Garrison, we'll also replace your suit. I'll have our tailor come to your suite first thing in the morning."

Jen's mouth gaped open at the lengths Borman was going before he even heard her side of the story. Like a toddler in a foul mood, Garrison had thrown a temper tantrum. That was the plain truth of the matter. Now, instead of being punished, he was getting a free stay and a new suit? Didn't anyone care that Garrison had ruined her uniform? Or that remnants of his drink dripped from her hair?

"And her?"

Jen froze beneath Ralph's withering glare.

"I can assure you, the River Delta treats all its customers with the utmost respect. We won't tolerate an employee who fails to live up to our standards." With another snap of his fingers, Mr. Borman signaled again.

Unaware that Kurt had left his post at the velvet rope and taken a position behind her, Jen flinched when the big man's hand grasped her upper arm.

"Let's go." His face set in impassive lines, Kurt propelled her forward as if she was one of the riffraff he regularly barred from the high roller section.

"But I—" she started to protest. Her mind raced. She'd spent months serving watered-down drinks and emptying ashtrays on the main floor of the casino. Smiling whenever one of those cheapskate customers rewarded all her hard work with a quarter or fifty cents. All for the chance to get here, to The Deluxe Room. Where whales on a winning streak didn't think twice about tossing a hundred-dollar chip on her tray. Now, after only six weeks of hobnobbing with the rich and famous, she was getting the axe? She hadn't done a single thing wrong. Borman couldn't—he wasn't actually firing her, was he?

The casino manager continued. "Kurt, you'll see that she turns in her uniform and employee ID before you escort her off the property?"

Apparently, that's exactly what's happening. Her heart sank.

"Yes, sir." When disbelief kept Jen's feet rooted to the floor, Kurt's grip on her arm tightened. "C'mon," he said in a gruff voice. "Let's go."

Hoping against hope that if she played along, she'd still have a chance to save her job, Jen let herself be led from the room. But as soon as they'd rounded a corner and couldn't be seen by anyone on the other side of the velvet ropes, she stopped dead in her tracks.

"Let go of me," she hissed through gritted teeth. Card sharks and cheats deserved to be paraded across the casino floor. Not her. She hadn't done anything wrong.

The man she'd considered a friend until five minutes earlier relinquished his grip. Holding her head high, she fell into step beside him. "What happens next?" she asked as she rubbed her arm, where bruises were already starting to form.

"I'll take you back to the employee lounge. You'll change into your street clothes. Take any personal items from your locker and hand me the key. Turn over your ID, too. They'll mail your final check to you in a week or so."

"Just like that?" Shock and indignation swelled in her chest. "I don't even get a chance to defend myself?" *Impossible!* There had to be a way out of this mess that didn't end up with her looking for a new job. "You know I didn't dump a drink on that man. He's an oaf, but I wouldn't do that. Not ever. When Mr. Borman reviews the security tapes, he'll see that I'm telling the truth." Hidden cameras monitored customers' every move from the moment they entered the casino until they were safely tucked away in their hotel rooms upstairs or left the property. The Deluxe Room was no exception.

"Doesn't matter," Kurt muttered. "You've been around long enough to know the way things work." He glanced down at her. "You gotta keep the big spenders happy. That's Rule Number One."

Hadn't she been doing exactly that?

"What are the odds that they'll take me back once Borman realizes I'm telling the truth?" she asked softly.

Her stomach sank when Kurt's massive head moved from side to side. "I hate be the one to break it to you, but that ain't never gonna happen. Borman won't risk letting you work anywhere in the River Delta. Not where them *Preservation* boys could run into you." Kurt shuddered. His voice dropped even lower. "They're not the only ones, either. That Peterman kid and his cronies watched the whole thing go down. They find out you're still working here after this, they'll all take their business elsewhere."

So that was it. Starting over at another casino wouldn't be easy, but what choice did she have? It wasn't like she could afford to be out of work. She didn't have some cushy inheritance to fall back on. Heck. She didn't even have a husband who'd share the bills and warm her bed. No, if she wanted to keep a roof over her head and put food on her table, she'd have to find another job, and fast. Which, all things considered, shouldn't be too hard. Dozens of casinos crowded Biloxi's strip of beachfront property. She tipped her head toward Kurt's.

"You know the bouncer over at the Horseshoe, don't you? Are they hiring?" The Horseshoe wasn't nearly as grand as the River Delta, but considering the state of her nearly empty checking account, she couldn't afford to be too picky. She'd even schlep drinks on the main floor again if it meant getting her foot in the door.

"Forget about it," Kurt's low rumble continued. "Once word gets out that the Delta let you go, none of the other casinos in Biloxi will hire you. They all stick together."

Thirty minutes later, Jen stood in the alley outside the employee entrance and watched as the River Delta's door swung shut.

"Crap," she whispered.

Despite temperatures in the seventies, she folded her arms across her ample chest to ward off a sudden chill. Landing that job in The Deluxe Room had been her ticket to happiness. High rollers were notoriously big tippers, and with the extra money she'd have earned rubbing elbows with the exclusive clientele, she'd hoped to finally get that white picket fence on her own.

It was time, wasn't it? Time to put down roots.

But if Kurt was telling the truth—and he had no reason to lie—that wasn't going to happen. Not here. Probably not in Mississippi at all. No, the time had come for her to pull up stakes and move on. Again.

She shoved one hand into the pocket of her jeans. Her checkbook balance was nearly in the red, and the wad of tips she'd taken from her uniform pocket would have to see her through until the River Delta sent her final check. At least she wouldn't have to pay rent. Hers was due at the end of the week, but there was no point in paying it if she wasn't sticking around.

The question was, where would she go next? Vegas? She pulled out her phone, intending to see how long it would take her to get there. A red dot on one of the icons alerted her to a missed call. Her pulse quickened.

Had Borman realized his mistake? Was he giving her back her job?

Bright hope surged through her as she switched to voice mail. A sense of utter defeat quickly dashed her dreams when the only incoming call was from her sister. Without even bothering to listen to it, Jen deleted the message. A moment later, she studied the route to Las Vegas while she tried to figure out if the money in her pocket would get her there.

Five

Diane

"It can't be time to get up, can it?"

Diane Sommer Keenan reluctantly opened her eyes. Enough light seeped from behind the window curtains to make the darkness retreat into the corners of the room. Without stirring, she stretched one arm behind her and felt for her husband's lean form. She frowned when her fingers found only cold, empty space. Had Tim gone for a morning run without waking her? How late was it anyway?

Hauling her own softly padded body up on one elbow, she grabbed the cell phone that lay facedown on the off-white nightstand. The time appeared above the family photo she'd chosen as her screen saver.

Six thirty.

So much for squeezing in a morning workout, she sighed. She'd barely have time to shower and dress and get to work before the eight o'clock staff meeting. She flung back the covers and swung her legs over the side of the bed.

"Ee-yow!"

One of her feet struck the edge of a small step stool with an unexpected whap. Pulling the foot onto her lap, she rubbed her poor heel. Now completely wide awake, she swept a gaze over the room and told herself to stop complaining. A bruised heel was a small price to pay for finally having the bedroom of her dreams, wasn't it?

When she and Tim had first married, he'd promised to replace their secondhand bedroom furniture within a year or so. That was before they'd both realized that building a dental practice didn't happen overnight. Then, thanks to things like air conditioners that broke down in the middle of sweltering Florida summers, as well as the expected—and unexpected—expenses of raising two kids, he'd never moved new furniture to the top of his priority list. Instead, they'd hauled the scarred dresser and the bed frame they'd had to prop up on stacks of books from their first apartment to their first house and, finally, here to Parkland Estates, where they'd lived long enough for David to start kinder-garten and finish high school.

Earlier this year, though, she'd landed a big promotion at Ybor City Accountants. In addition to a window office, her compensation package had included a sizable bonus. Though Tim had wanted to sock the money away for a rainy day or that dream vacation to France he was always talking about, she'd had other ideas. They'd argued, but with a stubborn determination, she'd stuck to her guns. A short time later, the broken-down bed frame sat at the curb while a couple of burly delivery drivers toted their new furniture up the curving staircase. To complement the ivory-colored dresser with its matching head-board, nightstands and chest of drawers, she'd chosen off-white curtains adorned with broad leaves. A custom-made abaca rug completed the look and turned their bedroom into a tropical oasis.

She sighed happily. So what if Tim still complained that he missed their old, saggy mattress. He'd get used to the new one. Just like she'd get used to using a step stool to climb in and out of the taller bed each day. Which she needed to do right now. As much as she enjoyed the new décor, if she wanted to keep that window office or better still, move into one on Executive Row, she'd have to get moving.

Five minutes later her slippers made soft, swishing noises on the gleaming hardwood floors of the two-story house in one of Tampa's most exclusive neighborhoods. As she headed down the first-floor hall to the spacious kitchen, she offered up a prayer that she could snag a cup of coffee and escape back upstairs to shower and dress before Tim returned from his run. She wasn't in the mood to deal with the guilt her husband of twenty-three years would heap upon her for skipping yet another workout—even if it was his own fault for not waking her. Lately, his litany of a million and one ways she'd failed to live up to his expectations had no end.

She reached the doorway to the kitchen and peeked inside. So much for the power of prayer. If God had even heard hers this morning, he'd answered with a big, fat "No."

Still wearing his running shorts and a sweat-streaked T-shirt, Tim hummed snatches from various show tunes as he stood at the kitchen stove, expertly flipping a piece of French toast on the griddle. In the breakfast nook that over-looked a picture-perfect backyard, glasses of milk, a pitcher of freshly squeezed orange juice and individual carafes of maple syrup crowded the table he'd set for three. She blinked wearily.

"What's all this?" she whispered. Tim only

made French toast for their daughter on game days, and this wasn't one of them. She was sure of it. She'd checked the calendar before she logged off last night. Or, to be more precise, this morning. She hadn't closed the Mason file until two.

She must have spoken louder than she'd intended because Tim swung toward her, spatula in hand.

"Remember the scrimmage that got postponed against Robinson last week? It's been rescheduled for today. Four o'clock. Caitlyn's the starting goalie."

"Oh, shoot." Diane pressed her lips into a dissatisfied frown. She'd wanted to be there to cheer their daughter on when Caitlyn made her first start in front of the net. Especially since, as the only sophomore on Plant High's varsity team, Caitlyn would probably ride the bench most of the season. "I hate to miss that."

As soon as he heard what she'd said, Tim stopped humming. His movements slowed. With exaggerated care, he turned a stiff back to her and set the spatula on the spoon rest. "You haven't been to a single one of Cat's scrimmages yet this season," he said, using the nickname he knew she detested. "Can't you at least take a few hours off to watch this game?"

She did her best to ignore the accusation in her husband's tone. It was too early to argue. Besides, he had her at a distinct disadvantage. He'd been up for hours, while she hadn't even had her first cup of coffee. A cup she desperately needed, not that he cared.

"You know it's more than that," she insisted. "With traffic, it would take me at least a half hour to get from the office to the high school. Then, two hours watching warm-ups and the game itself. Another half hour back to the office. By then, I might as well have taken the whole day off."

"Would it kill you to do that?"

Diane bristled at the accusation in Tim's voice. "Easy for you to say." The words flew out of her mouth before she could stop them. "You didn't spend ten years at home with the children or have to take an entry-level position when you went back to work. You haven't spent your entire career playing catch-up."

Immediately, she felt her face heat. It was a tired, old argument, one that didn't bear repeating. But why didn't her husband understand that he'd never dealt with the same kind of demands she faced? He'd opened his dental office shortly after they'd gotten married. For twenty-three years, weather permitting, he'd walked to work, where he'd flicked on the lights at eight each morning and shut them off at five each night. Except for tending to the occasional broken tooth, he didn't even work weekends. Two years ago, he started thinking about his eventual retirement and had brought an eager young dentist into the practice. Within six months, the two of them had divided the workload, giving Tim more free time than he knew what to do with. Since then his complaints about her busy schedule had grown more and more pointed.

She, on the other hand, had never worked harder or had more to lose than she did right now. Thirteen years of hard work and dedication had finally put her in line for a vice presidency. She'd either make it or the next time the company thinned the ranks of middle management, she'd be on the chopping block. Not that she'd ever wanted to work for a big corporation. That had been Tim's idea. Running her own small firm had been her goal. But faced with the very real possibility of one day having two kids in college, she'd traded her dreams in on a steady paycheck. One they'd need once Caitlyn started college in a few years. Which was why, much as she might want to, she absolutely could not play hooky to watch their daughter's preseason scrimmage.

LEIGH DUNCAN

Scrimmage—it wasn't even a real game. She'd already entered the twelve official matches into her calendar and planned to be in the stands for every one of them. Trouble was, Tim expected her to attend the scrimmages and daily practices, too. Then there was the club team Caitlyn played on during the "off" season. And the travel team Caitlyn's coach had oh-so-strongly suggested their daughter join. That one held matches all over the state, which meant either she or Tim was forced to devote at least one weekend day to driving back and forth from their home in Tampa to places as far away as Tallahassee and Miami. How was she supposed to do all that and excel at her job, too?

Trying to soothe things over between them, she said, "Everything in here smells so good. I hope Caitlyn's hungry."

The half smile that had first attracted her to Tim formed on his lips. "Our daughter is always hungry."

Glad they'd apparently left the argument behind, Diane took a step toward the coffeepot. "I wish I had time to join you, but I have to get ready for work."

"You missed dinner last night. You're not even going to eat breakfast with us?" Tim looked up from the slice of bread he'd been pushing

100

around in a bowl of egg batter. Irritation creased his brow.

"I told you last night I have a staff meeting at eight today. I should already be on the road." They'd chosen the house in Parkland Estates, in part, for its shady streets and close-knit community but also for the ease of getting downtown in a matter of minutes. In the time they'd lived here, though, the population of Florida's third-largest city had swelled to nearly three million. The additional traffic had added twenty minutes to her commute. "I'm going to be late as it is."

"Par for the course," Tim said with an angry jerk of one shoulder.

"You know this is one of the busiest times of the year for me," she said, slowly eyeing the coffeepot and wishing a cup would magically appear in her hand. In the weeks leading up to October fifteenth, every client who'd asked for an extension on their taxes last April had to file their returns. There were steep penalties for anyone who missed that deadline. As a result, everyone at Ybor City Accountants was working overtime. But Tim already knew that. It was another verse in a song she'd grown tired of singing.

"I thought, now that you're in management, your staff would take care of those kinds of things." Picking up the spatula, Tim added another perfectly browned piece of eggy toast to the serving platter.

"I do. And they have. But I'm the one who has to sign the papers that get filed with the IRS. I won't do that until I'm sure the government is getting every penny owed them and not a penny more." When Tim only grunted, she rushed to defend her position. "It's a good thing, too. Last night, I discovered an error in the Mason file."

She'd spent another hour fixing the problem after she realized one of her junior accountants had failed to include Schedule E's in the important client's return. That kind of sloppiness couldn't be tolerated. She planned to address it in today's staff meeting.

Her need for coffee growing more desperate by the minute, she started across the spacious kitchen just as Tim lifted the platter and headed for the breakfast nook. In the early years of their marriage, they would have made a game of the near collision. Tim might have wrapped one arm around her waist and spun her on her way with the grace of a dancer in one of the musicals he loved so much. She might have curtsied and waved an invisible fan through the air like any good Southern belle would. But not today. Today, she fumed silently when Tim only stood as still as a carved wooden statue until she moved past him. Not for the first time she asked when all the fun had gone out of their marriage. Would they ever get it back? Or was this the way life would continue for two people who'd spent nearly a quarter of a century together?

"Cat will be disappointed if you don't make it to her game."

"It's a scrimmage," she corrected. "Not a *real* game," she added for emphasis.

In the middle of pouring her coffee, she flinched when a loud thunk resounded through the kitchen as Tim let the platter fall the last inch or two onto the table. She gripped the handle of the coffee carafe and fought for control, but coffee still sloshed over the rim of her cup. A long-suffering sigh passed through her lips. She didn't want to get into a fight, but that's all she and Tim seemed to do lately.

"I. Can't," she said, hanging on to a civil tone for all that it was worth. Aware that Tim stood watching her with disapproval written all over his face, she offered an olive branch. "Look, I know I've been putting in a lot of overtime, but things should quiet down soon."

"Like I haven't heard that before." Tim's voice dripped sarcasm. "You said you'd take time off after you landed this latest promotion.

We were supposed to go to Cancun for our anniversary. That didn't happen. If anything, you're spending more time at the office than ever."

Diane studied her coffee. Even she had to admit that her husband had a point. She'd postponed the cruise until she got a handle on her new responsibilities at work, but she'd been operating in crisis mode instead of taking charge. "You're right. I know you're right," she admitted, hoping that would put an end to today's argument. But Tim had apparently worked up a head of steam, and he wasn't ready to let her off the hook with a simple apology.

"When you do come home," he continued as if she hadn't just agreed with him, "you hole up with your laptop and work way past bedtime. You haven't sat down and eaten dinner with us all week, and that's not fair to Cat or me. She misses you." Finally over his rant, he softly added, "I do, too."

Tears welled in her eyes. She wasn't one of those women who were so driven they thought of nothing but their careers. She missed spending time with her family, too. But she needed to make Tim understand the pressure she'd been under. Hoping for a little sympathy, she said, "It's just that, frankly, I've been a bit overwhelmed. And now, with the deadline for filing all those returns right around the corner, things have been extra crazy."

When a muscle in her husband's jaw twitched, she hurried to assure him, "But I'll try harder to get a better handle on my work schedule. To spend more time with you and Caitlyn. As a family."

"So you'll come to today's game?" Tim asked.

She shook her head. "Today's schedule is already set in concrete. I can't do anything about that." And the longer they argued, the longer she'd have to work tonight. "But I will make it to her next game. I promise."

Tim held up his palms in a gesture of surrender. "I—we need you to make us a priority in your life. If you don't, I'll…"

Diane's head rose. "If I don't, you'll do what exactly?"

"I don't know how much longer we can go on like this." Having said his piece, Tim headed upstairs to wake their daughter for school.

Standing at the counter, Diane deliberately stirred an extra spoonful of sugar into her coffee. Her husband's parting words had sounded an awful lot like some kind of threat. Surely, he wouldn't leave, wouldn't end their marriage over something as minor as a preseason scrimmage. She shook her head.

Tim was making too much out of one missed soccer game, but he was right about one thing—she needed to make some changes. For far too long now, she'd been reactive rather than proactive at work. She'd been running around putting out fires when she needed to force her staff to take responsibility for their own assignments. The Mason case that had kept her up last night was a prime example. She shouldn't have corrected that return herself. Once she found the error, she should have written "Fix this!" on a stickie and handed the file back to a junior accountant.

She lingered for several long seconds while she considered the changes she needed and wanted to make. Like the coach in her weight loss group said, she wouldn't be able to fix things overnight, but she could make a few steps in the right direction. Starting today. Once she had a better handle on where she wanted to go and how to get there, she carried her coffee upstairs, where she made a special point of taking a few minutes to wish Caitlyn success on the field later today.

An hour later, Diane was pulling into the Ybor City Accountants' massive parking garage when her sister's name appeared on the screen of her cell phone. With her promise to make more time for family still at the forefront of her mind, she took the call, although she did warn Amy that she only had a minute to talk.

"No problem," Amy assured her. "I'm really just checking to see if you're available to talk tonight. You, me, Belle and Kim? Kim's going to try and get Jen, but you know how that goes."

"You can say that again," Diane whispered. Their youngest cousin had always been a bit of a free spirit. "When?" she asked.

"Seven thirty."

Would she make it home in time for the call? She'd promised Tim she'd try to leave work in time for dinner. Diane mulled over the possibility for another few seconds before she said, "Sounds good. I'll get Caitlyn to pop in for a minute or two." Her daughter would love being included in the group.

"How is my favorite niece?" Amy asked.

"She's your only niece, so she has to be your favorite," Diane teased. "She's fine. Growing up way too fast. I'll fill you all in when we talk this evening." She pulled into a parking spot that had been reserved just for her and tamped down the pride that swelled at seeing her nameplate on the wall.

"Gotta go," she said, slipping the car into park and shutting off the engine. After she and

Amy said their goodbyes, she took a moment to organize her thoughts. In order to make it home on time, she needed to take charge of her day. "Starting today, I'll stop running from crisis to crisis," she told herself firmly. "Starting today, I'll be the one in control."

With renewed confidence, she walked into the headquarters building and took the elevator to the tenth floor, where her window office overlooked beautiful downtown Tampa. The moment she stepped out of the elevator, however, an unfamiliar mix of conversation and complaints enveloped her like clouds in an approaching storm. Throughout the large, open room, people leaned over the chest-high dividers that separated their work space from the next and chatted with their neighbors. Here and there, some of the staff remained at their desks, where they sat in front of black monitors while they ineffectively struck random keys on their keyboards. Diane knew of only one thing that would bring business to a standstill days before tax deadline. She went in search of answers.

"How long has the server been down?" she asked an admin who appeared to be on her way to refill her coffee cup. "Has anyone called the help desk?"

"It's been like this since I got here," the

woman replied in a tone that was far too nonchalant for Diane's taste. She moved on without addressing the second question.

"Geez," Diane swore softly. Computers were critical to the work they did. Without them, business had ground to a halt. As much as she'd resolved not to waste another minute putting out someone else's fire, this was one crisis that had to be dealt with, and quickly. She singled out one of her staff and directed the young accountant to inform the IT department of computer problems on the tenth floor. Then, repeating her affirmation under her breath, she squared her shoulders and resumed her trek toward her office. She'd barely taken three steps before another of her staff approached her with a different urgent matter. Try as she might, she couldn't gain any traction, and she fell into her usual rut of dealing with one problem after another for the rest of the day.

Rays of afternoon sunlight glinted off the rooftops of nearby office buildings by the time Diane finally settled into the chair behind her desk. She pulled a stack of papers from her briefcase and began reviewing one of her current projects. She'd barely made any headway with it when her phone chimed with her daughter's familiar ring. Shocked at how quickly another day had gotten away from her, Diane took the call.

"Hey, sweetheart," she said as she softly closed her office door. "How was the scrimmage?"

"You won't believe it, Mom!" her daughter gushed. "I got a save! Coach said she's planning to use me more in the regular season."

"Wow, sweetie! That's wonderful!" Caitlyn's excitement was palpable, and Diane fought down a twinge of remorse over not being on the sidelines when her daughter prevented the other team from scoring. "I'm so proud of you."

"Can we have tacos tonight to celebrate?"

Smiling, Diane leaned back in her chair. Her spicy chicken tacos were Caitlyn's absolute favorite. The urge to tell her daughter she'd hurry home to fix them surged through her. One look at the pile of papers in her inbox, though, forced her to take a more pragmatic approach. Slowly, she shook her head. "I'm sorry. I'll need a rain check on dinner tonight." Not only was she not going to make it home in time to cook supper, she'd be lucky if she pulled into the garage before Caitlyn went to bed.

"Oh, that's okay," Caitlyn said. "I know you're busy."

Unable to miss the disappointment in her daughter's voice, Diane ran her fingers through her hair. Okay, today hadn't turned out exactly as she'd planned, but she'd meant it when she said she'd make more time for family. There was no time like the present to make that happen. "How about Saturday instead?" she suggested. "Tacos and all the fixin's. You can even have a friend or two over."

"Really?"

"Absolutely," Diane promised. With the tax deadline a matter of days away, she'd planned to keep her nose to the grindstone for another week, but her daughter's happiness was every bit as important, wasn't it? "We'll ask Daddy to fire up the grill and make street corn, too." If her daughter loved anything more than tacos, it was corn on the cob drenched in spices and doused with cheese and Mexican crema.

"Oh, wow! That'd be awesome. I'll see if Sarah and Marty can come. I'll call them right now. Bye, Mom."

Bolstered by her daughter's reaction, Diane continued to smile as she withdrew the bottom item from her inbox and set about answering a query from one of the company's senior partners.

She was still working on the task when her alarm pinged with a reminder about the call with Amy. Diane tapped her pencil on the table. Finally, resisting the temptation to skip the family meeting, she searched through her email for the link to the video chat. While she waited for the connection to go through, she crossed her fingers. She hoped the others wouldn't mind too much when she had to bug out, but she couldn't afford to talk for long. As it was, Tim was already upset with her. Another late night wasn't going to help matters, and the longer she stayed on the phone with her sister and her cousins, the later it'd be when she finally got home.

Six

Amy

Amy grinned at the adorable twin kittens painted on the antique wall clock she'd hung in the kitchen of the small, two-bedroom house situated behind Sweet Cakes. She'd salvaged the clock, like many of the furnishings in her home, from the bargain bin at Goodwill. Seeing it never failed to make her smile, though in this case, it only took one look at the paws that counted off the minutes and hours to tell her she was running late.

Picking up her pace, she scooped the bread dough off the flour-covered counter and shaped it into a ball, which she slid into the bottom of a bowl that held a scant tablespoon of oil. Deftly, she turned the round shape over to bring a now glistening surface to the top. After untying her apron, she hung it on a nearby rack before she returned to the counter.

She poked at the ball with one finger. Too much yeast would make the bread rise too quickly, resulting in big, gaping holes in the finished product. Too little, and it'd turn out dense and tasteless. Her lips pursed. Judging from how quickly the dough swelled to fill the slight indentation, she suspected the new, gluten-free recipe wouldn't turn out right. She cupped her chin. Bread making was a balancing act, and finding the right ratio of ingredients usually involved lots of experimentation. But that was half the fun, wasn't it?

"If I cut the yeast in half for the next batch, will I need to reduce the psyllium as well?" She directed her question to Socks, the black-and-white cat who perched on the windowsill overlooking her herb garden.

When Socks gave only a languid stretch in reply, Amy washed and dried her hands at the white porcelain sink before she covered the bowl with a tea towel and slid it into the proofing oven. Her task finished for now, she moved to the small, built-in desk at the far end of the kitchen counter. She sat, powered up her laptop and kicked off the video chat. Her own image appeared on the screen, and she laughed. Her hair was its usual end-of-the-day mess. Swiping a streak of flour from one cheek and tucking a few loose tendrils of dark hair behind her ears, she did as much damage control as she could without a comb or a brush. The computer monitor blinked while she was still weighing the possibility of freeing the rest of her hair from the chignon she wore whenever she worked in the kitchen. A second later, Kim's face appeared in a box beside hers on the screen.

"Hey," Amy said. "How's it going?" Not that she needed to ask. Like a soufflé that had collapsed the moment it was taken from the oven, her cousin had carried a defeated air about her ever since her marriage had fallen apart. Judging from the half-inch growth of salt-and-pepper at the roots of Kim's blond hair and the frayed collar of her T-shirt, things hadn't improved.

"About the same as always." Kim tightened her ponytail and straightened like anyone would when they didn't exactly love seeing their own image. "How 'bout yourself?"

"Good," she said, deliberately not mentioning the reason for her call. She had decided to save that until the others logged on. "The bakery's doing well. We have more orders than we can fill. If this keeps up, I'll have to bring on more part-time help." She paused long enough to give Diane a quick wave when she saw her sister enter the chat. "Is Jen coming?" she asked, returning to her conversation with Kim.

"I doubt it. I left a message on her cell phone, but I haven't heard back from her."

Just as well, Amy thought. For someone who didn't come around much, Jen never hesitated to wade into any conversation and voice her own opinion. Usually a strong one. Talking about Aunt Margaret and the inn would be hard enough without throwing their prickliest cousin into the mix.

"Where is she these days?" Seated behind a wide desk and still dressed for work, Diane slipped on a pair of glasses.

"In Biloxi," Kim answered. "She's been working as a cocktail waitress at one of the casinos for about six months now."

"Six months? That's got to be some kind of record, doesn't it? Must be a new man in her life," Diane mused.

Amy inhaled sharply. Although none of them would mistakenly describe Jen as settled and stable, their cousin wasn't a tramp, either.

"Nope. She hasn't been involved with anyone for a while now," Kim said, coming to her sister's defense, though Jen herself readily admitted that she hadn't had the best of luck with relationships. "I think she just likes it there. She said she's saving up to buy a place of her own."

"Good for her," Diane said.

When Diane looked like she might loose another pointed barb, Amy groaned. Her sister and Kim might not know it yet, but it was important that they work together tonight. Something that would be harder to do if they got sidetracked into a discussion of each other's shortcomings.

Butting in with a question guaranteed to put a halt to the snide comments, she asked, "Are you still at the office, Diane?" Her sister usually made a point of getting home in time to have dinner with Caitlyn and Tim, but tonight she sat with her back to a window overlooking the city. Behind her, the last rays of the setting sun bounced off tall buildings.

Diane ran her fingers through hair quite a bit shorter than her usual chin-length bob. "The October tax deadline is right around the corner. That means I'm working longer hours than I like." Adjusting her glasses until they hid the dark shadows under her eyes, she tapped a thick stack of folders on her desk. "I have to go through all these before I leave here, so I can only visit for a few minutes. Are we just catching up, or did you have something specific to discuss, Amy?"

Amy winced as Diane gazed directly into the camera. She hadn't wanted to get into this quite yet. Sharing the news about Aunt Margaret's recent fall—and Scott's reaction to it—was going to be hard enough to do once. She dreaded the thought of repeating herself. "I was kind of waiting for Belle," she hedged.

"Who is late. As usual," Diane remarked dryly.

Amy stared at her sister. Diane wasn't usually mean-spirited, but something sure had her panties in a twist. Was work getting to her? Hoping to find a safer topic, Amy turned to Kim. Their cousin had been in the market for a new job. "What are you up to these days? Any nibbles on the job front?"

Kim gave her head a sad, slow shake. "Still pounding the pavement. I'm waiting to hear back from a couple of places. Meantime, I'm working temp jobs to tide me over."

"Don't give up. Anyone with any brains at all would be glad to have you." Diane's glasses slid down her nose. She peered over the dark frames that made her look even more serious than normal. "How are your accounting skills? If they're any good, I'll hire you," she offered.

Kim's nose scrunched. "It's not really my forte. I was an admin at Connors Industrial."

"If you need something until you find the right position, I can use you at the bakery part-time," Amy added. She hadn't actually planned to hire someone just yet, but she'd make an exception for her cousin. After all, what was family for if not to help each other out?

Kim's expression softened the tiniest bit. "Thanks. I might just take you up on that if something doesn't open up here soon."

"Hold on a sec, guys." Amy held up a finger as the images on her monitor flickered. "I think Belle's trying to join us." The screen blinked again.

"Ooooh, sorry I'm late. Hi, everyone!"

A voice recognized by millions around the globe drifted up from Amy's speakers. Instead of their cousin's image, though, only Belle's name appeared in her box on the screen.

"Belle, we can't see you," Amy coached. Catching Diane's eye in the monitor, she grinned. No matter how often they video-chatted with Belle, the routine never varied. Their famous cousin might be a superstar, but she'd never been computer-savvy. "Make sure you click the little video camera icon at the bottom of your screen."

"Where?"

"On the lower left," Amy directed patiently.

"The one with the red line through it? Got it."
Belle's face finally appeared. Looking quite
proud of herself, she pumped her fist. "Yay!"

Amy aimed a warm smile at the newest
arrival. From the red hair that spilled in gentle
curls out of a loose updo down to a pert nose and
babydoll lips, her cousin still looked and dressed
like a teenager. Okay, if she wanted to get picky,
Amy guessed she could point to the faint lines
around Belle's mouth and the tiny crow's-feet at
her eyes, but she wasn't that petty. She ran a
smoothing hand over her own face and wished
she looked half as good. "How in the world do
you manage to look so drop-dead gorgeous after
all these years?" she asked.

"Five hours a day at the gym and zero carbs,"
Belle answered simply. "What I wouldn't give
for a slice of pound cake." She rubbed her flat
stomach while her gaze shifted to the counter
behind Amy. "You're making something divine.
I just know it. What are you working on?"

Amy glanced over her shoulder at the tins of
flour and measuring cups strewn across the
granite. "I'm trying out a new buckwheat bread
recipe. Gluten-free." She bit her lower lip. In all
likelihood, this batch would fail to live up to
her standards. "It's still a work in progress."

Belle pressed a manicured hand to her chest.

"I'm dying here. Even your rejects would be fine for mere mortals like me. Next time I come to Florida, I have to stop in at Sweet Cakes for something decadent. I don't care if I gain ten pounds. It'll be worth every calorie."

Even though she knew Belle would eat one or two bites max before tossing the rest, the praise sent warmth coursing through Amy's chest. She sat back and watched as Belle complimented Diane's new hairstyle before drawing everyone's focus to Kim's dangly earrings.

"You simply have to tell me where you got those," Belle gushed. "I need to buy a pair just like them."

Another burst of warmth shot through Amy. Belle could stock a fair-size jewelry store with all the expensive earrings and necklaces she owned. The diamond studs she wore tonight were probably worth more than the engagement ring Amy had stashed away in her underwear drawer after her marriage broke up. Yet Belle had gone out of her way to mention Kim's inexpensive trinkets. That was something Amy had admired in her cousin ever since they were little kids—she had a knack for making those around her take pride in their own achievements and successes, no matter how minor and no matter how they compared to her own.

Once more checking the images on the screen, Amy noted that Diane had begun bouncing the tip of her ink pen on the top of her desk, a sure sign that her sister had grown impatient. Time was running out. If she wanted to discuss her aunt with the rest of them, she needed to get to it. She drew in a deep breath.

"I promised Diane we'd make this quick, so I'm going to just dive right in." Amy cleared her throat. Willing her cousin not to freak out, she said, "Belle, your mom fell this morning."

She waited for the collective gasp and wasn't disappointed. Barely a second passed before it rolled like a tidal wave out of her speakers. Also as expected, all three women started firing questions at her at once.

"She's all right," Amy soothed, doing her best to wipe the looks of concern from Diane and Kim's faces, to say nothing of the stricken one Belle wore. "I walked in just a few moments after it happened, and together, we were able to get her to her feet again and situated. Of course, she made me swear I wouldn't tell. But—" She rolled her eyes. "Some promises are made to be broken."

Belle, who'd paled, began to regain her composure. "You're sure she's all right?" she whispered hoarsely.

"Nothing broken. Nothing sprained," Amy

said with all the certainty she could muster. "I checked her out pretty good. Then I stuck around long enough to have a cup of coffee with her. A flock of monk parakeets has taken up temporary residence in the palm trees. We watched those for a while. I would have stayed longer, but she basically threw me out when she heard her guests stirring."

"That sounds like Mama." The wisp of a smile played around Belle's lips.

Now that she'd broken the ice, Amy plunged on with the rest of her news. "But here's the thing. I don't think this was the first time she's fallen."

"What makes you think that?" Kim wanted to know.

"I can't swear to it," Amy said, voicing her doubts aloud. "It's more of a feeling. But when I helped her to her feet, Aunt Margaret knew exactly what had to be done. How to pull a chair over. How I needed to support her. Without her telling me what to do, I couldn't have gotten her up off the floor on my own."

Belle moaned softly. "I had no idea things had gotten this bad. We talk every week, and she's never mentioned…" Her words trailed off as she clamped one hand over her mouth. Above it, her green eyes grew huge. "Do I need to hire round-the-clock care for her? Have we reached that point? Are we, are we running out of time?" Her voice thinned as it climbed an octave.

"Belle, I know you're worried," Diane said in a calm, soothing tone. "But let's let Amy finish before we jump to too many conclusions."

"Listen to Diane, Belle." Kim chimed in like only someone who'd grown up with the super-star would do. "Honey, I wish I were there with you right now to hold your hand. But hang on. If this were urgent, Amy would have gotten in touch with you right away."

"That is so true," Amy confirmed. "I would have told you when we spoke earlier today if I thought your mom was in immediate danger." She paused to let them all catch their breath. "There's absolutely no reason to think Aunt Margaret won't live another twenty years. Or longer. But I might not be around to help her if she falls again. And it's not fair to expect guests at the inn to take care of her. Not that there are a lot of those. So I was thinking we need to help her make a few changes." She'd thought of little else throughout the day and had come up with a list.

"What do you have in mind?" Diane reached for a slip of paper and began writing things down.

"First, we need to get rid of the throw rugs in the kitchen. We need to install grab bars in her bathroom. And I worry about those stairs off the deck. That railing is beyond rickety."

"Can't the handyman do all that?" Belle asked.

"Max?" Amy tapped her chin.

Kim cocked her head. "Who's Max? I thought Chester took care of odd jobs around the inn." The rail-thin gentleman in faded overalls had been a fixture around the place for as far back as any of them could remember.

"Chester sold his business and retired last year," Amy said, catching them up on some of the goings-on in Emerald Bay. "Max took over from him. He stops in at the bakery nearly every day. I'll ask him about the grab bars and the railings, but Aunt Margaret will probably fight having the work done."

"Tell her if she doesn't play nice, I'll come down there and do it myself," Belle threatened.

"Oh, no! I can't tell her that!" Amy threw up her hands. "Then she'd never let me talk to Max."

The joke sent a ripple of tension-relieving laughter through the group.

"Send the bills to me," Diane reminded. She balanced the inn's checkbook and filed both her aunt's and the inn's taxes.

"I'm not sure when I can get Max out there, but I'll work on it," Amy said slowly. "There's another problem, though…Scott."

"Scott?" A rare frown creased Belle's forehead. "What's he got to do with this?"

"You know he's been lobbying for Aunt Margaret to sell the inn ever since Mom died." Amy absently rubbed a knot in her chest. Five years had passed since the accident, and the loss still made her heart hurt.

"Running the inn is a lot of work," Belle said, considering. "It was different when Dad, Uncle Paul and Aunt Liz were alive. They shared the load together." Diane and Amy's dad had suffered his first stroke while Diane was in college. A second one had killed him a year later. Nearly a decade had passed since the heart attack that killed Belle's dad. "Personally, I think Mama should retire and enjoy her golden years, but she says the inn gives her a sense of purpose. Until she's ready to sell, Scott's going to have to hold his horses. Mama's going to stay right where she is." Belle shook her finger for emphasis.

"Here's the thing, though. She might not have a choice." When Belle's eyebrows climbed so high they disappeared into her bangs, Amy explained. "Scott has your mom's power of attorney." Though he hadn't said as much, she suspected Aunt Margaret had signed the paper in the aftermath of the accident. Amy brushed a sudden dampness from her eyes. Her mom and Aunt Margaret had been on their way back from church when their car went off the road. "With it, he can force your mom to sell."

Belle let out an ear-piercing screech. "Why on earth would she give him a POA?"

"I don't know, Belle. She was hurt pretty badly in the accident. Maybe she thought he was in the best position to make decisions for her. If, you know, she couldn't make them for herself." It had taken multiple surgeries and weeks in rehab before Aunt Margaret recovered enough to walk again. She still relied on a cane to get around.

"But why him?" Belle demanded. Her face flushed a bright red as her temper rose. "Why not me? I'm her daughter, for heaven's sake."

"Well, he is a lawyer," Kim pointed out.

"And he's only an hour away. You live in New York, and you're gone a lot," Diane added.

None of them dared mention how difficult it had been to get in touch with Belle the night of the accident. The pop star had been halfway through a monthlong overseas tour, performing each night in a different city, sometimes on different continents, when a police officer had knocked on Amy's front door. While word spread throughout Emerald Bay with the speed and force of a tsunami, it had been morning before someone tracked down Belle's itinerary, longer still for the news to reach her. Within hours, half the town had shown up at the hospital, but another two days slipped by before Belle stood at her mom's bedside. After that, she'd slept on a cot in Aunt Margaret's hospital room for an entire week. But with millions of dollars at stake, Belle couldn't abandon the tour completely. Once the doctors assured her that her mother was on the road to recovery, she'd hired private nurses for her mom and boarded a plane back to Europe.

"I get that, I guess," Belle admitted. "But you all have my number now." She'd made sure everyone in the family could reach her in case of an emergency. "My assistant knows to put your calls through. Day or night." She waited as one by one, her cousins nodded. Her hand on her chest, she took a few deep breaths before she said firmly, "Scott doesn't need a POA anymore. Leave that to me. I'll have Mama revoke it."

"That's between you and your mom and Scott," Amy said, preferring not to take sides against her brother. "Try not to get him riled up, though, okay? We might need his legal help later."

"Speaking of Scott, though, there is something else we need to think about." Diane tapped her pencil. "Even without a power of attorney, he could try to get legal guardianship over your mom, Belle."

"He wouldn't do that," Amy protested. Their brother had his own way of going about things, but his heart was in the right place.

"It happens far more often than you'd think. I've seen it myself several times." Diane made air quotes. "A well-meaning relative steps in to *help out* when an elderly relative gets sick. Once they control the purse strings, anything can happen. I'm not saying Scott's like that. Personally, I think our brother would rather cut off his right arm than cheat or harm Aunt Margaret. But if he thinks he's acting in her best interests…"

He could sell the inn, Amy finished silently. She folded her arms across her chest as if to ward off the thought. "Nothing's going to happen for a little while," she insisted. "Scott told me he'll be tied up with a big case for the next two weeks, at least."

"I'd have serious problems with him if Scott tried to railroad Mama into selling, but in a way, I have to agree with him," Belle said slowly. "Mama's too old to be running that place on her own. We need to convince her to sell the inn."

"But where would she go? What would she do?" Amy protested. Try as she might, she couldn't picture her Aunt Margaret idly sitting in a rocker for days on end.

"She'll come to New York and live with me," Belle said as if the matter wasn't up for discussion. "My condo is plenty big for the two of us."

Amy blinked. Did Belle honestly think uprooting her mother and moving her to New York was a good idea?

"Whoa. Time out!" Kim formed a *T* with her hands and held them up to her camera. "Let's not rush into something here. I'd feel better if one of us could scope out the entire situation before we jump to a conclusion that might not be entirely accurate."

"What's to figure out?" Belle asked. "Mama fell today. According to Amy, it's happened before, too. Sooner or later, she's going to get seriously hurt."

"Maybe. Maybe not." Kim leaned away from a kitchen table so rickety it shifted beneath the weight of her hands. "My neighbor down the hall had a few dizzy spells and was convinced she was dying. It turned out, she was taking too much blood-pressure medication. Maybe it's something as simple as that with Aunt Margaret."

"How would we know?" Diane asked.

"You live the closest to her. Can you check into that?"

Amy flinched when Belle's focus landed on her. She scooted her chair away from the screen. "Not me," she protested. "Aunt Margaret would be furious if I started poking around in her medicine cabinet. I can't ask her doctor. Privacy laws would prevent Doc Spears from answering my questions." She might have better luck with Lydia, the doctor's nurse, but at what cost? The woman was the biggest gossip in Emerald Bay. Sooner or later, word would get back to Aunt Margaret and feathers would fly. She shook her head. Nope, that wasn't going to happen.

"It's not just her medication, though, is it?" Diane asked. "That might be part of the problem, but what else? We need to know why she fell and what can be done to make her environment safer for her."

"I've worked on a health and safety team before," Kim volunteered. "It's not all that difficult. Periodically, we'd go through the building from one end to the other, looking for potential problem areas and making recommendations to avoid injuries. Maybe we should go that route with Aunt Margaret before we try to convince her to sell her home and move to the other end of the country. We can always talk to her about selling if that doesn't work. Unless one of you has a burning desire to take over the inn?" She let the question hang.

When no one volunteered to upend the lives they'd built in order to run the inn that had been handed down from one generation to the next, Amy said, "There's just one problem. Who's going to do it?" She looked first to Belle. As Margaret's daughter, she had the most to win or lose.

Belle stared down at her lap. A fat tear dripped down her cheek. "I can't. Not right now. I'm committed to this next album. We've been in rehearsals for weeks. We were—we are—we're going to be in the recording studio for the next month at least. If it were a matter of life or death, you know I'd be there, but—but even you said it isn't, Amy."

Something in Belle's explanation hit a false note that made Amy consider pinning her cousin with a demanding look. She quickly changed her mind. Probing into whatever was going on with Belle would steer the conversation down a different path from the one it was on. For now, they needed to focus on Aunt Margaret. Putting the talk with Belle aside for the moment, she studied her sister next.

"Don't look at me," Diane protested. "If I take on one more project, Tim will divorce me for sure."

Ouch. Amy couldn't help but cringe at the quiet note of despair in her sister's voice. It sounded like Diane's marriage was going through a rough patch. Coupled with the stress that came with tax time, that ruled her sister out for the time being.

Amy worried her lower lip while the others looked expectantly at her. She couldn't blame them. She lived the closest to Aunt Margaret. It made sense that the rest of the family would expect her to look after their aunt. And, as much as she was able, she did. Didn't she stop by to say hello practically every day? But she couldn't promise to do more than that. Not and run her own business.

"I was telling Kim earlier that Sweet Cakes is booked solid for the next three months," she said with a mix of pride and regret. "We'll be hard-pressed to fill the orders we have on the books as it is. This is definitely not a time for me to go on vacation."

That left Kim, and Amy eyed her cousin. "What do you think, Kim? Feel like spending a couple of weeks in sunny Florida?"

Kim took a breath so deep her chest visibly shuddered. "Technically, I don't have to be in

Atlanta right now. Not until I get a job offer, anyway. My rent here is paid through the end of the month. The only hitch is my car. I'm not sure it'll make it that far."

"I'll spring for a plane ticket," Belle offered before anyone else could beat her to the punch.

"You won't need a car while you're here," Amy added. "The inn owns several vehicles. I'm sure you'd be welcome to use any of them."

"You'd stay at the inn. The way reservations have fallen off, there's plenty of room. There's a full kitchen, too," Diane added.

Amy grinned. "Don't forget the best part. We'd get to hang out together."

"I don't know if that's a plus or a minus," Kim said, but the laughter in her eyes told everyone she was teasing. She tilted her head to one side. "You're making this awfully tempting."

A blinding flash lit up Kim's apartment. Seconds later, thunder rumbled through the speakers. Five hundred miles away, Kim glanced at the storm that raged beyond her window. "Two weeks in the Sunshine State. Free room and kitchen privileges in exchange for spending time with my favorite aunt. I can't see a downside." She paused for a second while more thunder rumbled. "Can you?"

Seven

Margaret

"Oh, for pity's sake." Margaret stared down at the purple blotches that ran along the outside of her arm from her wrist clean up to her shoulder. That's what she got for following doctor's orders. After helping Liz nurse Paul back to health following his stroke, to say nothing of standing at her sister's side when they lowered his casket into the ground a year later, she'd been willing to do whatever it took to avoid her brother-in-law's fate. So when Dr. Spears had recommended taking a low-dose aspirin as a stroke preventative, she'd dutifully added it to her daily regimen.

She gave her arm another glance. She would've put up more of a fuss if he'd warned her that her skin would turn the color of a ripe eggplant whenever she so much as brushed against something.

Granted, the fall she'd taken yesterday had been a bit more than that, but her backside had borne the brunt of it. That *was* black-and-blue. And ugly, she added, remembering the startling dark patch she glimpsed in the mirror as she stepped out of the shower this morning. Her arm, though—she hadn't realized the bruises on her arm would be quite so dramatic. They were bad enough that she'd tried the trick her mother had used on them as children. But pressing a banana peel over the dark spots and holding it in place with plastic wrap hadn't helped. The awkward bandage had only kept her awake last night. This morning, the marks had stubbornly insisted on showing through the foundation and powder she'd plastered over them.

"Well, phooey."

There was nothing else to do for it. Indian summer had sent temperatures climbing into the mid-eighties, but she'd have to wear a sweater anyway and pretend old age was finally getting to her. It wasn't the best solution, but it was better than having everyone from the people at church to the guests at the inn get all up in her business. She shook her head. She could just hear them now.

"Oh, Margaret, what happened!" one of the women in the Ladies Auxiliary would loudly exclaim while she chopped celery for the tuna salad they'd serve at today's meeting.

"We wouldn't dream of going off all day and leaving you here alone. We'll stay right here and keep you company," Jenelle Brady would insist right before George made plans to spend the rest of their vacation somewhere that didn't involve babysitting a clumsy eighty-year-old.

Then there was Amy. Much as she'd needed and appreciated her niece's help yesterday, Margaret knew full well the girl wouldn't let the matter drop. That went double if Amy caught so much as a glimpse of the bruises. The next thing she knew, her niece would be saying something like, "That cane isn't enough anymore, Aunt Margaret. Let's get your walker out of the attic and use it from here on out."

Well, thank you very much, but no thank you. She'd been chained to that ugly torture device for three long months while she was recuperating from the accident. She absolutely didn't want or need it now.

Determined to live life on her own terms as long as she was able, she reached past the summer-weight shirts and dresses in the front of her closet. Leaning heavily on her cane, she slipped a lightweight sweater from a hanger in the back. Thanks to Florida's temperate climate, she rarely needed to wear it. She tried not to wince as the nubby material rubbed her tender skin when she slipped her arms into the sleeves. A little pain was a small price to pay for maintaining her independence.

Taking care not to trip over the runner in the hallway—only the good Lord knew how Amy would react if she took another fall—she moved past the bedrooms and her apartment's single bath. Irene and Eunice would arrive at nine to change the sheets in the occupied rooms and give the inn their usual, thorough cleaning. Nowadays, their duties also included dusting and vacuuming her rooms, and she wanted to make sure she'd picked up after herself last night. Truth be told, the fall had taken a little more out of her than she'd let on, and she'd fallen asleep on the couch, her Bible in her lap. Had she folded the afghan? Or left it crumpled on the couch like a used tissue?

At the threshold to the living room, she took in the eclectic mix of furnishings with a sweeping glance. Until recently, she'd redecorated the guest suites on a regular basis—replacing a worn sofa here, a table and side chair there, providing all new bed linens when the old ones showed the least bit of wear. Often, the older pieces had found new homes right here in the family quarters. Her current sofa was one of them. It had seemed shameful to toss a perfectly good fold-out couch because of a stained armrest. Likewise, one tiny rip in the upholstery hadn't been a good enough reason to toss an otherwise pretty Queen Anne chair.

Okay, she'd admit the green plaid on the sofa clashed with the chair's yellow print, but so what? The off-white blanket spread across the back of the couch did a good job of blending the colors together. Besides, living with mismatched furniture was just the way it was when your family owned an inn. She and her brother and sisters had grown up understanding that. If it had been good enough for them when they were alive, she certainly wasn't going to raise a fuss about it now that she was the only one left.

A smile crept onto her lips. Oh, the times the four of them had had growing up in this apartment. Closing her eyes, she could almost hear the whispers of long-ago conversations, the laughter the girls had shared at their brother's antics. Not that they'd spent a whole lot of time together in these rooms. When they weren't in school or helping their parents with the many chores expected of them, she and her siblings had walked along the trails that crisscrossed the property. They'd gone swimming in the ocean or, her personal favorite, searched for buried treasure using an old map her dad swore had belonged to none other than the infamous pirate Henry Jennings.

Whatever had become of that map? she wondered. Three generations of Dane children had tried to decipher its clues and find the chest that, according to legend, held the Queen of Spain's crown, along with a king's ransom in gold and emeralds. No one had ever found it, of course. She'd long ago realized that the map was a hoax. The fortune in gold and jewels, too. If it had been real, someone would've found it long before now.

Still, it might be nice to frame that scrap of leather and hang it in the foyer. Trouble was, she had no clue where the map had gotten off to. Maybe one of the grandchildren—Diane's or Kim's youngsters—had taken it home with them after that last reunion. Oh, she didn't think they'd meant to steal it. They were good kids, each and every one of them. No. Whoever had taken it no doubt planned to figure out where X marked the spot and lead the hunt for Jennings's treasure the following year.

But then Eric died, and the annual Dane Family Reunion just sort of fizzled.

Eric.

She crossed the room to a bookcase dotted with framed photos of her husband. Tracing one finger over the face of the love of her life, she swallowed tears. Oh, how she missed that man.

Try as she might to push them away, the memories of that fateful day nearly ten years ago came rushing at her with the intensity of a tidal wave. She and Eric had just seen the last of the family off following another successful reunion. As their daughter's limo headed down the driveway, her husband had said he was going to make sure the grandkids had picked up all the lawn darts, horseshoes and croquet mallets before he mowed the lawn. She had yawned and told him a nap was high on her priority list. Though she'd loved every minute of it, two weeks of nonstop entertaining, of trying to keep the entire family fed, of bonfires and sing-alongs late into the night had plumb tuckered her out. Eric had kissed her cheek and given her the smile that still got her motor humming. He'd told her to go in and lie down; he'd join her in a bit.

Instead, she'd stood where she was for a minute while she enjoyed the view. A cool breeze had ruffled the hem of her sundress. She'd savored the warmth of the sun on her face as Eric bent down to pick up a forgotten croquet wicket. At first, she'd thought he was fooling around when he keeled over completely. But when he lay on the grass without moving, she'd known. In that instant, her heart had broken.

"A massive heart attack," the doctor in the emergency room had told her after the paramedics had rushed them to the hospital. "Probably dead before he hit the ground."

Things had changed after Eric's death. She'd changed. Unable to face living in the cottage that had been her home ever since the day she and Eric said "I do," she'd moved into the family quarters in the main house. For months on end, she'd gone through the motions, an empty shell of her former self. She didn't know what she would have done without Liz those months. Her sister had been her rock, her strength, insisting she eat when she had no appetite, making her exercise when she had no energy, forcing her to deal with their guests as if the light hadn't gone out of her world.

It had worked, though. Little by little, she'd reawakened. The hurt never left, but eventually, she found out how to live with it, to appreciate the memories of all she and Eric had shared together. As the weeks turned into months and the months into a year, she started looking forward to the spring and the annual family get-together.

But Eric's death, coming as it had on the final day of the reunion, had cast a pall over the event. As the next Memorial Day approached, one family member after another discovered an unforeseen conflict in their schedules. In the end, only Belle, Diane and Kim had come, though Amy had popped in from time to time. The trio had stayed for only a few days before heading home. After that, she flat hadn't had the energy to organize another Dane Family Reunion.

Giving herself a little shake, she stepped away from the bookcase. The inn might not be operating at full capacity these days, but that didn't mean she could spend all day traveling down Memory Lane. Checking to make sure her sweater hid every vestige of her bruises, she headed for the inn's kitchen. Amy would be here soon with the bakery order. She wanted, needed, her niece to know she was all right.

Her cell phone rang just as she stepped from the family quarters into the main hall, where framed photos of native bushes and trees dotted the walls. She fumbled in the pocket of her slacks for the device and checked the caller ID. A mixture of love and apprehension spread through her the moment she saw a familiar name on the screen. Hurriedly, she pressed the phone to her ear. "Kimberly! What a surprise."

"It's so good to hear your voice, Aunt Margaret. How's life been treating you?"

"Good," she lied. She tugged the sleeve of her sweater a little lower. "How's life in Hot 'Lanta?" With no ocean breezes to cool it, the landlocked city baked beneath the sun.

"Miserable, as usual. That's actually why I'm calling. I need a little vacay. I thought I'd head to the beach for a couple of weeks. I know it's the start of the busy season, but do you have any rooms available?"

A snort of laughter escaped Margaret's mouth. Reservations had shrunk so much of late that the rooms upstairs sat vacant and unused for months on end. A fact Kim knew full well. "You can pretty much have your pick of the suites on the second floor."

Though the prospect of seeing her niece again send a bolt of joy arcing through her, the timing seemed suspicious. Had Amy broken her promise and spilled the beans? "You haven't by any chance spoken with your cousin Amy, have you?" Margaret held her breath.

"As a matter of fact, she called me while I was stuck in traffic yesterday. We only had a minute to talk, but hearing her voice made me homesick.

I realized how much I've missed the beach. How much I need the peace and calm of Emerald Bay. How much I want to spend time with you. That's okay, isn't it?"

"Of course, it is. And I'll look forward to seeing you just as much." Margaret slowly let the air seep out of her lungs as Kimberly's answer eased her fear that she'd become a topic of discussion. She hesitated, torn between curiosity and the kind of good manners that said she should keep her nose out of her niece's personal life. Deciding to leave the manners to someone who didn't care for Kim as much, she asked, "Can you, um, afford to take that much time off work?"

"No." Kim laughed. "But I'm going to do it anyway."

Margaret pressed her lips tightly together to keep from saying something she shouldn't. If that scoundrel Frank had been half the husband he should have been, Kim wouldn't have to work so hard. As far as she was concerned, Natalie and Joshua were the only good things to come out of that marriage, and there were times she wasn't sure about that grandniece and - nephew of hers. They sure hadn't stood up for their mother in the divorce, had they? But Kimberly deserved to have someone in her corner. If she could be that someone, she'd do it.

"Come on down, child," Margaret soothed. "You know you're always welcome here."

"I can be there tomorrow, if that's all right."

"Tomorrow?" She couldn't hide her shock. She'd hoped to have a little more time to prepare for her niece's visit.

Kimberly must have heard the note of concern in her voice because she said, "The next day, if the inn's full up."

"No, no, tomorrow's fine." Margaret hurried to offer reassurance. She really didn't have any preparations to make since the housekeepers, Irene and Eunice, kept all the rooms ready for guests. "I'll put you in the Topaz Suite, where you can have some privacy," she announced.

"That's awesome, Aunt Margaret. But don't go to any trouble, okay? And don't worry about sending a car for me. If Amy can't come get me, I'll take the shuttle." A service ran from the Melbourne Airport to Vero Beach with stops in Sebastian and Emerald Bay.

They stretched their goodbyes over the next minute or two before Margaret pocketed her phone. She stood for a moment, her hands resting lightly atop her cane, and let anticipation warm her. Her own daughter had been the star she and Eric revolved around. They'd made sure their little girl wanted for nothing. Liz and Paul had doted on their three, showering them with love and discipline like any good parents would. But Shirley? Margaret would never speak ill of the dead aloud, but her youngest sister hadn't had a maternal bone in her body.

Practically from the day Kimberly was born, the little waif should've been given more love, more kindness, more everything. Kim had only been eighteen months old when Shirley dumped the baby on the inn's doorstep and took off with her latest boyfriend without shedding so much as a single tear. From then on, Shirley's car would roar up the driveway every few months and speed away in a cloud of dust, leaving her daughter—usually hungry and wearing soiled diapers—behind. After Jen came along, the children's visits had lasted longer and longer until, finally, a whole summer passed without anyone hearing a word from the girls' mother.

Margaret sighed. Lord, how she and Eric had tried to make up for her sister's shortcomings. They'd showered those girls with affection, outfitted them for school each year, made them a part of their family. Temporarily at first and then, after Shirley died, permanently. Small wonder that Kimberly had her own special corner in Margaret's heart.

And now, she supposed, she'd best get moving if she was going to have everything ready for her niece's arrival tomorrow. First on her list of things to do, she'd ask Amy to bake Kimberly's favorite cake. A trip to the grocery store was in order, too. She couldn't expect Kimberly to exist on the canned soups and crackers that made up her normal supper fare.

Movement through the sidelights of the front door startled her as she stepped into the foyer. She squinted to get a closer look and caught glimpses of a tall man in a suit and tie through the leaded glass. Had a new guest shown up without calling first? She gave her head a gentle shake. Guests didn't normally arrive dressed as if they were headed for the office. And they never showed up before she'd had her first cup of coffee in the morning.

If not a guest, then who? She was still trying to figure that out when the visitor's weight shifted. Suddenly, the puzzle pieces fell into place.

Scott. What was her nephew doing here at this time of the morning? More to the point, what was he doing here at all?

Aware that she'd locked up before she'd retired the night before, she quickened her pace to the front entrance. Only the two suites on the first floor were currently occupied, but the doorbell was likely to disturb everyone's sleep. She flung the door open before Scott could ring it. Ignoring the burst of heat and humidity that rolled into the foyer, she blurted, "Scott, what on earth are you doing here?"

Her sister's eldest smoothed the tie he wore despite temperatures that promised the day would be a scorcher. "Can't I just drop by when I happen to be in the neighborhood?" he asked. "Or do I need an appointment these days?"

"You know you're always welcome." Hanging on to her cane with her bruised arm, she enfolded her nephew in a one-armed hug. "I'm just surprised to see you here this early. Is something wrong? How's Fern? And the girls?" Margaret had hoped Isabella and Sophie would follow in their father's and aunts' footsteps and work at the inn each summer, but Fern's family owned a house on Tybee Island. Scott's girls spent their summers there.

"Everyone's fine, Aunt Margaret. I'm going to be tied up in court for the next couple of weeks, and I wanted to make sure everything here was okay before I got too busy with this case."

Margaret let out the breath she hadn't realized she'd been holding. "Well, don't stand

149

there letting all the air-conditioning out. Come on inside." Goodness knew—as Diane repeatedly pointed out—the electric bill was high enough already. She waited until he joined her in the foyer before she continued. "I was on my way into the kitchen for a cup of coffee. Can I get you one? Or a glass of tea?"

"Tea would be awesome. But don't trouble yourself, Aunt Margaret. I can get it."

Aware that he followed at her heels all the way down the long hall that led past the living room and dining room, she led the way to the back of the house. There, while she poured her first cup of the day, Scott grabbed a glass from the cupboard, filled it with ice and helped himself from the tall pitcher of sweetened tea in the fridge. By the time she'd doctored her coffee and carried it to the table, he was already nursing his second glass.

"No one makes iced tea as good as yours, Aunt Margaret," he declared after draining half the liquid.

"Tea is one of life's simple pleasures." Margaret hung her cane from the back of her chair and sat. "Now why'd you really come all this way this morning?" She didn't for one minute believe he'd just happened to be in the neighborhood. Scott's home and law office were in Vero Beach, a half hour's ride south of Emerald Bay.

Scott set his glass on the table. His eyes narrowing, he pointed to her wrist. "That looks painful. What happened to your arm?"

"My arm? How did you..." Caught off guard, she glanced down at her hands. While she'd been busy fixing the coffee, the cuff of her sweater had hiked up, exposing her blue-mottled flesh for all the world—and most unfortunately, her nephew—to see. Her face warmed as she tugged her sleeve down to cover the bruise. "It looks far worse than it is," she insisted.

"But what happened?"

She stared into Scott's unblinking blue eyes. From the time he'd been a little tyke running around in short pants and diapers, he'd been like a dog with a bone whenever something caught his attention. In most respects, the trait was a real asset. Once he'd set his mind on something—like studying the law—he never let go of it. His dedication had only intensified as he aged, and she had to admit, it had served him well. He was known for defending his clients to the bitter end and then some, which made him one of the most sought-after attorneys in the state.

She sighed. There were other times, times like now, when Scott's inability to let things go could be a royal pain. There was no point in lying to him, either. Along with a dogged persistence, he possessed a knack for ferreting out the truth.

"If you must know," she said grudgingly, "I tripped over a rug and went splat yesterday. I guess my arm took more of a beating than I thought it did. But it's fine. Really." She flexed her wrist to prove her point.

"Aunt Margaret, it's too much. You shouldn't be working so hard at your age. I've said it before and I'll say it again—you need to sell this place and get yourself a small house somewhere in town. Or, with the money you'd make, you could live very comfortably in Emerald Oaks. Wouldn't it be nice to have other people at your beck and call for a change? Why don't you let me put your name on their waiting list?"

Same song, forty-second verse. Scott had been hounding her to sell the old homestead ever since the accident that left her dependent on that no-good cane. Lucky for her, two could play this game, and she was just as stubborn as he was.

"You know good and well I have no intention of selling," she said, giving him her firmest look. "My parents—your grandparents—built this inn. They wanted it to be a legacy, passed down from one generation of Danes to the next. As long as I'm grass-side up, that's the way it's going to be." This would be a good time to stomp the floor with that infernal cane, she thought. Wishing she hadn't hung it on the back of her chair, she paused for what her daughter called "dramatic effect."

"I worry about you, Aunt Margaret. All alone in this huge place." Scott gestured toward the living room and the suites beyond it.

"I'm not alone," she corrected. "Amy stops by every morning. Irene and Eunice are here every day to clean. When I want company, there's always a guest or two somewhere nearby." She glanced at Scott to see if her words had had any effect. The firm set of his jaw line hadn't eased a bit. She might as well have saved her breath for all the good her argument made.

"This time you tripped and you say you're all right, but we both know you're not." Scott continued as if she hadn't spoken a single word. He glanced pointedly at the sweater she'd worn despite the warm day. "One of these days, you'll fall and get seriously injured. Break a hip. Or die, even. What kind of nephew would I be to let that happen?"

Margaret let her voice grow softer. "There ain't none of us going to get out of this world alive, Scotty." She patted his arm. "I should know. I'm the last one in my family to still be here."

"I know. And I want to keep you around as long as possible." Scott covered her age-spotted hand with his own. "You might live a lot longer if you'd be sensible about this house. That's all I'm saying. I, for one, would like you to stick around another decade or so. I'd like my grand-kids to have the chance to know their great-aunt Margaret. I know the others feel the same."

The boy knew exactly what buttons to push, she'd say that much for him. For a minute there, she'd felt herself waver. But if he thought she'd change her mind, he had another thing coming. She cleared her throat.

"I'm not planning to toddle off into the sunset just yet, Scott. Till I do, I'm staying put." To emphasize her point, she freed her hands. Letting her nephew stew for a bit, she added a spoonful of sugar to her coffee and slowly stirred it.

Much as Scott and the others might think she didn't, she knew that twenty acres of prime, beachfront real estate would fetch a pretty penny in today's market. One glance at the inn's property taxes—a bill that climbed higher every year—told her that much. She also recognized how unlikely it was for the entire family to agree to keep the inn open after she was gone. In keeping with her parents' wishes, Belle would inherit a third of the estate. Scott, Amy and Diane would get Liz's share. The final third would go to Kimberly and Jen. She sipped her coffee.

"When my day comes, it'll be up to you and the others to do whatever you want with the place. But I hope you'll hang on to it. There aren't many of these old Florida homes left anymore." From Miami to Jacksonville, hotel chains had swept in and bought up as many of the mom-and-pop inns and motels as they could get their greedy hands on. Then, instead of preserving the historic buildings, they'd razed them and erected towering hotels so much alike they could have all been cut out with the same cookie cutter.

"Old Florida monstrosities, you mean," Scott argued. "No one wants to stay at a place like this anymore. Today's guests want big-screen TVs in their rooms. A fully equipped gym. Free Wi-Fi and breakfast."

"We serve breakfast every day," she protested. "There's Wi-Fi, too. Right there in the business center." She pointed down the hall to the little alcove where guests were welcome to plug in their laptops and browse the internet to their hearts' content.

"They want to use their laptops in their own rooms, Aunt Margaret. And they want more than a few stale rolls for breakfast. Geez. Even the Best Western offers a breakfast buffet. Why would anyone stay here when they can get all that at half the price at a cheap hotel?"

Ouch. Now Scott was just being mean. She firmed her resolve, intent on putting him in his place.

"I'll have you know Amy brings us fresh sweet rolls every day. And don't forget, the inn has its regulars. The couple in the Diamond Suite is one of them," she pointed out. Granted, George and Jenelle were among a dwindling group of couples and families who returned year after year. But the hospitality business was cyclical. Right now, people were crazy about their cell phones and laptops. Sooner or later, though, the pendulum would swing, and they'd rediscover the value of a simpler way of life. When that happened, people would be thrilled to rediscover the Dane Crown Inn.

"The fact is, Diane says the inn isn't breaking even and it hasn't been for some time. You should cut your losses and sell now while there's some interest in the property. Don't wait until the place is falling down around your ears and no one wants it."

Okay, enough was enough. She had better things to do than waste her morning arguing with Scott. Standing, she took her cane from the back of her chair and leaned on it. "Thank you for your opinion, Scott. I hear what you're saying, but I've already given you my answer."

"At least think about it." Scott's voice dropped to a low whisper as he rose until his six-foot-two frame dwarfed hers. "You can't continue to live here alone. It's not safe. The fall you took yesterday proves that."

Not liking the certainty in Scott's tone one little bit, she pulled herself erect. She'd hoped to surprise her nieces and nephew with the news of Kimberly's visit, but based on Scott's attitude, that might not be her wisest move. Tipping her head up to scour his face with her gaze, she played her final card. "If you're worried about my safety, stop. I won't be alone for much longer. Kimberly will be here."

Scott's bushy eyebrows drew together. "My cousin Kim?"

"Yes, your cousin. Do you know another one?" She didn't wait for an answer but forged ahead. "I got off the phone with her just before you arrived, as a matter of fact. She's flying in tomorrow and will be staying on indefinitely."

Okay, she might have stretched the truth with that last little bit, she admitted. Kimberly hadn't actually said how long she planned to stay in Emerald Bay. But she'd sure made it sound like her trip was open-ended. And if Kim didn't know when exactly she'd return to Atlanta, neither would Scott.

Clearly perplexed, Scott folded his arms across the barrel chest he'd inherited from his father. Muttering more to himself than to his aunt, he said, "Maybe having her here will be a good thing. Maybe she'll be able to convince you to sell this place and let other people take care of you for a while." Finished thinking out loud, he checked his watch. "I can't stay. I have to be in court in an hour. Likely I'll be tied up for a couple of weeks." Though he slung one arm around her and pulled her in for a goodbye hug, he remained adamant. "But we're not finished with this, Aunt Margaret. I expect you to think about what I said. Talk it over with Kim. You need to seriously consider selling this place—and soon." With that, Scott carried his glass to the sink and, after thanking her for the tea, showed himself to the door.

Margaret stood where she was and stared after her nephew until she heard the front door click shut behind him. This wasn't the first time she and Scott had had this conversation, but he'd never been so adamant about it, never pushed her so hard to make the decision to sell her home of more than fifty years. Though she hated to admit it, she'd sensed some kind of veiled threat behind Scott's words today. But that was ridiculous, wasn't it? Scott wouldn't, he couldn't force her to sell, could he?

A sudden chill struck her. Tears pricked at the corners of her eyes. Glad for her sweater, she pulled the front edges closed.

Eight

Kimberly

"All right," Kim said with a resigned sigh. Though she was pretty sure Natalie was bluffing, she wouldn't stake her daughter's life or her own sanity on it. The girl was bright, articulate, college-educated, but she'd made her fair share of knuckleheaded decisions in the past. "Let me know how much your ticket costs." She paused for a moment before deciding she'd better spell out all the details. "Economy, not first class. I'll Venmo that much and no more."

Kim slipped the phone into the pocket of her backpack and sank against the headrest. She actually had to give her daughter credit. Natalie had merely threatened to hitchhike from Vail to New York, and she'd caved. *That child,* she tsked.

Natalie had probably been counting on her to react exactly the way she had. But seriously, much as she hated the thought of raiding her savings, especially after Belle had so generously paid for her own flight to Florida, what else was a mother to do? The thought of her petite twenty-four-year-old climbing up into the cab of a semi on a dark, lonely stretch of highway was the stuff nightmares were made of.

The doors of the shuttle swished closed. Throughout the van, passengers stowed bags and bundles as the vehicle pulled away from the curb. Glad no one sat next to her, Kim plopped her backpack onto the empty seat. She latched her seatbelt and settled in, hoping for a nap during the two-hour ride to Emerald Bay.

Heaven knew, she could use one. She'd spent most of the night doing laundry and packing. By the time she'd cleaned out her apartment's refrigerator and taken out the trash, she'd had just enough time to shower and throw a few last-minute items into her suitcase before her phone dinged with a text message letting her know her ride was waiting downstairs. She'd been on the Traveler Treadmill ever since.

As the van merged into the flow of traffic exiting the airport, fatigue spread over her like a warm blanket. She let her eyes drift shut. She'd barely started to relax when the driver abruptly hit the brakes. Jolted upright, she held her breath while her van cut across two lanes before rolling to a stop in front of the baggage claim exit. The driver opened the door for a well-dressed man holding a briefcase. Behind her sunglasses, Kim watched as the newcomer boarded the van with an easy grace.

"Thanks for stopping, Ben." The man brandished a ticket at the driver. "I don't know what I would have done if I'd missed you." In the sixteen-passenger van, his deep baritone drifted all the way to Kim's seat at the rear of the bus.

"You'd'a waited four hours for the next shuttle, I reckon. Or called somebody to pick you up. Go ahead and take a seat, Mayor. We're about full up, so sit wherever you can find a place, if you don't mind."

"Anywhere's fine, Ben. I sure appreciate this."

Mayor clasped the driver on the shoulder before he headed down the aisle. Like a kid on a school bus, he searched the faces of those already seated looking for friends who might invite him to join them. Avoiding eye contact, Kim tracked his progress while she hoped against hope that he'd find a place in one of the rows up front. Not that the guy was hard to look at. The gray at his temples and the laugh lines around his mouth to give him the distinguished look of a man moving easily into his fifties. Holding a finely crafted leather briefcase out in front of him, he exuded an air of deep Southern roots and old money as he moved down the narrow aisle. From the number of people who exchanged greetings with him, he seemed to be both well-known and well-liked. So, no. He didn't give off a sketchy vibe or anything. It was just that, after spending several hours in a cramped middle seat on the plane, she'd been hoping to stretch out a bit. That didn't look like it was going to happen when Mayor reached the last row without finding an empty spot.

Just as she'd feared, he glanced down at her. "Do you mind?" he asked. He nodded to her backpack, which was occupying the otherwise vacant spot on the bus.

"Sorry. Sure." Kim tugged the heavy bag to the floor, where it landed with a thump.

"Thanks." He shucked his suit jacket and lowered himself onto the seat. "I'm Craig."

Not sure whether she was more surprised that he'd bothered to introduce himself or that his name was, apparently, not Mayor, she answered with a nod. "Kimberly."

"Where are you headed, Kimberly?" Craig

stowed his briefcase under the seat in front of them and buckled his seat belt. He draped the jacket neatly over one knee.

"Emerald Bay. You?" she asked, hoping he'd be getting off when the shuttle bus made its first stop.

"Small world," Craig said. "I'm going there, too. Have you been there before?"

"My aunt has a place just outside the town limits. I spent most summers with her as a kid. Then, when I was in high school, we moved there." Which was probably more information than she needed to give but, much as she was looking forward to a nap, she couldn't be rude. The good Southern manners Aunt Margaret had instilled in her dictated that she engage in at least a few minutes of polite conversation. Besides, there was something about Craig that looked oddly familiar. Trying not to stare, she gave him a quick once-over. She noted the tan that was standard issue for anyone who'd lived their life beneath Florida's sunny skies. His lean build reminded her of long-distance runners. Or baseball players, she corrected as an image of cheerleaders and bleachers flickered at the edge of her memory.

"You must have gone to Emerald High like I did." Beneath his starched white shirt, Craig's chest puffed out the tiniest bit. "Class of '90. Go Pirates! Arr!" he said with a grin.

"Arr!" She echoed the standard school greeting.

So she and Craig had been in the same class—go figure. She ran a hand through her hair, stalling for time as she tried to place him. But it was no use. In the thirty-plus years since graduation, the memories of her classmates had grown too hazy. Even if she could recall what they'd looked like as teenagers, time had no doubt changed them as much as it had changed her. She'd bet money that Craig bore little resemblance to those long-ago pictures of him in his cap and gown.

To make things even harder, she'd only attended Emerald High for a couple of years. Not long enough to make many friends. She'd deliberately lost touch with those once she'd realized how badly Frank was taking advantage of the people they knew. Except for family, that was. She couldn't exactly cut ties with the people she loved. But she had warned them against putting money into any of her husband's so-called investments.

"Wait a minute," Craig said after a long pause during which Kim fought the urge to squirm beneath his scrutinizing gaze.

"Kim? Kimberly Dane?" Craig asked as recognition dawned in a pair of gray-blue eyes. He snapped his fingers. "I thought you looked familiar. You're one of Margaret Clayton's nieces, aren't you?"

"I'm surprised you remember me." Heat crept up her cheeks. Her memory of him was as blank as a freshly erased blackboard.

"You're kidding, right? Everybody pays attention when a new girl moves into a town as small as Emerald Bay. Especially when she's pretty. The guys were tripping all over themselves to ask you out." His grin widened. "You turned them all down. Shot me down, too."

"You asked me out?" And she'd turned him down? What had she been thinking? She inhaled. She knew exactly what she'd been thinking back then.

"Yep. To the movies. I had it all planned out. We were going to see *Beetlejuice* and stop for an ice cream cone on the way home."

"That sounds nice." She squeezed her eyes shut. A barely there recollection of a tall, gangly youth swam into her conscious. "Craig, um, Morgan?" she asked as the memory solidified.

"That's me." Craig aimed a thumb at his chest.

"Sorry I didn't recognize you. You've..." She stopped herself before she could say something totally inane about how nicely he'd aged.

"Nothing to be sorry about." Craig waved off her apology. "But I'll let you make it up to me if you finally heal my wounded, teenage pride."

"What do you want me to do?" She steeled herself, prepared to turn down the expected invitation for drinks or dinner. She'd had her reasons for not dating in high school. Things had changed a lot since then, but she had no more interest in going on a date with Craig Morgan now than she'd had thirty years ago.

"Let me know if there was any truth to the rumor that circulated back then," he said with a smile that gave her a glimpse of perfectly straight white teeth. "All the guys swore you wouldn't go out with them because you were in love with the captain of the football team at your old school. True or false?"

"False." Kim laughed bitterly. The truth was much less interesting and something she rarely talked about. For some reason, though, she wanted Craig to know her decision all those years ago had had nothing to do with him. "Truth was, my mom died the summer between my sophomore and junior years."

The cancer had struck without warning. Or at least, not with the kind of signs a sixteen-year-old might recognize. One day her mom had been smoking a cigarette with one hand and downing cough syrup with the other. Six weeks later, Kim had held her little sister's hand while they watched her uncles and their friends lower her mom's casket into a grave. For a long time afterward, she'd existed in a fog of anger and grief.

"It was a rough couple of years," she finished, sparing Craig the worst details of how she'd watched her mom slip away. Between coming to grips with her death and trying to earn enough credits to graduate, she hadn't had the time or interest for dating.

Beneath his tan, Craig paled a bit. "Gosh, Kim. I'm sorry. I had no idea. None of us did."

"It's okay. It was a long time ago." The copious amounts of love her aunts had showered on her had helped her put that part of her past behind her. It was time to change the subject, and she let her brows furrow as a question that had been nagging at her resurfaced. "Wait. Why'd the driver call you Mayor? Are you…" She took a breath. "Are you the *mayor* of Emerald Bay?"

"Guilty as charged." Despite the tight space, Craig bowed from the waist. "But don't let the title fool you," he added once he was more upright. "Some people might say the position makes me a big fish, but honestly, that's only because Emerald Bay is a very small pond."

Huh. Funny and humble. Craig Morgan might be one of those rarest of all creatures—a truly nice guy. Was he married? If so, she hoped his wife knew how lucky she was. Kim stole a glance at his left hand and wasn't at all surprised to see metal glinting on his third finger. Looking away quickly, she pretended to be interested in a towering bridge on the left until the tiniest twinge of disappointment faded.

They chatted about this and that, getting acquainted like relative strangers who had little in common other than the fact that they'd grown up in the same small town. Meanwhile, the van made its steady way south along US 1. The road paralleled the Indian River, and Kim caught glimpses of seagulls soaring over the water. Between the mainland and the distant shore, sailboats moved swiftly beneath crystalline blue skies dotted by puffy white clouds. From time to time, she spotted fishermen who prowled the shallow waters closer to the shore in their hunt for elusive trout or catfish.

The time passed quickly, and before she knew it, the road turned inland. As they neared a sprawling city, scenic views gave way to housing developments and businesses that crowded either side of the highway. At last, the van pulled into the parking lot of a grocery store.

LEIGH DUNCAN

From his seat behind the wheel, Ben announced, "Palm Bay, folks. Look around your seats and make sure you've got everything."

"So how long will you be in Emerald Bay?" Craig asked once the van was underway again.

"Two weeks. Three at the most." Kim was pretty sure it wouldn't take any longer than that to assess her aunt's situation and put some safety measures in place at the inn.

"Must be nice to be able to take such a long vacation. Me, I don't often string more than two or three days together."

Kim laughed. "It's not a vacation, exactly. I'm here to help my Aunt Margaret."

"That's—" Craig paused. "Really nice of you," he finished.

"I owe her far more than that," Kim confessed. "Aunt Margaret practically raised me and my sister after my mom died." She could never hope to repay her aunt and her late uncle for all they'd done for her and Jen. Long before their mom took sick, Aunt Margaret and Uncle Eric had opened their arms and their hearts whenever her mom dropped her and her sister on their doorstep. For Kim, those visits meant going from scrounging through near-empty cupboards for something to eat into the land of milk and honey. From being responsible, not

170

only for herself but for her baby sister, into life as a kid again. From Charles Dickens to Norman Rockwell.

"I'm sure Ms. Clayton will be glad to have you. I don't get out to see her near often enough." Craig's brows knitted. "She's got to be lonely, rattling around in that whole place all by herself so much of the time."

"She's never completely alone," Kim protested, eager to put Craig's concerns to rest. "You know Amy Peterson? She owns the bakery in town?"

"Sweet Cakes?" Craig patted a flat stomach. "That place will be my downfall."

"Amy's my cousin. Her mom was Aunt Margaret's sister. They visit almost every morning when Amy delivers the inn's order of baked goods." Despite her words, a sharp guilt pricked at Kim's conscience. Her cousin's brief chats couldn't possibly take the place of having another family member living under the same roof. "The housekeepers and the gardeners are always around. Plus, the guests are in and out all the time," she finished lamely.

"I could be wrong, but it's gotta be hard for the inn to compete now that a couple of the hotel chains have opened just west of Emerald Bay." Craig gave his head a sad shake. "That's one reason the town council and I fight so hard to keep the big chains out." Stretching, he shifted his position on the hard seat. "Local businesses wouldn't survive long if we let one of the big box stores set up shop in our backyard. To say nothing of how quickly a big chain would put A Likely Story out of business."

"No one in their right mind would want that," Kim agreed. She made a point of visiting the tiny bookstore on the corner of First and Main whenever she was in town. Next to her family's inn, it was probably her favorite place in the whole world.

Their conversation had moved in fits and starts, stopping altogether whenever the van rolled to a halt to let passengers off in tiny towns like Grant and Micco. Finally, Ben drove across yet another bridge, this time into Sebastian. Halfway through town, he pulled into a Walmart parking lot, where nearly everyone else disembarked.

As the van left the outskirts of Sebastian behind a few minutes later, Kim stared out the window where low-slung strip malls and doctors' offices gave way to older homes surrounded by palm trees and scrub oak. A giddy excitement passed through her at the thought of walking up the front steps of the Dane

Crown Inn. It wouldn't be long now. Another half hour and she'd be home.

"Is it my imagination, or is there a lot more traffic than there used to be?" she asked when, several miles south of Sebastian, cars still crowded the roadway.

"You're not mistaken. Between all the new activity going on at the Space Center and an influx of people who want to retire someplace warm and tropical, the whole area is booming. That means more jobs, which is a good thing. But it also means more traffic, more pressure on schools and hospitals."

Kim nodded. "My aunts and uncles used to talk about 'the way things were' when they were growing up. And not in a good way." According to them, the east coast of Florida had been a sleepy little slice of paradise best known for fishing camps and mosquitoes prior to the sixties. Then, JFK kicked the space program into gear. The arrival of engineers and technicians and their families had spurred the growth of schools, roads, housing and businesses. Apparently, the area was experiencing another boom now.

"And yet, with all the new growth in the area, Emerald Bay stays the same. No one wants to build there?" Her cousin Scott swore the inn and the twenty acres surrounding it could fetch millions in today's market. Was he right?

"Oh, they do. The town council and I fend off developers every day who want to turn our small town into the next Orlando. So far, we've been able to resist those who'd destroy Emerald Bay's charm and way of life." Craig finished with a self-deprecating shrug of one shoulder.

"With all the newcomers in the area, you'd think the inn would have more business, wouldn't you?" she mused to herself. Thinking of her family's home sent a burst of pride through her. With its wide verandas out front and the huge deck on the back of the house, the inn offered guests a glimpse of old Florida without sacrificing any of the amenities they expected, like air-conditioning and cable TV. True, the inn didn't have a pool, but who needed one of those when the ocean lay just feet from the front steps? As for those exercise rooms filled with fancy equipment, what guest wouldn't prefer a bike ride along the beach with the wind blowing through their hair and the sound of the waves to keep them company? "You have to admit it—there's no place quite like the Dane Crown Inn."

Craig cleared his throat. "Since you mentioned it, um, how long has it been since you've visited Emerald Bay?"

"It's been a couple of years," she admitted. Until the layoff at Collins, she'd flown home every six months like clockwork. But after losing her job, she'd struggled so hard to make ends meet, she hadn't been able to spare the time or the cost. She waited, expecting Craig to say more. When he didn't, she tipped her head to study his face. His tense expression made it clear he had something on his mind. She mentally shrugged her shoulders. He probably just wanted to know what it was like to share a house with perfect strangers. So why didn't he ask?

"What?" she prompted.

"I probably shouldn't say anything," he said, his features smoothing.

She couldn't very well let that cryptic comment go unchallenged. "No, really. What is it?"

Craig waited a long beat before, his voice softening so much she had to lean forward to hear him, he said, "It's just that the inn used to be a real showcase. In recent years, though, it's become a bit of an eyesore."

An eyesore?

Kim stiffened. "That wasn't what I expected to hear," she admitted, uncertain whether to burst into tears or claw Craig's eyes out. It was one thing for her and her cousins to point out the inn's flaws, quite another ball of wax for a relative stranger to speak so harshly about it. She cast another look in Craig's direction. Maybe he wasn't such a nice guy after all.

Some of what she was feeling must have shown on her face because Craig backtracked. "It's none of my business, really. I mean, the property is technically outside the Emerald Bay town limits. But a lot of people think it's nothing short of a miracle that your aunt has been able to keep the place open. Do you mind my asking what the family plans to do with it?"

"Actually, I do. Mind, that is." She stared out the window. When she'd last visited, the inn had needed a fresh coat of paint, but otherwise her family home had reminded her of a gracefully aging Southern belle. With the emphasis on "graceful." Had things really gotten that bad in just two years?

She wouldn't have to wait long to find out, she realized as the driver steered onto a towering bridge that spanned the Intracoastal Waterway.

Her eyes narrowed while she considered what game Craig might be playing. Was he belittling the property, hoping to drive the price down if and when it did go on the market? She'd heard that potential buyers sometimes resorted to those kinds of tactics.

She squared her shoulders. If that was what Craig was doing, he was barking up the wrong tree. Aunt Margaret was the sole owner of the Dane Crown Inn, and from what Kim had heard, her aunt had no intention of selling.

"Final stop, Emerald Bay," Ben announced.

Beyond the windshield, Kim glimpsed the familiar wooden sign depicting shiny green stones that spilled from a treasure chest onto a sandy beach. She took a deep breath and let it out slowly as Ben pulled into the parking lot of a strip mall and stopped. Their arrival had saved her from having to choose between stomping down the aisle to one of the now-empty seats or giving Craig the silent treatment for the rest of the trip. Instead, she hefted her backpack. Aiming for a perfect blend of Southern charm and ice, she said, "It's been nice talking to you."

Ignoring the man who'd insulted her family, no matter what his motives, she slung her bag over one shoulder and marched off the bus.

Aware that Craig trailed her out of the van, Kim stepped aside without looking over her shoulder once she reached the pavement. When she heard his feet hit the ground, she stood still, hoping he'd apologize for his bad manners. Instead, his footsteps never even slowed as he strode directly to a car that waited in the parking lot, its engine idling. Without so much as a glance in her direction, the mayor climbed inside. The last Kim saw of it, the vehicle was pulling onto the main street.

A vague disappointment washed through her at the way things had ended between them. Their high school acquaintance might have deepened into friendship if he'd been a wee bit less opinionated. Of if he'd kept those opinions to himself. But he hadn't, so that was that.

"His loss," she muttered, taking a much-needed second to settle herself.

The mayor's comments faded into an only slightly irritating memory as she scanned the parking lot for her ride. The late afternoon sun cast the western side of the street in shadow while red-golden rays of light bounced off window fronts to the east. A warm breeze brushed her skin. It rustled the fronds of the ornamental palm trees planted along the sidewalks. The air in Emerald Beach carried a salty tang of the ocean mixed with the heady aroma of honeysuckle and jasmine. She drank in the unique smell like a shipwrecked sailor gulped fresh water. Letting the sights and sounds of the small town work their magic, she tipped Ben when he unloaded her suitcase.

Nearby, Amy leaned against a van that bore the image of a large cake on its side. Kim grabbed her bags and hurried toward her cousin.

"Hey-yay!" She waved.

Seconds later, two arms firmly enveloped her in a warm hug. "I can't believe you're here!" Amy squealed.

"Me, either!" she answered, laughing. Some things never changed, and the scent of butter and sugar clung to Amy like an aura. Tears stung Kim's eyes. She squeezed her cousin tightly. "It's been too long," she whispered.

"You bet your sweet petunias it has," Amy said.

When they finally stepped back, Kim held the shorter woman at arm's length. Though Kim had packed on ten pounds while she was going through the divorce, Amy looked as thin and trim as she always did. How she managed that while spending her days creating delectable desserts, Kim had no idea. She homed in on Amy's unlined face.

"You haven't changed a bit, have you? What's your secret?" she demanded. Despite slathering herself with Pond's cold cream each night, lines were slowly making inroads around her mouth and eyes.

"You're too kind." Amy laughed. "Who was that French actress? The one who said, 'After a certain age, a woman has to choose between her fanny and her face'?"

"Catherine Deneuve?" Kim suggested. Her mom had been a big fan.

Amy patted her rear. "I guess I made my choice."

"You say that like you've gained as much weight as I have." Living on TV dinners and cheap pasta wasn't helping her diet. "Whatever you're doing, it's working for you. You're still as beautiful as always," she said with heartfelt assurance.

"You, too."

Knowing Amy meant well, Kim forgave her cousin for telling a fib while she swept hair that had lost its natural shine over one shoulder. She'd tried everything to combat the side effects of the aging process, even hormone replacement therapy. Unfortunately, that had led to serious complications, so she'd had no choice but to learn to live with dry skin and lackluster hair.

"What do you think? Should we head to the inn, or do you need a bite to eat first?" Amy asked.

Kim's stomach grumbled. Hours had passed since she'd taken a few bites of her breakfast sandwich before boarding the plane. But whether she was hungry or not, Aunt Margaret was probably standing at the front window, waiting impatiently for their arrival. "I think we'd better head on out."

"That's fine. I have cupcakes in the van." Amy waggled her eyebrows. "There's a red velvet one with your name on it."

"Yummmm." Her taste buds tingled with anticipation. "You're the best." It had been a while since anyone had gone out of their way for her, but she should have known Amy would remember her favorite flavor. Brushing a stray tear from her eyes, she gave her cousin another quick hug.

Riding shotgun a few minutes later, she slowly peeled the wrapper away from a rich confection that smelled divinely of chocolate. She nibbled a tiny bit of the icing and nearly groaned as the combination of butter, cream cheese and sugar melted in her mouth. Determined to enjoy every crumb, she peered through the windshield as Amy pulled out of the parking lot.

She was pleased to see that Emerald Bay had maintained the look and feel of a sleepy beach town. The same two surf shops she remembered from previous visits anchored either end of the small business district. A string of familiar-looking mom-and-pop shops lined the sidewalks on either side of the street. Lights glowed from the hardware store. She was about to conclude that nothing had changed since her last visit, but as they passed Campbell's Drugs, where she and her cousins had spent countless hours when they were much, much younger, she noted the vacant look of a store that had served its last customer.

"What happened to the drugstore?" she asked.

"Mr. Campbell finally retired last year," Amy answered while she waited for the town's only stoplight to change from red to green. The white-haired gentleman had inherited the pharmacy from his father.

"You mean the soda fountain's gone?" When they were kids, she'd looked forward all week to Sunday afternoons when, after the last of the inn's guests left, Aunt Margaret would dole out quarters to her and each of her cousins. Change jingling in their pockets, they'd hop on their bikes and race into town. Sweaty and red-faced, they'd run down the narrow aisles of the old drugstore to the tiny lunch counter. There, they'd perch on round barstools and treat themselves to ice cream sodas.

"Yeah. It's a shame really. Mr. Campbell tried to sell the business, but he didn't get any takers." The light turned green, and Amy proceeded through the intersection.

"I'm surprised. The drugstore was always busy. You'd think someone would snap it up."

Behind the wheel, Amy shook her head. "Not with a CVS and a Walgreens only a stone's throw away."

Perplexed, Kim frowned. "Craig Morgan told me the town council had made it their life's mission to keep franchised businesses out of Emerald Bay." Had he been lying about that? If so, what other lies had he told?

"You've met our mayor, have you?"

When Amy took her eyes off the road just long enough to pin her with a questioning look, Kim pretended the passing scenery had caught her attention. On the other side of the road, palmetto and sea grass climbed sandy dunes. Every once in a while, she caught a glimpse of the blue ocean in the distance.

"We ended up sitting beside each other on the airport shuttle," she finally said when Amy kept darting looks her way. "Turns out, we were in the same class at Emerald High."

"Oh, yeah?" Eyes back on the road, Amy passed the surf shop that marked the end of the business district. A small apartment complex, built around a courtyard filled with towering bamboo and umbrella plants, came next. After that, several one-story homes constructed from sturdy concrete blocks sat on wide lots. "I never knew him in school—he was a couple of years ahead of me. I didn't realize you and he were friends back in the day."

"We weren't. Not really. We didn't really have much in common back then." She paused. Craig had lived his entire life in Emerald Bay, while she'd grown up with a mom who considered "permanence" a dirty word. The frequent moves she'd insisted on had left gaps in Kim's education. When she'd finally arrived at Emerald Bay High, she'd struggled to catch up with the other kids. Between her studies and working at the inn every weekend, she'd had no time for extracurricular activities. Craig, on the other hand, had taken all advanced classes. He'd been a member of the student council, a star on the high school baseball team, president of the Honor Society.

"We still don't have anything in common," she finished firmly. As near as she could tell, the differences in their lives had only widened as they'd aged. She glanced at Amy and relaxed when her cousin gave a noncommittal nod.

"Back to your question, though," Amy said. "The big chains would love to get a toehold in Emerald Bay, but most folks around here want to keep things the way they are. Craig and his crowd have worked hard to do that, but they can't control what goes on beyond the town limits. The county's rules are more pro-development." Surrounded by Indian River County, which stretched from the Sebastian Inlet southward past Vero Beach, Emerald Bay, like most towns and cities in the state, was a self-governing island. "IRC let a developer buy two lots just to the north of us. He put a Walgreens on one corner, a CVS on the other. They've literally cornered the market on prescription drugs around here."

"Which is why Mr. Campbell couldn't find a buyer." Three drugstores was at least one too many for the area.

"Yep. You got it. He still owns the building. I've heard some talk about dividing it into several smaller stores—like the Threadneedle Mall in Cocoa Village."

Recalling a dress she'd bought from a consignment shop in the little town north of them, Kim smiled.

"Enough about small-town politics. You'll probably get an earful of that while you're here,"

Amy declared. "I want to hear what's up with the kids." She stopped herself with a chuckle. "I guess they aren't kids anymore, are they?"

"Josh is twenty-five. Practically middle-aged."

"No! How did that happen? The last time I saw him he was barely in his teens."

Kim sighed. "I haven't seen him since he moved to Chicago. From what he says, his job is very demanding." Josh's college internship had led to a position in Motorola's home office. "When we do talk, he sounds happy. He has a girlfriend, and I think things are getting serious."

"Ooooh, do I hear wedding bells? I'd love to bake their wedding cake." Amy grinned.

"I'll remind you when the time comes."

"That makes Natalie, what? Twenty-two? Twenty-three?"

"Twenty-four and still finding herself." Using one hand, Kim enclosed the last two words in air quotes. "She's decided graphic design isn't her life's passion after all." After getting her degree from the Savannah College of Art and Design, which offered one of the top programs in the country, Natalie had lasted a mere six months at her first job. She'd quit, intending to open her own design company, but that idea had quickly fizzled. "Now she's a social influencer, which, as near as I can figure out, means she goes to a lot of parties and eats at expensive restaurants, then posts pictures of where's she's been and who she's seen on Facebook and TikTok."

"Where do I sign up?"

When Amy's laughter filled the van, Kim joined in. Too much time had passed since she'd been around someone who looked at life through the same lens as hers. It felt good to share a laugh or two about the values and goals of the next generation. But when her cousin asked about Kim's relationship with her daughter, she sobered.

"She's still Daddy's Little Girl. Still blames me for the divorce. I don't hear from her too often."

"Let me guess—just whenever she needs something."

Ouch! The pointed remark stung, but she wouldn't lie to her cousin.

"You know you shouldn't let that girl guilt you into anything. It's not good for either of you," Amy said softly.

"I know." Kim studied the floor of the van. "It's just that, for now, that's the way it has to be." She'd rather have a lopsided relationship with her daughter than none at all. Amy didn't have children. She'd understand that if she did.

She glanced up. Amy had tucked her lower lip between her teeth. Knowing her cousin was literally biting back more well-meaning advice, Kim grinned. "You can say whatever's on your mind, you know."

"Nah. I got nothing," Amy answered, giving her head the slightest shake. "There's other, more pressing stuff we should go over before we get to the house."

Not unhappy with the chance to talk about something else, Kim said, "Shoot."

"Apparently, Scott stopped by to see Aunt Margaret yesterday." Amy waited a second to let the news sink in. When she continued, her tone had hardened. "He strongly suggested she sell the inn. He even threatened to put her name on the waiting list at Emerald Oaks. I didn't get there until after he'd left, but Aunt Margaret was all kinds of upset."

"Did you read him the riot act?"

"I tried," Amy said. "He's working some big case. I've left several messages, but he hasn't returned my calls."

"I'd hate to be him when he does." Two years younger than her older sibling, Amy had never let her big brother intimidate her.

"You got that right," Amy agreed. "Aunt Margaret does not need his bull-in-the-china-shop approach. I don't mind telling him to butt out and let us handle this."

"But that's not the goal, is it? We're not trying to convince her to sell, are we?" Kim stiffened. That hadn't been the plan they'd discussed. She'd meant it when she told Craig she wouldn't be a part of an effort to strong-arm their aunt into doing something the older woman didn't want to do.

"That didn't come out the way I wanted it to," Amy offered, her voice carrying just the note of reassurance Kim needed to hear. "I'm certainly not in any hurry to sell the place. Diane and Belle aren't, either. We just want to make the inn as safe as possible so Aunt Margaret can live there as long as she wants. If and when she does change her mind and wants to move, of course, we'll help her do it."

Relieved, Kim let out a long, slow breath just as the road curved away from the bay that bore the same name as the town. Ahead on the left, a sign swung between two pylons. The sight sent a heady anticipation rushing through her, and suddenly, she felt like she had when she was a little girl eagerly standing on tiptoe to peer over the front seat of her mother's car. When she was five, the golden crown painted on the sign shone like a welcoming beacon. Today, though, one of the support posts canted to the side. As a result, the sign tilted so badly it gave the faded crown a slightly cockeyed look. Chipped and flaking, the white letters that were supposed to welcome passersby to the Dane Crown Inn were in even worse shape.

So much disappointment burned in Kim's stomach that she regretted eating the cupcake. "What happened there?" she asked, pointing to the weather-beaten sign.

"It was damaged in a hurricane, I think." Amy shrugged one shoulder and sighed. "I asked Diane to order a new one."

Kim idly rubbed her forehead. Most of the tropical storms that formed off the African coast fizzled into rain showers before they ever reached land. But when the conditions were right—or wrong, as the case might be—the storms strengthened tremendously during their trek across the Atlantic. The worst ones were ranked and given names. Powerful Category Fives, like Dorian, Michael or Irma, wrecked devastation wherever they struck, while most people who'd lived in Florida for any length of time considered a Cat One a mere nuisance.

"That's odd. I usually pay close attention to the weather during hurricane season. I don't remember a really bad storm this year." Kim frowned.

Amy stroked her chin. "Now that I think of it,

there wasn't much damage. Campbell's Drugstore lost an awning, but since it had already closed, no one cared. Everyone else in town got their repairs made right away."

"Do you think the order got lost or…" Kim hesitated.

"Or?" Amy prompted.

"Maybe she didn't order it? Could it have slipped her mind?" She didn't want to blame Diane, but several months was a long time to wait on something as important as a sign. She drummed her fingers on her thigh. "Didn't you say there's a new handyman in town?"

"Yeah. Max."

"Let's ask him if he can repair this one tomorrow. A little paint, a little straightening, and it'll do till we get a new one."

"Great idea," Amy agreed. She patted her chignon. "I knew you were the right person to help out with Aunt Margaret. Because you haven't been here in a while, you'll see everything with fresh eyes. Take a new approach to getting things done."

"Oh, I don't know about that," Kim demurred. "You'd do the same thing."

"Uh-uh," Amy corrected. "I musta driven past this very spot every day for the past six months. I'd see that sign listing to the side like that and think, 'Oh, Diane's getting a new one,' and then I wouldn't think of it until the next time I drove past."

Kim's mouth slanted to one side. She could totally see that happening. After all, how many times had she overlooked Frank's failings before she'd finally realized that he wasn't the man she thought she'd married?

A hundred yards farther down the road, Amy signaled for a left turn and pulled into the median crossover. She waited for a pickup truck to roar past before, giving the van a bit more gas, she drove onto a driveway made of crushed coquina.

Eager for her first glimpse of the old homestead, Kim leaned forward until her seat belt tightened across her chest. Through the trees, sunlight glinted off the tin roof of the main house, and she drew in a breath filled with anticipation and hope. As the van emerged from a copse of trees onto the circular drive, tension eased from her shoulders and she relaxed into her seat. The Dane Crown Inn was certainly not the eyesore Craig had described. From the little he'd said, she'd half expected to see missing window shutters, gaps in porch railings and a caved-in roof. But the deep, wrap-around porches still provided plenty of shady spots to sit and enjoy the ocean breezes on lazy summer afternoons. Not a single shutter hung at a crazy angle. The roofline was intact.

"We're here," Amy said as they bumped over a parking lot that hadn't been scraped and leveled in far too long. Braking to a stop, she shut off the engine. "Let's leave your bags for now. I want to get inside before Aunt Margaret decides she needs to find out what's taking us so long."

"Sounds good." Kim already had her door open. Her feet hit the ground soon after. She tried to avoid stepping on the weeds that grew between the walkway's pavers but gave up the effort once she realized that the bricks themselves had grown slick with moss and algae. Nearing the main house, a sharp twinge of dismay shot through her as she studied the once-pristine flower beds. Her uncle Eric would roll over in his grave if he saw them. The man had absolutely hated weeds. He'd set her and Belle to work pulling them whenever he spotted so much as a single dandelion. Now clumps of beggar lice and sandspurs ran wild wherever she looked.

She took a calming breath and made a concerted effort to unclench her teeth. Weeds and overgrown bushes were one thing, but they were just cosmetic. A couple of willing gardeners armed with chainsaws and hoes could put things to rights without too much trouble. The house itself posed a bigger problem. Here and there, bare wood showed through where the wind and sun had scraped away the white paint. Sure, the porch railings were intact, but even from this distance she could tell they weren't as sturdy as they needed to be. As for the outbuildings, she'd merely glanced at the cottages scattered around the property and had known they were in dire need of a general sprucing up. And she hadn't even stepped inside yet. Who knew what she'd discover there?

She swallowed. Maybe she shouldn't have been quite so abrupt with Craig. Oh, he'd been wrong to call her family estate an eyesore. It was still far from that. However, unless someone intervened—and soon—the old Southern belle was well on her way to becoming one.

Nine

Kimberly

"I'm sorry. I planned to go to the grocery store today. Maude Anders and I always go together, but she had a doctor's appointment in Fort Pierce." In the quiet kitchen of the Dane Crown Inn, Aunt Margaret huffed. "I shoulda just driven myself."

The image of her aunt behind the wheel of a car sent a knife plunging straight into the middle of Kim's stomach. Her eyes widening, she glanced across the kitchen table at Amy. Her cousin's face bore the same shocked expression she felt on her own. As far as she knew—as far as anyone in the family knew—Aunt Margaret had never driven a car. Not once. If, by some miracle, she made it out of the driveway without hitting a tree, she'd almost certainly get pulled over

LEIGH DUNCAN

before she completed her errand. Did she even have a license?

Betting she didn't, Kim leaned in to give the older woman a gentle squeeze while suggesting a safer alternative. "Aunt Margaret, now that I'm here, I'll be glad to drive you wherever you need to go. We'll go into town and get groceries tomorrow." Like a bridesmaid lifting a glass in a toast, she took a cupcake from the box Amy had brought and held it aloft. "In the meantime, we won't starve."

"But it's not right," Aunt Margaret complained. "You flew all the way down here without getting a proper supper." Seated in one of the kitchen's hard-backed chairs, she gave Amy a pointed look. "I thought you'd eat at the diner in town."

"It's okay," Kim said, hurrying to absolve her cousin from blame. "Amy asked if I wanted to stop, but I told her I couldn't wait another minute to see you. I knew you'd be standing at the window, watching for us." She nudged her aunt's elbow. "I was right, wasn't I?"

"Well, yes," Aunt Margaret admitted. "It's not every day one of my nieces plans a sudden trip to Emerald Bay." She paused for several heartbeats. "There's, um, nothing wrong, is there, dear?"

"Not a thing," Kim said firmly when a pair of piercing blue eyes searched her face. Nothing that finding a new job, resolving her issues with her children, and assuring her aunt's safety wouldn't fix, she added silently. For the time being, though, she'd done all she could about the first two items on her list. Which meant, for as long as she stayed in Florida, she'd concentrate on the last one.

"You don't have any big plans while you're here?" Aunt Margaret asked next.

"Nothing much. I'll take some long walks along the beach. Work on my tan a bit." She held out her arm so everyone could see how pale she was. Next to her aunt's sun-darkened skin, hers looked pasty. "Other than that, I'm looking forward to spending some time with you and with Amy." Kim sipped her wine.

Which was all true but not the main reason for her trip. Sure, she'd enjoy the occasional afternoon sunbathing. With the sandy beach practically at the inn's front door, only a fool would pass up that opportunity. But her aunt's well-being was her number one priority. For the next couple of weeks she'd quietly comb through the inn on the hunt for trip-and-fall risks. Anywhere an electrical line snaked from a wall socket across a stretch of flooring, she'd rearrange the furniture to eliminate the hazard. She'd make sure the bath mats had non-slip backs. She'd have the new handyman install grab bars in every shower. If guests tracked water onto the floor after a thunderstorm, she'd replace the current floor mats with absorbent ones before it rained again.

The only problem with her plan was Aunt Margaret herself. The woman guarded her independence as fiercely as a mother lion guarded her cubs. If she even suspected someone was mollycoddling her, she'd dig in her heels and refuse to cooperate.

Somehow, Kim would have to convince her that a few minor changes were worth the effort and expense. After all, they'd been lucky so far. When Aunt Margaret had fallen in the past, she'd escaped serious injury. Sooner or later, though, that luck would run out. Plus, there was the not-so-little matter of Scott. Before he'd even known about the falls, he'd wanted to move his aunt someplace where other people would dictate her comings and goings. One more accident, and he'd make good on his threat.

No one wanted that to happen. Not Belle or any of their cousins. Certainly not Aunt Margaret. Which was why, starting tomorrow, Kim was determined to take whatever steps were necessary to safeguard her aunt's welfare. She'd succeed, too. With so much at stake, she couldn't fail.

But that was a task for tomorrow. Tonight was all about unwinding after her trip. She longed to catch up on the changes in Emerald Bay—to learn which of the neighbors had put their houses on the market, to find out if there were any newcomers in town, to hear how things were going at Sweet Cakes. Most of all, she wanted to spend some quality time with two of the people she loved most in the world.

Although, she admitted several hours later as she surveyed the crumbs and napkins that littered the kitchen table, some real food to balance out all the cupcakes and wine would have been nice. Not that she'd expected Aunt Margaret to prepare a huge spread in her honor. She knew better. Her elderly aunt had never been much of a cook, and judging from her thin figure, she barely ate enough to keep body and soul alive. No, the kitchen had always been Aunt Liz's domain, and before she died, Amy's mom had done a great job of keeping the family and guests at the inn fed. Knowing that, Kim's mouth hadn't watered with anticipation for the chicken 'n dumplin's or the hearty beef stew that had been her late aunt's go-to dishes.

But she wouldn't have turned down a grilled cheese sandwich. Or maybe some tuna salad.

One glance at the empty refrigerator and the equally bare shelves in the pantry, though, and Kim knew even meager fare had been too much to hope for. Which was one of the reasons she so readily put making a trip to the grocery store at the top of her list of things to do tomorrow morning. She took a peanut butter cupcake from the box and broke it in half. After handing the other piece to her cousin, she took a bite.

"Just so I know, Aunt Margaret, how many people are staying here right now?" she asked once they'd covered the local news and she'd provided the others with a few carefully edited highlights from her life in Atlanta.

"We have two sets of guests this week. George and Jenelle Brady from Ohio," Margaret answered, stringing the words together like one long name. "Nice couple. They go beachcombing every morning and ride bikes in the evenings. They're in the Diamond Suite."

Kim nodded. With a separate living area and a full bath, the first-floor accommodations were the inn's largest. "And the others?"

"Sarah and Phillip Norman. I don't see much of them. They're on their honeymoon," she said, her eyes twinkling. "I put them in the Garnet

Suite." At the far end of the hall from the Bradys, the newlyweds' room featured a sumptuous poster bed and its own private entrance.

"How about the cottages?" Kim asked. In case she went for a walk in the morning, it'd be nice to know who else she might run into on the path down to the beach.

"Helen March is here," Amy piped up. "She's on deadline."

"No one else?" Kim asked when neither her aunt nor her cousin offered any more information. "What about the Sonnabergs and the Johnsons? When do they arrive?" Close friends, the two couples had spent their first winter at the Dane Crown Inn while Kim was still in high school. They'd rented side-by-side cabins every year since.

Aunt Margaret gave her head a sad shake. "When I hadn't heard from them by Labor Day, I called Marcia Johnson. She said they'd decided to try someplace on the West Coast."

"Aunt Margaret, you didn't tell me they'd canceled this year," Amy chided softly.

Across the table, Kim saw her own concerns reflected in her cousin's eyes. Family-run inns like the Dane Crown relied on repeat business to remain afloat. If long-term guests like the Sonnabergs and the Johnsons were staying elsewhere, the inn's outlook might be even worse than she'd suspected. She tapped her fingers on the tabletop.

Noticing the room had gone quiet, Kim looked up from thoughts that had veered in a discouraging direction. "Sorry," she apologized with a yawn she didn't have to fake. "I was up all night getting ready for the trip. I guess it's catching up with me."

Amy scooted her chair away from the table. "I've already stayed longer than I should. I didn't want to be a party pooper, but I still have cakes to bake before I turn in tonight."

Kim rose with her. "Let me walk you out, Amy, and I'll grab my bags."

"Girls, I don't mind telling you, it's almost my bedtime." Aunt Margaret eased out of her chair. Her cane in one hand, she picked up one of the wineglasses with the other. "Let me just tidy up first."

"Leave those for now." Kim took the glass from her aunt's hand and returned it to the table. "I'll clean up before I go to bed. After all, I need to earn my keep while I'm staying here." She grinned. "Earn your keep" was a refrain she'd heard quite often when she spent summers at the inn. "Do you still lock the front door at ten?" When her aunt nodded, she checked the clock over the stove. It was nearly that now. "Good. I'll take care of closing up."

"Just like you did when you lived here. In case I haven't mentioned it already, I hope you'll be here for a nice long visit." Aunt Margaret cleared her throat. "Now everything's just where it always was. I wasn't able to check your rooms—I can't manage the stairs like I used to—but Irene and Eunice keep all the suites in move-in condition."

"Don't worry about me. I'll be fine," Kim said firmly. Pretending she didn't notice how much her aunt relied on her cane to steady herself, she gave the older woman a warm hug and tried to recall if Margaret had always been so thin when she felt the bony outline of ribs. Seconds later, she listened to the slight shuffle of steps fade when her aunt's door closed. Turning to Amy, she said, "I feel like I should have gone with her. Made sure she got all tucked in for the night."

"Are you nuts?" Amy asked with a laugh. "She might seem small and vulnerable, but she'll fight you tooth and nail if she thinks you're trying to boss her around."

"Thanks for the warning." Kim nodded. For now, she'd keep the real purpose behind her visit under wraps. How long that would last, though, she couldn't say. Her aunt's body might be frail, but Margaret Dane Clayton had never been anyone's fool. Sooner rather than later, she'd figure out what her niece was up to. Once she did, they'd have to have a heart-to-heart chat.

Outside, the gentle roar of the ocean nearly drowned out the nightly chorus of frogs and crickets. Their songs were occasionally punctuated by a male alligator's deep-throated bellow. Kim peered into the darkness beyond the solar lights that ringed the parking lot. "He's not close, is he?"

"Relax. He's probably in the river. It's not mating season, so he won't wander far." Alligators rarely traveled more than two miles from the nest where they hatched. The exception being in the spring, when the males traveled far and wide in their search for a mate.

Despite that bit of reassurance, Kim shivered. "Some people fear spiders. Others are phobic about snakes. I hate alligators," she explained.

"They're not my favorites, either," Amy agreed. "Remember when we were kids and we thought nothing of swimming in the river? You couldn't pay me enough to dip my toes in that water now. Too many gators." Once considered an endangered species, the fearsome creatures now thrived throughout the state.

"One gator is one too many," Kim pointed out. She shivered again. "Let's talk about something else before I end up giving myself nightmares."

"Okay. Shoot." Amy pulled a key fob from her pocket and aimed it at the van she'd parked at the end of the walkway. A soft glow filled the vehicle and spilled out onto the ground when the tailgate rose.

"How's Aunt Margaret doing, really? She has to be worried about the inn, right? I mean, only two couples in the house? And only one of the cottages in use?" Kim's brow furrowed. Thirty years earlier Amy's dad had put crews from his construction company to work erecting three identical cabins on either side of the main house. Guests and family alike had been clamoring to stay in them ever since. Or at least, they had until recently. "I knew things had slacked off, but I didn't realize business had gotten this bad."

"Yeah. I was as surprised as you were to learn that the Sonnabergs and the Johnsons canceled their reservations. That's gotta hurt the bottom line."

Kim rubbed eyes that had grown gritty and tired after her long day. "I wonder how much Aunt Margaret was counting on those rentals to help cover her expenses this winter."

"It's been ages since I've been inside one of the cottages," Amy admitted. "Judging from the outside, though, I'd say they all need some TLC."

"If I have a chance, I'll take a look at them while I'm here." It couldn't hurt to apply the same safety measures to the cabins as the main house. Kim threaded her fingers through the ends of her ponytail while she thanked the powers that be for the ocean breezes that kept the mosquitoes at bay. "I was actually thinking about how everyone fought to stay in those cottages during the family reunions." Aunt Margaret and Aunt Liz had finally resorted to a lottery system in order to put an end to the squabbles.

"Oh yeah?" When they reached the back of the van, Amy pulled Kim's suitcase out of the storage area.

"You know, for a long time, I thought maybe if Frank and I had stayed there instead of in the main house, things might have turned out differently for us."

"Whoa, Girl! That's quite a leap." The comment must have totally surprised Amy because she dropped the suitcase. It fell the last few inches, making a solid thunk when it landed on the brick pavers. "Oops. Sorry."

"Don't worry about it. I didn't pack anything breakable."

"I thought your marriage broke up 'cause Frank was a cad."

Kim chuckled. She could always count on Amy to cut straight to the chase. "It did. He was. He still is. But it took years for me to figure that out. The rest of you, though, you had him pegged from the moment you met him."

"Ohhh, that was a disaster." Amy shook her head. "You'd been married, what? Five years by then?"

"A little over." She and Frank had exchanged vows in front of a justice of the peace in January. The first few months of their marriage had been pure bliss, and she'd been looking forward to proudly introducing her husband to the rest of her family at the start-of-the-summer reunion. By the time mid-May rolled around, though, she'd realized the nasty case of the flu she hadn't been able to shake was actually morning sickness. Barely able to roll out of bed most mornings, she hadn't had the heart to argue when Frank had insisted they forgo the annual get-together so they could save money for their unexpected bundle of joy. The next year, he'd declared that the beach was no place to take a newborn, so they'd skipped the family gathering again. The following year, history had repeated itself when she was pregnant with Natalie. The year after that, she'd been so overwhelmed by the daily grind of juggling a newborn, a toddler and a full-time job that even the thought of packing up and going to the beach had given her heart palpitations. The fifth year, though, she'd known her family would soon disown her if she and her little brood didn't show up. So they'd gone.

And Frank had hated every minute of it. Worse, he'd been a complete jerk about it. Granted, sleeping in the same room with their children hadn't been ideal, but, as Kim had pointed out, not even a place as large as the inn could accommodate the entire Dane family without some compromises. Frank, however, didn't believe in compromise. Or at least, he felt he shouldn't be the one doing the compromising. He'd taken one look at the Jack-and-Jill bathroom they shared with the suite next door and had launched an endless campaign to go home.

Which hadn't exactly endeared him to the rest of her family.

"I've often wondered, if we'd stayed in one of the cottages, would he have been happier? Fit in better?"

"I don't think so." Amy shook her head. "That husband of yours was an equal-opportunity dolt. He wouldn't have liked it here even if we'd given him the best suite in the house or put lobster on the menu every night."

"True." According to Frank, Emerald Bay was too remote, the meals Aunt Liz and her staff slaved over too bland and the beach too beachy. As if too much sun and sand could ever be a bad thing.

"You never brought him to another reunion," Amy hinted.

"He refused to come. I think that was the beginning of the end for us." Kim straightened. She'd never told anyone the whole truth about Frank. Her voice dropped to a whisper. "He wanted me to leave the kids at home and go with him on a cruise to the islands. Or spend a week in New York. Or jet off to Paris, just the two of us. Can you imagine?"

"He didn't know you at all, did he?" Amy asked. Darkness surrounded them when she closed the van's rear hatch.

"Apparently not." Her mom had thought nothing of leaving her and her sister behind while she took off with her boyfriend of the month. Kim had stood at the window watching her mother leave often enough that she'd vowed to do better by her own children. "I tried to find some middle ground. I told him we could attend the reunion one year, take a family vacation the next. All four of us, that is. That part was non-negotiable. He wouldn't hear of it. So I agreed to take the kids to the reunion while he took his own vacation."

"That couldn't have been easy," Amy commented.

"No," Kim answered with a laugh. She and Frank had fought like cats and dogs about it. In the end, though, she'd stood her ground. The next summer, she and the kids had made the trip on their own, and they'd had a great time, she explained. "When I got home, Frank was so happy to see us that I thought that was the end of it. I even thought he might reconsider and come with us the next time. But I was wrong." She shook her head. "So wrong. The very next day, while I was still trying to dig myself out from under a mountain of laundry, Frank took the kids to a theme park for an entire week."

A long moment passed when the only sound came from the frogs and crickets. At last Amy asked, "A whole week?" She whistled softly. "What an as—"

Kim held up a hand to stop her cousin before Amy could finish her thought. "Trust me. I've called him enough names for the both of us. Don't waste your breath."

"Still, what he did, that wasn't fair."

"No kidding," she agreed. "From then on, he'd offer Josh and Nat a choice between going to a theme park with him or coming here with me." She paused. "Of course they chose the theme park. What kid wouldn't?"

"That's why you always came to the reunions by yourself?" When Kim nodded, Amy said, "Oh, honey. I thought he was giving you a well-deserved break. That's what everyone thought."

"I know." Kim hung her head. Amy would be well within her rights to ask why she hadn't left Frank over this one thing alone, why she'd stayed with him for as long as she had. At the time, she'd justified his behavior by telling herself that lots of families took separate vacations. It wasn't until years later, when she spoke with a therapist following the divorce, that she realized how much her own childhood had influenced this decision, like it had so many others.

"You know I never met my father, right?" she asked. As reluctant as she was to split open a vein and spill, Amy was closer to her than her own sister. She ought to know the truth.

"Yeah, I... No one ever talks about it, but yeah. Aunt Shirley lived life according to her own rules."

"That's one way of saying it," Kim said slowly. To put it plainly, her mom had slept around a lot. "To this day, I don't even know my father's name. I think, because of that, I desperately wanted Josh and Natalie to know their dad. So desperately, in fact, that I convinced myself that an imperfect husband was better than no husband at all. Among my many regrets, that's the one that hurts the most." She'd done her best to give her children a sense of stability, to teach them the importance of family, to help them value the simpler things in life. Frank, who thought nothing of uprooting his family on a whim, who showered the children with expensive gifts and trips to places they couldn't afford, had undermined her efforts at every turn.

Sensing that she'd come full circle in her thinking, she straightened her ponytail. "I better get inside," she said. "I wouldn't want Aunt Margaret to lock me out of the house." Plus, she still needed to clean up the kitchen before she turned in.

"Yeah. And I've got some baking to do yet." Amy's head lifted. "Hey. Thanks for telling me all that. You didn't have to, you know."

"I know." Kim leaned close enough to wrap her arms around her cousin. "I wanted to. I've missed being here, hanging out with you and the others, telling each other all our deep, dark secrets." She breathed in, drinking in the smell of vanilla and sugar that clung to Amy.

"It'll be nice having you around for a bit. I've missed this, too," Amy said, returning the hug with a quick squeeze of her own. Her keys jingled when she cupped Kim's back with one hand. "Okay. I gotta run. Talk tomorrow?"

"You bet." Kim hefted her suitcase and retraced her steps toward the back door. The salty tang of the ocean, the sweet smell of night-blooming jasmine and the faintest trace of orange blossoms filled the air. She drank it in, convinced that coming home had been the best decision she'd made in a long, long time.

"Or maybe not," she corrected when dust bunnies scattered as she dropped her suitcase and backpack onto the Topaz Suite's hardwood floors a half hour later. She gave the sitting room and the bedroom beyond it a quick scan. The polished surface of a side table had lost its gleam beneath a film of dust. The pillows on the love seat leaned drunkenly to the side. The covers on the canopy bed were rumpled. Her gaze rose to the ceiling, where cobwebs created a lacy pattern around the bulbs in the overhead light. She spotted a few more webs in the corners.

So much for keeping the upstairs rooms move-in ready. She pummeled the back of a club chair and sneezed when a cloud of dust rose from the faded blue upholstery. When she'd spent her summers working at the inn with her cousins, they'd treated every suite—empty or not—to a thorough cleaning at least once a week. This room looked as if it hadn't seen a broom or a mop in months.

Wearily, she eyed the bed. Had the sheets even been changed after the previous guest's departure?

Unwilling to take the chance, she marched down the hall to the second-floor linen closet. Flinging the doors wide, she breathed in deeply and was instantly rewarded with the good smells of detergent and bleach. She gathered a stack of sheets, pillowcases, towels and washcloths from the piles of fresh linens and, returning to her suite, made quick work of stripping and remaking the king-size bed. In the bathroom, she disposed of the dubiously clean towels, replacing them with fresh. She showered, ran a comb through her wet hair and, deciding to leave the dust where it was for the time being, turned out the lights and crawled between the sheets. Before she drifted off to sleep, she promised she'd have a word with the housekeeping staff first thing in the morning.

Ten

Belle

"I look ridiculous in this getup," Belle insisted. Standing in front of the full-length mirror that doubled as the closet door in a standard room at the Best Western, she flung her arms out to the sides. She rolled her eyes when the foot-long fringe dripping from the sleeves of a rhinestone-studded jacket shook while the ruffles along the plunging neckline of her shirt shifted to reveal far more of the girls than she wanted to expose. As if that wasn't bad enough, Lisa had insisted she wear torn denim. Belle brushed a loose thread from the jeans with a sigh. She was all for a few strategically placed rips, but these showed far too much skin before they disappeared into a pair of hot-pink boots no self-respecting cowgirl would ever wear.

No country singer making her debut stage appearance either, for that matter. She'd bet dollars to doughnuts none of the thousands of hopefuls who came to Nashville each year could afford to throw down fifteen hundred dollars for a jacket. Nor would they drop a cool five thou on a pair of Lucchese boots. No. She knew from personal experience that singers waiting for their big break slung hash and waited tables to pay the rent. They hustled from one open mic night to another, all the while praying they'd earn enough in tips to splurge on a burger after the show. If she expected to convince anyone she was just starting out—and that was the goal, wasn't it?—she'd be far better off wearing a plaid shirt and a pair of jeans fresh from some thrift store's bargain bin.

"Lisa, let's rethink the whole wardrobe," she said with a sigh. "In fact, let's cancel the gig. We can try again once we've had more time to prepare."

Ever since Jason had sprung the booking on her, she'd been too busy studying song lyrics and trying to wrap her head around the nuances of country music to even think of what she'd wear on stage. She'd left that little detail to Lisa. Which ordinarily worked out perfectly because Lisa had excellent taste in clothes. In this case, though, the agent had dressed her in a cross between Dolly and Reba. As much as Belle respected those powerhouse singers, she was pretty sure she needed to earn her chops before she adopted their signature looks. Or covered one of their songs.

"Belle, darling," Lisa said with the practiced patience of someone who made their living by dealing with temperamental superstars. "You're gorgeous. This outfit is exactly what you need to wear in order to convince the audience you're ready to explode onto the country scene. Now put on that wig so we can head to the bar. You want to be waiting in the wings when they call your name."

"It's not right, Lisa. It's too rushed. Too soon. I haven't had enough time to learn the lyrics. Geez. Jason doesn't know what he's asking—walk out on a stage I've never seen and perform with a guitar player I haven't even met?" Another fly in the ointment—the bar supplied its own stage musicians. No one from her band could appear with her. "I'm telling you, this is not going to go well."

Lisa folded her arms across her chest. "It has to. There are no other options. Jason has asked for a show of good faith. Winning over the crowd tonight will go a long way in proving you're a team player. For a guy like him, that's more important than I can dare to say."

Belle swallowed a final protest, but that didn't stop her from seeing all the ways the gig could go wrong. Only three days had passed since the record label executive had canceled her tour and put her album on hold. Though she'd immediately plunged into a study of country music, she'd barely scratched the surface. Oh, sure, she could croon along with the songs on the radio, but that was a far different thing from performing them on stage. How was she supposed to stand in front of an audience and belt out a hit when she hadn't had time to learn everything there was to know about it?

"My fans will hate me. They'll think I'm abandoning them. Anyone who loves country music will know I'm a fake," she'd argued when Jason called to tell her he'd booked her into a Nashville venue.

"No one will know it's you," the executive had countered. "I've listed you under an assumed name. It's an open mic night. Covers only, no original material—that should take some of the pressure off. No one there will be expecting perfection."

She'd pointed out a few more reasons her appearance in a Nashville honky-tonk was doomed to failure, but she might as well have been talking to a wall for all the good it had done. Minutes later, the man who signed her paychecks had tired of even pretending to consider her opinions. When he'd tossed terms like "failure to perform" and "breach of contract" into the conversation, she'd known she had no choice. Which was why she was standing in the middle of a cheap hotel holding a curly blond wig.

"Couldn't we have at least brought one makeup girl with us?" Normally a bevy of hair, makeup and fashion stylists crowded around her before a performance. They made sure she looked like a million bucks before she stepped one foot out of her dressing room. But was that happening tonight, when her career, her future was at stake? No. Tonight, instead of warming up her voice or running over her song lyrics, she was struggling to position a wig over the skin-tight cap that plastered her naturally auburn hair to her scalp.

"And run the risk of someone recognizing you?" Lisa looked askance. "Or worse, tipping off a reporter from *CMT* or *Taste of Country* and having them show up at the bar?"

Belle huffed. Her foray into a different kind of music needed to be handled with finesse. The last thing she wanted was to open a gossip rag tomorrow and see her picture over a caption that read "Pop Star Goes Country." To minimize that risk, she and Lisa were doing their best to keep her presence in Nashville a secret. They'd taken a commercial flight rather than the record company's private jet. A nondescript rental had replaced her usual car and driver. Instead of booking the Presidential Suite at a five-star hotel like she always did, she and Lisa had taken adjoining rooms at the Best Western, which, she had to admit, was the last place in town anyone would expect to run into her. The preparations didn't stop there, either. Tonight, Lisa would wait in the car at least two blocks from the bar, leaving Belle, like any other struggling artist, to walk the rest of the way on her own.

She gave the wig a final tug and anchored it in place with pins. All their precautions would hopefully keep her name out of the papers, but none of it had dissolved the hard knot of uncertainty in the pit of her stomach. And if there was one thing she was certain of, it was that unless she delivered the performance of a lifetime tonight, her career and her future were over.

"Next up, folks, making her first appearance on stage, let's all give a warm Nashville welcome to newcomer Rosie Dawn."

A smattering of applause rose from the sparse crowd in the Whiskey Street Blues Club, a bar so far from Nashville's famed Music Row, hardly anyone had ever heard of it. Which, according to Jason, made Whiskey Street the perfect place for Belle to make her country debut. So here she was, waiting in the wings of a half-empty bar for her turn to go on stage.

"Rosie? Rosie Dawn?" Mark, the emcee, looked pointedly toward the black curtains that hung between the front of the house and the darkened back stage where a dozen hopeful singers milled about. When there was no response, Mark shaded his eyes and scanned the audience. "Are you out there?"

"Hey. That's you, isn't it?"

Belle felt a gentle nudge at her shoulder. She turned to see a man with broad features gesture her forward. "Better get the lead out, or you'll miss your big chance."

"Geez." Some country star she was. She hadn't even recognized her own name. She shot a grateful smile toward the man who was next in line to perform. "Thanks."

Pivoting toward the stage, she repeated the

same pep talk she gave herself before every performance.

I have the voice, the talent, the drive to be the best. People love me for it. I can do this!

She paused to consider the new path she was on while she called upon every ounce of poise and professionalism she'd accumulated during thousands of appearances all over the globe.

Despite a firm reminder that for tonight, at least, she was Rosie Dawn, Unknown Talent, disappointment welled within her when no one cheered as she stepped onto the stage. Not for the first time, she wished Lisa had come to the bar with her. Then at least one person in the audience would give her a proper welcome. But having the talent agent at her side doubled the chances someone would recognize her, despite her disguise, so she and Lisa had decided it wasn't worth the risk. Now, though, used to the thunderous applause that greeted her wherever she performed, Belle felt an unfamiliar rush of stage fright when her footsteps echoed hollowly in a room that had filled with an uneasy hush.

Had someone in the crowd recognized her beneath the flowing blond wig and the rhinestones that gleamed from practically every inch of her jacket? She hoped not. Everyone, from her record label to her millions of fans, demanded perfection from Belle Dane. Something she prided herself on delivering. Rosie Dawn, on the other hand, was just starting out. If *she* forgot the lyrics or lost her rhythm in the middle of a song, people would chalk it up to a bad case of nerves. But if anyone discovered that Rosie and Belle were one and the same before she nailed down the nuances of this new style of music, the gossip rags would have a field day. That would be a disaster, she told herself just as one of the chunky heels of her boots caught on a board. To her horror, she stumbled forward a couple of steps.

Someone in the audience tittered.

"Oh, dear," she whispered, praying her near-pratfall wasn't a sign of things to come.

In desperation she locked eyes with the emcee and came face-to-face with a stark reminder of what it felt like to be just starting out with no star power whatsoever. Instead of rushing to her aid like someone in her usual cadre of employees and roadies, Mark fixed her with an unsympathetic gaze. His blank expression said it all. She, along with the hopefuls who still waited offstage, had been granted fifteen minutes behind the mic. Fifteen minutes and not a second more. Her timer had begun the moment Mark had first called her name. Not only that, but he wasn't going to make an exception. Not for a wannabe so wet behind the ears she couldn't make it across the stage without tripping over her own two feet. Certainly not with a half-dozen others just like her watching and waiting for their own chance to break into the music business.

She swallowed and gave the man a curt nod to let him know she understood. She'd already wasted thirty precious seconds. She wouldn't waste a second more. Rushing the rest of the way across the stage, she aimed her brightest smile and her friendliest wave at the crowd.

"Howdy, ya'll!" she called, unleashing the full effects of the faintest Southern accent that, as befitting a pop star, she'd spent years training out of her voice. "I'm Rosie Dawn, and I'm so glad to sing for you tonight at the Whiskey Street Blues Club that I'm fallin' all over myself."

Just as she'd hoped it would, making a joke at her own expense earned her a few laughs.

"Thanks so much, Mark, for having me here," she said while she adjusted the mic until she could reach it without standing on tiptoe. When she was satisfied, she looked around for the guitar player she'd been assured would be on stage to accompany her. Spying him on a nearby stool, she fought down a surprised gasp. Pimply-faced and sporting more ink than a newspaper, if the kid was a day over eighteen, she swore she'd eat her recently purchased cowboy hat.

With only three days to get ready for her first country gig, she'd spent every available minute nailing down song lyrics. There simply hadn't been enough time to learn those and master the melodies on her guitar, too. And don't get her started on making the switch from an electric to an acoustic instrument. She'd no more accompany herself on one of those than she'd… She stopped herself. It was no use saying she'd never sing in a country bar 'cause here she was, doing exactly that. Which meant she had to rely on the kid unless she wanted to struggle through her set a cappella. Praying her music had somehow made it into the boy's hands, she shot him a hopeful glance.

"Ready?" she mouthed. Following the cover-only rule, she planned to kick things off with Reba's "Fancy" and close out the set with a Dolly Parton ballad. She'd handed in her carefully marked selections when she'd first arrived at the bar.

With one worn cowboy boot braced against the floor, the other hooked over the footrest, the kid nodded. Belle steadied herself with one final deep breath. Then, she gave the thumbs-up sign and prepared to launch into a rousing rendition of a young girl's rags-to-riches story.

Instead, the guitar player strummed the

opening bars of what was supposed to be her second song. Caught off-guard by the switch, Belle missed her cue. With no time to regroup, she did her best to shrug off the mistake and waited, expecting the kid to repeat the beginning chords the way her band did on those rare occasions when she failed to stick an opening. When he kept on playing as if she'd joined in at the right place, she had to jump in mid-song. The result was messy, amateurish and certainly not the start she'd envisioned. But she hadn't spent thousands of hours on stage without learning a thing or two about grace under fire. She stuck with it.

By the end of the first verse, she'd gained her footing. By the end of the third, she felt almost as much at ease as she did whenever she performed the song that had turned her name into a household word. She rounded into the final verse and handled the soaring high notes at the end of the chorus like the pro she was.

Pleased with how she'd finished despite the rough start, she waited for the audience's reaction. And got...nothing. Her heart lodged in her throat when, for a long beat, the muted buzz of conversation continued without a break. Just when she was beginning to think she'd have to move on without any response at all, someone in the back clapped. After another second or two, a few more people joined in.

Tough crowd.

Determined to win this one over, she sucked down a steadying breath. This wasn't her first rodeo, she'd told herself. These people might think they were listening to Rosie Dawn, newbie. They probably thought she'd dissolve into a puddle of tears or run from the stage if they treated her badly enough. Little did they know, they were dealing with Belle Dane. *She'd* performed before presidents and kings and queens. She'd paid her dues by singing for tips on street corners. She'd worked hard to get where she was today, and it'd take a lot more than a demanding audience on the backside of Nashville to get her down. No, sirree, Bob.

Throwing her shoulders back and pulling herself to her full height, she launched into what should have been her first number. This time the audience, sparse as it was, paid more attention. Midway through the final chorus, she even spotted a couple of people in the bar tapping their feet in time with the music. When the final notes of the song faded, an enthusiastic applause filled the silence.

Belle curtseyed, half expecting the crowd to demand more. Knowing she'd nailed the song, she beamed at Mark when the emcee joined her on stage. She stuck one hand in her jacket pocket where she'd tucked the music for a third number even though the rules had clearly stated there'd be no exceptions to the two-song rule.

"Well, now," Mark said as he ratcheted the mic stand back to its original position. "Wasn't that nice?" he asked, damning her with the faintest of praise. Meeting her eyes, he aimed his chin toward the wings.

Wait, what? Belle blinked at the unmistakable signal for her to exit the stage. She stood, her feet rooted to the spot, as heat climbed onto her face. Nice? He thought her performance was nice? He wasn't even going to ask her to sing another number? Did he not know who she was? Apparently the answer to all her questions was a resounding no, she realized when Mark patently ignored her.

"Now, folks, our next singer needs no intro-duction," the emcee said. "Ladies and gentlemen, let's give a warm welcome to Nashville's own Terry Wilcox."

Before Belle hardly knew what was happening, a heavyset man dressed in black stepped from behind the curtain. Though her feet felt like they were encased in concrete instead of leather, she managed to get them in motion.

Recognizing the man who'd helped her earlier, she whispered the expected "Break a leg" as she passed him. She couldn't help but wince at the "Better luck next time" he gave her in return.

Had her performance really been that bad? she asked as she stepped into the wings. She shook her head and felt her wig wobble. It must have been. Otherwise, she'd still be on stage, not beating a hasty retreat after hearing the Nashville equivalent of "Don't call us; we'll call you." She had to face the truth. She, Belle Dane, had bombed. For the first time in decades, she'd left the stage without being asked to sing an encore. Not only that, but everyone in the bar—from the other wannabe country stars to the guy serving the drinks—couldn't wait to see her go.

Which she was going to do right now, she decided. Ignoring the others who still waited for their chance at stardom, she marched straight to the exit. Seconds later, she stepped out into an alley that stunk of dashed hopes and ruined dreams. The only saving grace was that no one knew who she really was. And if she had anything to do with it, they never would.

After giving up on sleep, Belle pulled what had to be the world's most uncomfortable chair in front of a table not much bigger than a postage stamp. Movement in one corner of the room caught her eye, and she stared at the curtains. The foam-backed drapes billowed and sank according to the vagaries of an air conditioner that cycled on and off at random. While she'd tossed and turned in the unfamiliar bed last night, the window box had stubbornly refused to produce a breath of air. But this morning when she'd welcome a little bit of warmth, it was doing its best to cool the room to polar levels.

Shivering, she snuggled deeper into the robe she'd pulled on over her jeans and T-shirt. She held onto her coffee cup for warmth while she ran one finger over her laptop's touchpad. Beneath the computer, the table wobbled atop legs that were so uneven, she hadn't dared set the paper cup on the scarred surface out of fear that some of the liquid would splash onto the keyboard. Not that it was the best coffee in the world. She'd had that. This wasn't it. As bitter as arugula, the nasty-tasting brew had grown lukewarm while she scrolled through blog sites and digital magazines on the hunt for any mention of last night's open mic at Whiskey Street. So far she hadn't found anything, but she kept at it, determined not to stop until she'd read all the news that had come out of Nashville in the past twelve hours.

She took a sip and forced herself to swallow. Bitter or not, she needed all the caffeine she could get. After the fiasco at Whiskey Street last night, she hadn't slept a wink. All night long, the performance had played in her head like a broken record or, better yet, like one of those Facebook reels that kept playing and replaying until you moved on to the next one. No matter how hard she tried, she still couldn't figure out what went wrong.

True, the kid on the guitar hadn't done her any favors. Kicking off the set with the wrong song had gotten things off on a decidedly wrong foot. But didn't she deserve a pat on the back for making an excellent recovery? Besides, that second number had gone perfectly, even if she did say so herself. So why had Mark rushed her off the stage? And why had Terry Wilcox wished her "better luck" on her next performance? The whole experience would have left her scratching her head if she hadn't been wearing that hideous wig at the time.

In the hall, someone rapped sharply on her door. Startled, she jumped, nearly spilling what was left of her coffee. Her mind raced. At six forty-five, it was too early for housekeeping. Much too early for Lisa, too. But who else could it be? The paparazzi?

Had someone recognized her when she'd dashed downstairs earlier? She considered the possibility and immediately rejected it. Other than a lone clerk behind the reception desk, she'd neither seen nor spoken to anyone during the five minutes it had taken her to sneak down the back stairwell, pour herself a cup of coffee in the lobby, and climb the three flights back to her room.

Her cell phone buzzed. She pulled it from the pocket of her jeans and read an incoming text from Lisa.

Let me in.

Her tension ratcheted higher. Lisa didn't "do" mornings, not without a good reason. Belle hurried to the door. Flinging it open, she gaped at the pale figure bathed in the hallway's flickering fluorescent lights. The hair on the left side of Lisa's head was mashed flat. On the other side, one clump stuck up like a rooster's tail. Still in her pajamas, the woman who'd landed more than one seven-figure deal for Belle barged past her.

"Have you read it?" Lisa demanded with a hoarse croak.

"Read what?" Belle stiffened. Bad publicity,

that had to be it. Nothing less would get Lisa out of bed at this ungodly hour. But where? Who? She'd been crawling through blog posts for an hour without finding a single mention of her name.

"The *Gossip Rags* article."

"No, I…" She'd begun her search with the A-list publications like *Town & Country* and *Country Daily*. *Gossip Rags*, with its smaller distribution and decidedly shoddy journalism, lay closer to the bottom of the barrel.

"Jason has. He sent me this." Lisa brandished her cell phone like a weapon.

Belle managed the briefest of glimpses of the image on the screen before Lisa jerked the device away. Holding it at arm's length, she read aloud: "Pop Star Falls Flat."

"Oh, no," Belle whispered.

Lisa looked up from the screen only long enough to issue a warning. "You haven't even heard the article yet." Her eyes on the screen, she read, "Members of the audience at the Whiskey Street Blues Club were appalled last night when none other than famed pop star Belle Dane literally tripped onto the stage during an open mic session meant only for aspiring artists. Ms. Dane, who tried to hide her identity behind a fake name and a blond wig, insulted country music fans all over with a disrespectful rendition of 'Early Morning Breeze,' which, as we all know, was the flip side of Dolly Parton's 'Jolene.' Bedecked in rhinestones and a pair of garish pink boots, Ms. Dane didn't stop there. For her next number, she cut loose with her own version of Reba's 'Fancy.' Ms. Dane was apparently so enamored with her own voice that she muscled through the song without giving Teddy Baynard his break. This was more than a faux pas, folks. It was an outright slap in the face to the man behind such hits as 'A Quiet Country Morning' and CMA's number one chart single 'Gotcha!' This reporter has only one thing to say for the likes of Ms. Dane. Hit the road, Belle, and don't come back now. Y'hear?"

"Oh, my word. That kid with all the ink was Teddy Baynard?" Belle's stomach sank. Even someone as brand-new to the Nashville scene as she was knew the musician/composer's name. If he'd recognized her—which he no doubt had—he'd probably messed with her audition on purpose. Still, the author of the article hadn't played fair. Sure, she'd gotten off to a rocky start. She'd be the first to admit that, but she'd proven her chops by sticking with it. And she'd never, never, ever intended to insult anyone. Much less the reigning royalty of the country music scene.

She had nothing but the utmost respect for the artists whose songs she'd covered.

"It gets worse." Lisa's voice turned positively funereal.

"How? How can it get worse?" It was bad enough already.

"The article only went live an hour ago. More than fifty people have already responded. One of them posted a video."

Lisa angled the phone so they could both watch the train wreck unfold. As Belle stepped onto the darkened stage, the hundreds of crystals glued to her jacket reflected the glare of the lights in a glow so bright, it hurt her eyes to look at it. She groaned as the figure on stage lost her balance halfway to the mike.

"The planks were uneven. My boot caught on one of them. I'm used to wearing heels." Belle stopped herself. Making one lame excuse after another wasn't going to undo the past.

"Shhh," Lisa said. "Just watch."

Zipping her lips, Belle leaned closer to her agent. Together, they stared at the tiny screen. She heard the guitar player strum the opening bars of the wrong song, watched herself rush to catch up with the man who should have been taking his cues from her. Instead, he barged ahead without paying her the tiniest bit of attention. The video ended just before she found her footing with the first song.

"That looked much worse than it actually was. There's no snippet of the second number?" She couldn't prevent the note of hopefulness that crept into her voice, although she was pretty sure she already knew the answer. "Pop Singer Nails It" was never going to be a headline on a third-rate blog like "Gossip Rags."

Lisa flipped through the comments. "No. That's it." She paused for a moment. "I thought you said attendance was low at Whisky Street last night."

Belle pictured the empty tables scattered throughout the bar. "Twenty people, maybe. Another dozen or so who signed up for the open mic."

"Hmmm."

"What?"

"In the five minutes we've been standing here, another fifty people have commented on your performance." Lisa tapped the screen with a chipped fingernail. "All of them claim to have been there."

"That's not possible," Belle protested. "I swear, the place was practically empty."

"Some of these comments…" Lisa blew out a puff of air. "Fake Southern accent…"

"Fake?" Belle inhaled sharply. "Do they not know I was born and raised south of the Mason-Dixon Line?"

Lisa continued as if Belle hadn't said a word. "Dolly Parton wig… Who does she think she is… A mockery of everything we love about country music…"

"They're really starting to pile on, aren't they?" Belle had seen this kind of thing happen before on social media. One person made a negative comment. The next thing you knew, twenty more people had added their two cents.

As if she was watching an accident happen in slow motion and couldn't tear her eyes away from it, Lisa kept reading. "I saw Belle Dane in concert last year. She stunk… Like all those aging rock stars… When are we gonna see some real talent… People like her should step aside, make way for younger, more talented…"

Belle's knees gave out beneath her as the comments shifted from last night's performance to her hit singles and recent performances. With a soft grunt, she collapsed onto the chair, where she cupped her head in her hands. "Oh, this is a disaster," she moaned. For three decades, she'd been so careful, so protective of her reputation. While other superstars had taken advantage of their wealth and privilege, she'd walked the straight and narrow. She'd been circumspect about the men she dated, the parties she attended. She'd never even given any of her staff a reason to run to the tabloids and tell tales out of school. But if this kept up, she'd be ruined.

"No. This is bad, but it's not a disaster," Lisa corrected.

"Really?" A tiny seed of hope took root in Belle's chest. Maybe things weren't as bad as they seemed.

"Really. Wait till later today when the other bloggers and magazines pick the story up and run with it. That'll be the disaster," Lisa said, sounding an awful lot like an always down-in-the-dumps character in one of Belle's favorite children's books.

"You don't really think they will, do you?" she asked, although a heaviness in her chest said she already knew the answer. Social media was as lawless as the Wild Wild West. Anyone with a grudge or a grievance could duck behind a wall of anonymity and take potshots at the rich or famous, and no one could do a thing about it.

Lisa studied her phone while she scrolled further down the list of comments. "There's no doubt about it. This is news. I'd be surprised if the video doesn't go viral."

The coffee Belle had drunk earlier threatened

to make a return appearance. "Is there, is there anything we can do to stop it? Force *Gossip Rags* to take the post down? Claim defamation? Threaten to sue?"

"Not much chance of that, I'm afraid." Lisa plopped down onto Belle's unmade bed. "We can't even deny you were there. Not as long as that video exists." She pointed to her screen, where the movie had started over at the beginning. "Without it…" She shrugged.

Belle shook her head. Video or no video, she wouldn't tell an out-and-out lie. That wasn't her style. If she'd made a mistake—and apparently she had made a big one—she'd own it.

"I guess there's nothing for it then. I'll have to issue an apology and hope this all blows over quickly." She'd watched other rock stars crater their careers and bounce back afterwards. With Jason and Lisa beside her, she'd weather this storm, too. "Set up a press conference at four this afternoon. I'll—"

Her cell phone chimed a distinctive ring. She held the device up to Lisa. "Jason," she whispered, as if the man on the other end of the line was already listening. "What does he want?"

"Only one way to find out." Lisa gave the cell phone a pointed glance.

Great. Barely seven in the morning and her

agent was already in her hotel room. Now the head of her record label was on the phone. This didn't bode well.

Straightening, Belle pressed the green button and put the phone to her ear. "Good morning, Jason," she said into the mouthpiece.

She listened without trying to get a word in edgewise while one of the most powerful men in the recording industry demanded her immediate presence in his office. When he was finished, she turned to Lisa.

"He ordered me not to say a word to the press before we can have a sit-down and figure out the right strategy to deal with all this. I told him we'd be there later this afternoon. That's doable, isn't it?" She looked to Lisa for answers.

"We'll make it happen." The agent was already punching numbers on her phone. "You pack while I call the airport and charter a flight back to the city. I'll arrange for hair and makeup to meet you at the condo."

Belle stifled a groan. Though she'd taken steps to safeguard her privacy, all the news agencies knew where she lived. If the situation worsened, reporters and cameramen would camp out at the entrance to the building that overlooked Central Park. She'd be a prisoner in her own home for at least one news cycle. Maybe longer.

She ground her teeth and refrained from pointing out that none of this was her fault. "Going country" hadn't been her idea in the first place. Neither had donning a disguise and dropping in on an open mic session. But would Jason acknowledge his part in this disaster? She took a breath. Only time would tell, and that was a commodity she had precious little of.

Hurriedly, she tugged her overnight bag onto the bed and began stuffing clothes into it.

Eleven

Kim

*T*he sky slowly filled with broad strokes of pinks and reds while Kim watched the sunrise from the top of the wooden stairs that cut through the dunes to the beach. "Red sky in the morning, sailors take warning," she whispered before she tightened the lid of a now-empty travel mug. She stood and dusted sand from the back of her shorts. She and Aunt Margaret would need to get an early start to their day unless they wanted to get caught out in the rain later this afternoon.

Of course, that would be after she addressed the little matter of the general state of cleanliness in the inn with Irene and Eunice. There wasn't a doubt in her mind that the two-person crew had been taking advantage of her aunt's inability to manage the stairs. While a quick survey of the rooms on the first floor had been somewhat reassuring, she'd wager that no one had treated the upstairs to a thorough cleaning in at least six months, maybe longer. In good conscience, she couldn't let that continue. For the next couple of weeks, until she headed back to Atlanta, she'd see that the housekeepers did their jobs properly. They could start by giving her own suite a much-delayed spring cleaning.

She stretched, working out a few kinks. Walking on wet sand, feeling the breeze in her hair while salt spray misted her face had been far more invigorating than using the treadmill at the gym. Or, as she'd been resigned to ever since the layoff, taking long walks along the city streets. In Atlanta, she'd worn headphones to block out the noise. But here, her headphones had hung unused around her neck while she drank in the roar of the ocean and the high-pitched calls of seagulls.

She bent to pick up the tennis shoes she'd kicked off after her two-mile hike. She'd have preferred not to wear them, but only someone who didn't know better walked barefoot along the beach in semidarkness. You never knew what the high tide might wash ashore. This morning alone, she'd spotted bits of broken glass and some debris from a passing cruise ship among the usual offering of shells. Several jellyfish had washed up on the sand as well. Their long tentacles could deliver a nasty sting.

But no Spanish treasure, she added with a quiet chuckle. The possibility was real enough. Plenty of accounts documented the journey of the eleven Spanish ships that had set sail from the New World loaded with gold and emeralds for the king, only to sink in a hurricane off the coast of Florida. Hundreds of millions of dollars in lost treasure had already been recovered. Gold coins and gems still occasionally washed ashore, but neither she nor any of her cousins had ever been lucky enough to find a single emerald or piece of eight. That hadn't stopped them from searching, though, and oh, how they'd looked. Most afternoons—after they'd finished their work at the inn for the day—they'd rushed to the beach, where they often spent hours scouring the sand for anything of value.

When they tired of that, they'd borrowed a leathery old map from Aunt Margaret and tried to find where X marked the spot. She nudged a small shell from the deck onto the sand below. While the treasure might be real, the map was an entirely different matter. One of her uncles had most likely created it along with the story of shipwrecked survivors who'd buried their loot somewhere on the inn's property before they fell prey to marauding pirates. Though there was almost no chance the map led to a real treasure, she and her cousins sure had fun looking for one.

Tennis shoes dangling from her fingertips by their laces, she gave the sunrise a final glance. Halfway down the path that led to the inn, fan-shaped palmetto leaves blocked her way. She pushed them aside, careful not to scratch herself on the razor-sharp blades. In the open, grassy spaces, more than a few pepper trees had sprung up among the palmettos. Kudzu vine had all but overrun the fences where blackberries used to grow. No one had trimmed the palms for so long that brown, dead fronds ringed the green tops like upside-down crowns.

"Another thing for the list," she murmured as she added chatting with the gardeners about weeding and pruning to the things she wanted to accomplish before she headed home.

"There you are," Aunt Margaret called when Kim walked into the house a few minutes later. "I knew you'd head for the beach this morning."

Kim smiled. Her aunt was obviously pleased with herself.

"Enjoy your walk?"

"So much." Kim sighed. She brushed her feet on the mat a second time to avoid tracking sand on the floors. "I miss watching the sun come up over the horizon when I'm in Atlanta."

"No beach there," Margaret pointed out.

"If there is, someone's done a pretty good job of hiding it." She bent to place a kiss on her aunt's cheek. "Did you sleep well?"

"As well as these old bones would let me." Margaret rubbed her shoulder. "Old age ain't for sissies. Aches and pains get ya out of bed at night. Then your mind starts to fretting, and you can't get back to sleep." She yawned. "I can't remember the last time I slept through the night."

"Anything in particular bothering you?" Kim asked. She'd do whatever she could to solve the problem if she could. A second later, she mentally delivered a swift kick to her backside. How could worries not trouble her aunt? Every day Margaret had to feel the pressure to sell the only home she'd ever known and move into assisted living. Kim swallowed. Was that the best they could do for Aunt Margaret—stuff her away in an old folks' home? After all she'd done for them, didn't she deserve more? Tears stung Kim's eyes.

She looked away so her aunt wouldn't see them.

"Oh, honey, don't waste your vacation worrying about me. You're supposed to be enjoying yourself."

"I have a confession to make," Kim said. "Yes, I needed to get out of Atlanta for a bit, but I chose to come here mostly so I could spend some time with you." She massaged her aunt's thin shoulders with a much lighter touch than she'd used when they were both twenty years younger. As tempting as it might be, she couldn't overlook how tense her aunt seemed. Trying to get her to open up, Kim prodded, "Now is there anything in particular I can take care of for you?"

"Nothing and everything," Margaret said. She patted Kim's hand. "That felt good, child."

Kim didn't need to be told twice that her aunt was done with both talking about her troubles and the back rub. She let her hands drop to her sides. "Let me know if there's anything I can do to put your mind at ease," she offered.

"Have a cup of coffee, hon? I made a fresh pot."

"No thanks. I had some at the beach." Kim crossed to the large farmer's sink, where she washed and rinsed her travel mug before placing it in the drying rack. "Do you still want to go to the grocery store this morning?"

"I think we'd better, don't you?"

"Probably." Other than a few cans of soup, the pantry didn't hold much. As for the freezer, it was practically empty except for a couple of trays of cookies, which her aunt would put out for guests each afternoon.

"I'm in the mood for beef stew," she suggested. "Or I have a great recipe for chicken bourguignon. Maybe I'll fix both. What do you think?" She watched her aunt closely to see if either idea hit home. Loaded with veggies, the two dishes were filling and nutritious. As an added benefit, she could freeze individual portions for future meals.

"You don't really want to spend the whole time you're here slaving over a hot stove, do you?" Margaret's tone said she considered the idea of cooking an onerous chore.

"Oh, please," she pleaded. "I live on takeout and frozen TV dinners in Atlanta. It would be a treat to work in a real kitchen again." It had been years since she'd done more than stick something in the microwave to reheat or thaw it, and she missed cooking. When her children were younger, she'd often spent her weekends prepping meals for the rest of the week. Chopping the vegetables and making the sauces had filled the house with such tantalizing aromas. Later, serving her family tasty meals that were good for them had given her a much-needed sense of accomplishment.

Margaret waved a hand in surrender. "If that's what you want to do…"

"Thanks!" Kim smiled as if Margaret had granted her a big favor by turning her loose in the kitchen. But she'd seen the bright spark of interest in her aunt's blue eyes when she'd mentioned the chicken dish and was already planning to serve it for dinner the next day. She paused for a second as if something had just occurred to her.

"Would you mind if we stopped for an early lunch while we're out? At Sweet Cakes? Or the diner?" she suggested.

"Amy dropped off our usual order of breakfast rolls while you were on your walk. Or there's plenty of canned soup in the pantry. You're welcome to help yourself to whatever you want."

"After all those cupcakes last night, I think I need to put something solid in my stomach." Though Kim gave her tummy a playful pat, she craved real food.

"Well, all right then," Margaret said, letting herself be talked into a meal in town. "Let me see to the guests this morning, and then we can go. Say around ten?"

"Sounds good. If you don't need me to do anything right now, I think I'll run up and take a shower. I love the beach, but I don't particularly want to wear it all day." Laughing, she brushed a few grains of sand from her arm.

On her way out the door, she turned and, as casually as possible, asked, "What time do Irene and Eunice get here?"

Her aunt checked her watch before she answered. "It varies, but they're usually here by nine. Why do you ask?"

"I noticed a cobweb in the corner of my room." Actually, there were several, but what her aunt didn't know wouldn't hurt her. "I thought I'd ask them to get it down for me."

"They better not be slacking off on those upstairs rooms. Not if they know what's good for them." Margaret frowned so hard, the lines between her eyebrows deepened.

Kim didn't have a doubt in the world that her aunt meant exactly what she said. The summers she and her cousins had worked at the inn, Margaret had hounded them until every floor gleamed and there wasn't a speck of dust to be found. She'd be terribly disappointed to learn that Irene and Eunice hadn't maintained her high standards.

"No need. I'll speak to them. I'm sure it was

just an oversight," she said, offering her aunt an assurance she wasn't quite certain she felt. She'd give the cleaning staff one chance to make things right. If they didn't, she'd find someone else to do the work before she headed back to Atlanta. "Let me jump in the shower. We'll make out a list for the grocery store when I'm done."

Margaret's usual smile returned quickly. "You always did like your lists, didn't you?"

"Marking things off is half the fun of grocery shopping." Not only did it ensure she bought everything she needed, it kept her from buying on impulse and ending up with a cart full of ice cream and candy bars instead of TV dinners and salad. As an afterthought, she added, "Oh. I tidied up the front porch on my way out earlier."

"You didn't have to do that. You're on vacation," Aunt Margaret reminded her.

"Old habits die hard." She laughed as she started up the stairs. She hadn't been more than five years old when Aunt Margaret had assigned her the special task of plumping the pillows and watering the potted plants each day. She'd repeated the chore so often as a child that she couldn't walk out the front door as an adult without making sure everything on the porch was in order. That, along with speaking with the cleaning crew and the gardening crew, was the least she could do to make life easier for the woman who'd opened her home to her and her sister when they had no one else in the world.

"Okay, what'll it be—the diner or Sweet Cakes?" Kim asked after she'd helped Margaret to the car and gotten her settled in the passenger seat. She'd been surprised by how heavily her aunt had leaned on her arm as they walked from the house to the parking area. At the time, she'd simply thought Margaret was being extra cautious on the uneven pavers, but when the elderly woman softly confessed that she was so leery of falling she rarely left home, Kim had nearly wept. Several long seconds had passed before she'd pulled herself together long enough to pat her aunt's arm and offer a few words of encouragement. Even as she said them, though, regret for all the years she'd been away filled her. As a small consolation, she'd insisted her aunt choose the place they ate today.

"The bakery." Dressed in linen slacks and a polka-dotted blouse, Margaret folded her hands primly across the top of the purse she held in her lap. "I'm in the mood for some of Amy's chicken salad."

"That does sound yummy," Kim agreed, although she suspected her aunt would be just as happy with a simple fried bologna sandwich from the diner. "Does Amy still use Aunt Liz's recipe?" She'd never tasted any that was even half as good, which explained why it had been so popular at the inn.

"She's a smart girl. She won't mess with perfection," Margaret answered firmly.

"The bakery it is, then," Kim said, latching her own seat belt. When she started the engine, though, her aunt suddenly stiffened.

"Wait! I—I've changed my mind. I don't want to go after all." Margaret's voice took on an odd tremble. Letting go of her purse, she fumbled with the door handle. "This car hasn't been driven in years. We should have a mechanic look it over. It's not safe."

Kim gulped. Her aunt's reaction bordered on panic, and small wonder. Except for church on Sundays and the occasional shopping foray with her friend Maude, Margaret had been cooped up in the inn for who knew how long. Not only that, but it had only been a few years since her aunt had been badly injured in the same car accident that had taken her sister's life. Given the circumstances, anyone might have second thoughts about trusting their fate to an unfamiliar driver.

She swiveled in her seat to face the thin figure in the passenger's seat. "You know Uncle Eric taught me how to drive," she said in the most reassuring tone she could muster. "He was an excellent teacher. I've never had an accident. Never even gotten a speeding ticket. As for the car, I checked all the fluids and the tire pressures before I brought it around front." Though she hadn't thought so at the time, learning how to perform routine car maintenance had been one of the few benefits of having a ne'er-do-well for a husband. "It started right up, so I don't think we'll have any problems."

"You're sure?" In the passenger seat, Margaret's body stilled.

"Yes, ma'am. I am." When her aunt still didn't look convinced, Kim offered a compromise. "I'll be glad to take you back inside, if that's what you want, Aunt Margaret. I can get the groceries by myself. I'll even pick up sandwiches for us at Amy's. But wouldn't you like to get out for a change?"

Kim held her breath while she waited for her aunt's decision. She'd do whatever Margaret wanted, of course. Personally, she hoped they'd stick with the original plan. Not only would it do her aunt good to see other people, but her little chat with Irene and Eunice had had the desired effect. The two women had promised to have the inn glowing by the time she and Margaret returned from their shopping trip.

"Well, I did get all dressed." Margaret plucked at the fabric of her polka-dotted blouse. "You won't race or anything, will you?"

"Turtles will pass us. Trust me." Kim let out a long, slow breath. Before her aunt could change her mind again, she slipped the car in gear. Shells crackled and crunched as the tires rolled over the crushed coquina driveway at a slow and steady ten miles an hour. The sound was oddly comforting and, by the time they'd reached the main entrance, Aunt Margaret had lost her tight grip on her purse. Still, Kim let several cars go by until there was absolutely no traffic approaching from either direction before she pulled from the drive onto the main road. Even then, she refused to hurry and stayed well below the posted fifty-mile-an-hour limit.

"There, that wasn't so bad, was it?" she asked after she'd parked the car in the small lot behind the bakery rather than in one of the parking spaces that lined the busier highway out front.

"You must think I'm a silly old goose," Margaret said plaintively.

"No. Not at all." She took a breath. Her aunt needed reassurance, and she was just the person to give it. "If you must know, I'm very proud of you. I'm also very grateful that you trusted me enough to get us into town and back."

"Well, we're not back yet," came the quick retort that showed a spark of her aunt's usual quick wit. "I might just decide to spend the night with Amy."

Cackling softly, Margaret opened her car door and planted her cane on the ground. Kim laughed along with her as she dashed around the back of the car to help her aunt to her feet.

Walking into Sweet Cakes with her a few minutes later, Kim started to look around for her cousin but was immediately distracted. The last time she'd visited the bakery, the walls had been covered in pink-and-white wallpaper that had given the place a distinctly feminine air. Dainty white tables and chairs with plump, round cushions had added to the ambience. In the years since, though, her cousin had gone bolder and brighter. Below a chair rail, paint the color of beach sand gave the walls a fresh, clean look. Above it, colorful fish and sea creatures swam beneath foam-dotted waves in a mural that was nothing less than stunning. In one corner of the room, the artist had painted the skeleton of a wooden ship resting on the faux ocean floor. In another, an old wooden chest spilled its treasure onto the sand. In between them, brass fixtures had transformed the long, glass-fronted display cabinets into more seafaring chests, though the goodies in these included a tantalizing array of cookies, cakes and decadent desserts.

"Wow!" Kim whistled softly. "Impressive." The decor wasn't what she'd expected to find in a bakery, but she had to admit it was a perfect fit for Emerald Bay.

"Amy said she wanted to draw people of all ages into the store," Margaret murmured.

"I'm sure intrigued. I bet kids love it, too." It was just the sort of thing that would keep children entertained while their moms lingered over coffee and pastries. She drew in a deep breath and was rewarded with the rich scent of caffeine mingled with sugar and spice. Her tummy gurgled. "What say we order something yummy?" she asked.

When Margaret nodded agreeably, she guided her aunt to a resin-topped table that held an array of seashells atop fans of white coral. Sturdy wooden chairs had replaced the tufted cushions. Her aunt chose one painted a lavender color, while Kim sat in a teal one that faced the open room. They'd no sooner sat down than a slender young woman hurried over with a pad and a pen.

"Hey, Ms. Clayton. I'm so glad to see you here today. It's been too long," the waitress gushed. "C'mon and give me a hug." Without waiting for permission, she leaned down and threw her arms about Margaret's shoulders.

"Hello, Deborah. It's good to see you, too." Her aunt returned the hug with a quick squeeze before she extricated herself. "Do you remember my niece, Kimberly?"

"My word! Of course I do," Deborah exclaimed. "You used to babysit me and my brother when we were little. Amy told me you were in town for a visit. It's been a while since we saw you, hasn't it?"

"Too long, I'm afraid." Kim glanced at her aunt. "Two years? Two and a half?"

"About that." Margaret nodded.

A fresh ripple of guilt washed over Kim. Fighting it off, she searched for something else to talk about. Asking about Deborah's family seemed safe enough, but for the life of her, she couldn't recall the name of the woman's son. She settled for a polite, "How's the family? Your boy's not a baby anymore, is he?"

"Danny? He's good." Deborah's voice filled with a mother's pride. "Sixth grade now. He takes after his daddy—all football and sports." She tapped her pen on her notepad. "You just missed Amy. She likes to make the bank deposit before the lunch rush." She leaned closer, her voice dropping to a whisper. "You're lucky you came in early. Saturdays are always busy. We'll be swamped in about twenty minutes. Can I get y'all something to drink?"

"I'll have sweet tea," Kim said. She looked at her aunt.

"Coffee for me, thanks. Black. None of those fancy flavorings in it, either." Margaret turned to her. "Why mess with a good thing?"

"You got it." Deborah tapped her pen on her pad. "We're running a special on flatbreads with your choice of toppings today. Would you like to see a menu? Or do you want something from the display case? We have some bread pudding that'll knock your socks off," she suggested with a smile and a wink.

"So many choices." Margaret smiled. "I think I'll stick with chicken salad. How about you, Kim?"

"I'll have the same. On a croissant, if you don't mind," she added, staving off any more questions before Deborah could ask them.

"Sounds good." Deborah slipped her order pad into the pocket of her apron. "I'll have those out for you in a jiff."

As Deborah had predicted, the shop began to fill while they waited for their food. Soon a line had formed at the register, and people crowded the tables in the cafe section. Conversation ebbed and flowed as longtime residents of the town exchanged greetings and the latest news about who was in the hospital or which car had been spotted parked outside a bar late last night. Margaret beamed with pleasure when several of her friends stopped by their table to say hello. When one of them asked if she'd make it to the potluck and prayer service at the church on Wednesday, Kim happily offered to drive her, a move that pleased everyone, her aunt most of all.

Kim's glass of iced tea was still three-quarters full and her aunt's coffee had barely cooled before Deborah returned with their orders. Kim paused for a moment to drink in the buttery scent of a flaky croissant so large it hung off either side of her plate. Leafy, green lettuce and slices of bright red tomato formed the perfect bed for the thick chunks of white meat, grapes and celery that swam in a sea of creamy mayonnaise. A mound of what looked like homemade kettle chips stood to one side.

"Oh, my goodness!" She glanced from the huge sandwich to her aunt. "Maybe we should have split one?"

"Speak for yourself, deary." Margaret wrapped her thin arms protectively around her plate.

Kim grinned. Prepared to do justice to the excellent food, she lifted half her sandwich. The first bite nearly made her moan with pleasure. The combination of the flaky roll, rich filling and crisp lettuce was a match made in heaven. She chewed slowly, savoring the flavors. When she'd swallowed, she whispered, "Oh, that's every bit as good as I remembered."

"Just like Liz used to make," Margaret murmured.

Kim tilted her head so she could steal a look at her aunt. Judging by the tears in Margaret's eyes, her aunt missed her sister fiercely, but that didn't keep the older woman from smiling as she took her next bite. Reassured that all was well, Kim plucked one of the smaller kettle chips from her plate and popped it into her mouth. Salty and crisp, the chips made the perfect side dish.

"Oh, look who's here," Margaret said when they'd each taken a few more bites. She blotted her lips with her napkin.

"Someone we know?" Kim looked up from the wedge of sandwich she held in her hands. She scanned the now-crowded bakery for a familiar face and saw no one she knew until, on her second pass through the room, she spotted a man headed straight for their table.

"Oh!" The faint gasp escaped her lips before she could stop it. She'd hardly been aware of Craig's features on the bus yesterday, but his rugged good looks were hard to overlook now that he'd exchanged his business suit for a pale blue shirt tucked and belted into faded blue jeans. Though his chest had thickened in the years since high school, and she'd swear his shoulders were broader than she remembered, he still sported the same trim waist and slim hips. As for the rest of him, the gray at his temples only served to enhance the wide planes of cheekbones that tapered to a cleft chin. Laugh lines framed lips that formed an easy smile whenever he stopped to exchange a bit of small talk with one of the dozens of people who crowded the bakery. Or when he looked her way, as he was doing now.

Kim lowered her sandwich to her plate while she gave herself a stern reminder that she was not interested in Craig Morgan. Oh, he'd been pleasant enough to talk to on the bus, and she'd enjoyed reminiscing about their high school days. She'd even begun to think she might like to renew their friendship while she was in town. But then he'd gone and ruined it all by insulting her family's home. When he'd poked his nose into their business, he'd clearly overstepped his bounds. Why had he done that? Was he like Frank, who'd had an ulterior motive for every move he made throughout their marriage? If so, what nefarious plot did Craig have hidden in those sleeves he'd rolled up to his elbows? And why was he seeking her out now?

"Good afternoon, ladies," he said when he'd neared their table. "Ms. Clayton." He brushed the brim of an imaginary hat. "Kimberly."

"Hello, Craig," Margaret said warmly before she shot Kim a speculative glance. "I didn't realize you two knew each other."

"Craig and I were in the same class at Emerald Bay High," she explained, opting for the shortest possible version of the story while she hoped Craig would finish what he had to say quickly and leave them to enjoy their lunch. Not that she'd finish hers—she'd lost her appetite the moment she saw him.

"We got reacquainted when we rode back from the airport on the shuttle together," Craig pointed out.

"Well, wasn't that nice. I always did like to have someone to talk to when I had to make a long trip," Margaret said. When Kimberly didn't add anything to the conversation, she swung back at Craig. "How's your mama? I hear she had the flu last month."

"Whoo." Craig whistled. "It hit her hard, ma'am. But I'm glad to say she's on the mend. I think she might make it to church next week. She's sure looking forward to it."

"You give her my regards, now, and tell her I've been praying for her."

"I will surely do that, Ms. Clayton. I know she'll appreciate it."

Kim, who'd remained silent during the interchange, hoped Craig had said what he had to say and would move on. Instead, he lingered at their table, his focus on her aunt. Wondering why, Kim pushed one of the chips around on her plate.

"It's nice to see you taking a little break," Craig said after a beat. "How are things at the inn? Has business picked up lately?"

The hairs at the nape of Kim's neck prickled at the new topic. Concerned that her aunt might give the man an honest answer, one that would provide him with ammunition to use against them in some way yet to be revealed, Kim cupped her fingers over Margaret's. "Fine," she said, answering for both of them. "We're doing just fine. Aren't we, Aunt Margaret?"

"Yes," her aunt said, although she didn't

sound all that certain. Questions formed in the narrowed blue eyes she aimed at Kim. Her focus swung like a pendulum from Kim to Craig and back again as if she wanted to know what was going on between them but was too polite to ask.

Kim didn't have that problem. "If that's all, Craig…" Letting her words hang between them, she gestured to the uneaten portion of her sandwich.

"There is one more thing before I let you ladies get back to your lunch." Craig pulled a glossy trifold from the back pocket of his jeans and slid it across the table toward Kim.

"What's this?" she asked without reaching for it.

"Our talk on the bus was weighing on me. I didn't like the way we left things, so after I got back to the house last night, I did a little research." He nodded to the paper. "This is some information about the National Registry of Historic Places I thought you might find interesting. It turns out the NRHP offers grants for restoring older buildings and homes of historical significance. The first step is getting the property on Historic Registry's list. It's not easy—there are several hoops you'd have to jump through—but this will tell you what you need to know to get started." Leaning down, he tapped the brochure. "If you're interested at all in fixing the place up, that is. Make it a little less…"

"Like an eyesore?" Kim tossed his own description back in his face.

Her gaze sharpening, Margaret gasped. Her face shifted into an expression that was one part stricken, two parts outright indignation. Drawing out his name until it stretched across two full seconds, she said, "Craig Morgan, do you mean to stand there and tell me that the Dane Crown Inn, which has been in business longer than you've been alive, doesn't live up to your standards?"

As if realizing he'd just insulted a friend of his mother's, Craig paled beneath his suntan. He took a half-step away from the table, his shoe scuffing the bakery's hardwood floor. "No, ma'am. I didn't mean any disrespect. I…"

When Craig's pleading look landed on her, Kim felt an instant pang of pity for the man. Craig might have grown up to become the mayor of Emerald Bay, but when it came to dealing with unhappy women, he was still just as shamefaced and tongue-tied as the day Aunt Liz had caught him and Scott rolling green oranges into the path of cars on the highway.

"I shouldn't have said that. That was, um…" He continued to stammer.

Kim could think of several words to finish Craig's sentence. Aware that her aunt was listening in, she chose one of the milder ones. "Mean-spirited?" she suggested.

"I didn't intend to be," Craig said while a red flush climbed onto his cheeks. "I was sorta hoping you'd forgive me for that."

"I suppose we ought to forgive him, shouldn't we, Aunt Margaret?" Kim gave her aunt's hand a quick squeeze. "I'm sure Craig meant well. Didn't you, Craig?" She aimed a pointed look in his direction.

"Yes. Definitely. I'm so, so sorry for speaking out of turn." Shooting Kim a grateful look, he took a breath. "And now, if you'll excuse me, I think I've intruded on your lunch long enough, Ms. Clayton." He bowed slightly from the waist. "Kimberly." He stepped away from their table but not before touching his fingers to his chest in a gesture of gratitude.

When he'd gone, Kim braced for her aunt's version of the third degree. She was surprised when Margaret merely picked up the remaining half of her sandwich, took a bite and chewed thoughtfully. "I suppose I should cut him some slack. After all, he did lose his wife recently."

"Lost? She died?" Kim's heart thudded slowly. On the bus, she'd noticed the ring Craig wore on the third finger of his left hand and assumed he was married. He hadn't said anything to the contrary.

"Oh yes. A little over a year ago." Margaret carefully blotted her lips. "It was one of those freak accidents you hear about but you never think will happen to anyone you know."

Puzzled, Kim stared at her aunt, willing her to go on.

"She stopped to get money out of the ATM at one of those drive-throughs, and she pulled a little too far forward."

Kim nodded. She'd done the same thing herself on more than one occasion.

"Anyway, she fell out of the car when she opened the door to get her cash. Hit her head on the cement. People called the paramedics right away, but she never woke up."

"Oh, my." Air whooshed out of Kim's lungs at the thought of losing someone she loved in such a senseless, tragic accident. She couldn't imagine the shock and pain Craig must have felt or how, a year later, he was coping as well as he was. She'd probably still be a basket case if something like that had happened to one of her children. "The poor, poor man," she whispered.

"He went through a rough patch. That's for sure," Margaret agreed. "And I feel sorry for him—the whole town does. That doesn't make it all right for him to criticize the inn, though." Her lower lip trembling, she asked, "Unless you agree with him?"

"I do not," Kim answered with as much reassurance as she could offer. Craig's remarks had been too cutting, too harsh. But given all that he'd been through recently, she was willing to give him a pass. Still, she couldn't deny that the Dane family home was aging in a not all that graceful manner. "The inn isn't ready for the wrecking ball—far from it—but it does need a few improvements." She fell silent, willing to let her aunt choose whether they continued the discussion or not.

"What sort of changes did you have in mind?" Margaret asked.

Kim chose to begin with the simpler repairs. "I noticed a couple of porch balusters had worked loose. You probably need to have someone fix those and examine all the railings. After that, repainting the inn and the cottages would give the place a fresh look." She didn't mention the general cleanliness of the upstairs or how vines and weeds had overtaken the grounds. She'd already spoken with the cleaning and the gardening crews earlier. Both teams had promised to up their game.

"Well." Margaret expelled a breath. "That sounds easy enough. It has been a while since we've had the house painted. We can speak to Diane about hiring someone." She traced a circle on the tablecloth with her index finger. "What else?"

Kim hesitated. The property needed more work—so much more work—but she refused to overwhelm her aunt with a laundry list of improvements and repairs. Safety, however, was another matter entirely, and with that in mind, she'd intended to remove the throw rugs that posed a hazard to her aunt or the inn's guests. When she pulled up one in the library room, though, she discovered a threadbare carpet beneath it. The rugs in the kitchen hid buckling floorboards. Deep gouges marred the hardwood in the dining area. "I couldn't help but notice the scatter rugs throughout the house," she said slowly. "You should probably have the floors refinished and the carpets replaced."

"I know. I was hoping to do that when business picked up, but..." Margaret's shoulders rounded in defeat. "Diane handles everything more than the day-to-day expenses. We could ask her if there's enough money to cover new flooring."

"I'm sure she'd rather pay for new carpets than have a guest trip over one of the throw rugs and get hurt." She let the rest go unsaid. Her aunt was well aware of how much she stood to lose if someone sued. To say nothing of what could happen if she herself took another spill.

Margaret pushed her plate aside. Taking her time, she blotted her lips. "I suppose there wouldn't be any harm in it if you spoke to your cousin about fixing a few things around the place. What's the worst she could say? No?"

"Me? You want me to talk to Diane?"

"Please?" her aunt wheedled. "If we get the place fixed up, maybe Scott will stop hounding me about moving into Emerald Oaks."

Kim drained the last of her iced tea. When she'd agreed to come back to Emerald Bay, she had one simple task to accomplish. Just make sure the homestead was safe enough for her aunt to continue living there—that was all she was supposed to do. The entire job was supposed to take a week, two, tops. After that, she'd be free to return to her life in Atlanta.

Now her aunt was changing the ground rules, and Kim didn't have to be a genius to see what came next. First, she'd talk to Diane about the finances. Then, assuming there was enough money in the bank to cover the cost of repainting, her aunt would cajole her into overseeing the repairs. All of which would take a whole lot longer than the short time she'd planned on staying in Emerald Bay.

Would she ever return to Atlanta? Did she even want to?

Twelve

Margaret

"Oh my, that's a lot of groceries." Margaret stared into the trunk of the car. It hadn't seemed like so much while she pushed the cart through the store as Kim methodically added one item after another to a growing pile. Now that they were home, though, the bags of fresh produce, canned goods and her niece's selections from the meat department took up every inch of available space.

"You're sure you can carry the eggs?" Kim reached for the straps of the flimsy bag Margaret had carried home on her lap.

"Yes, but—" Deftly avoiding her niece's fingers, Margaret slipped the handles over her own wrist. "Don't you want me to carry something else?"

"That's okay. It might take a couple of trips, but I'll get the rest." Kim eyed the full trunk. "Let me walk you in. Then I'll come back for these."

"I'm perfectly capable of making it into the house on my own steam." Margaret struck the pavers firmly with her cane. Kim meant well, but her niece hadn't let her out of her sight the entire time they were at the diner and the grocery store. The constant hovering was getting on her nerves. There were things she needed to take care of without someone looking over her shoulder.

Leaving Kim to heft an armload of bags from the trunk on her own, she carefully picked her way toward the house. Navigating the uneven pavers was trickier than she expected, and she slowed her steps to a snail's pace. When her feet nearly went out from under her despite her precautions, she sent up a silent prayer that they'd left the side door unlocked. Though she'd deny it to her death, the closer she got to the house, the less confident she felt that she could remain upright while, still juggling the eggs and her cane, she rooted around in her purse for the keys.

Finally reaching the door, she gripped the handle tightly and gave it a twist. When the door sprang open, her breath stuttered and then smoothed. Glad she hadn't been forced to search for her keys or worse, landed on her butt, she headed inside.

The instant she walked from the laundry room into the kitchen, she noticed the fragrant scent of cleansers and lemon oil. She sent her gaze scurrying over the freshly mopped floors before she gave the gleaming kitchen counters a searching look. Were they cleaner than usual? The few smudges she'd noticed on the windows earlier had been wiped away, leaving the glass so clean, it sparkled. From upstairs came the quiet roar of a vacuum that nearly drowned out the soft scuffing noises Kim's shoes made against the tiles or the quiet rustle of the bags she carried.

"Irene and Eunice are still here?" Practically aching with fatigue after the long day out and about, Margaret blinked slowly. The maids normally left by one or two. It was nearly three, according to the wall clock, and they were still hard at work.

Kim shrugged as she lugged several full bags of groceries onto the counter. "Oh, didn't I tell you? They asked if they could treat each one of the upstairs suites to a spring cleaning. Of course, they can't get them all done at once, so they're going to concentrate on one or two every day."

"They talked to you about it?" Irene and Eunice had worked at the inn for at least a dozen years. Why had they spoken to Kim instead of her?

"You don't mind, do you?" Kim asked over her shoulder. Without waiting for an answer, she headed back to the car for another load. A second later, a door slammed shut behind her.

Margaret considered how to answer the question while her niece retrieved the rest of the groceries from the car. She'd started letting the maids leave early so they could meet the bus after school and spend a couple of extra hours with their children each day. But that had been years ago. Weren't Irene's boys in high school by now? And Eunice's were the same age, weren't they? The teenagers could probably fare quite well on their own for a couple of hours.

Reusable bags hanging off her arms like ornaments dripping from a Christmas tree, Kim picked up the conversation where she'd dropped it on her way out the door. "You don't mind about Irene and Eunice, do you?" She added the bags to the pile already on the counter.

Margaret shrugged. "Not really. As long as none of our guests complain, they can work as long as they'd like." After all, the women received a weekly salary in exchange for keeping the inn spic and span. Far be it from her to interfere if they wanted to work a few extra hours.

"I didn't think you'd mind," Kim said. She began emptying the bags. Soon cans and boxes littered the counter beside a small mountain of fresh produce. "Oh, darn," she said as she surveyed the plunder. "I'm fixing that burgundy chicken dish tomorrow, and I forgot the wine. I'll have to run back into the town and get some. Want to ride along?"

Slowly, Margaret gave her head a thoughtful shake. She and Kim had practically bought out the store after their lunch at the bakery. By the time she and her niece put everything away in the pantry and the refrigerator, the sun would be sinking over the treetops in the west.

"If you don't mind, I'll stay here this time. The Garrisons visited the Mel Fisher Treasure Museum in Sebastian today. I need to get the afternoon snacks ready before they get back." Shoving her hand into her pants pocket, she crossed her fingers. She wasn't lying to her niece. Not exactly. Each afternoon, she did warm a tray of cookies and put out a pitcher of lemonade for their guests. But she had another pressing matter to attend to before supper. One she'd rather accomplish without Kim's hovering presence.

"That's okay. I won't be long. Is there anything else you think we might need?"

"I don't know where we'd put it if there was." Margaret peered over Kim's shoulder as the younger woman shoved aside bottles of juice, flavored waters and dairy products on the top shelf of the refrigerator in order to make room for a carton of half-and-half. A ready-made casserole, tonight's dinner, occupied another shelf. Crisp heads of lettuce, scallions, an array of bell peppers and broccoli filled the vegetable bin. As if that wasn't more than enough food to have on hand, onions and plump heads of garlic hung in a basket over the sink while a line of tomatoes ripened on the windowsill. She couldn't remember the last time so many boxes of cereal and canned goods had crowded the pantry shelves.

"Okay, then." Having found a place for the half-and-half, Kim moved to the sink, where she washed her hands. "I might swing by to see Amy since we missed her at lunch, but I won't be long."

"Take as long as you want, child. You're on vacation."

Kim grinned. "Thanks for the reminder. I keep forgetting."

Seconds later, Margaret enjoyed the feel of

her niece's arms wrapped around her in a warm hug. She patted Kim's arm. "I'm glad you decided to visit me instead of choosing some-place else to spend your time off," she whispered before the embrace ended.

"Me, too," came a heartfelt reply. Picking up the keys and her purse, Kim retraced her steps across the kitchen to the pantry and the exit beyond. "Back soon. Bye!" she called on her way out the door.

No sooner had the lock snicked shut behind her niece than footsteps sounded on the stairs. Less than five minutes later, Irene and Eunice ambled into the kitchen carrying plastic bins that held an assortment of cleaning supplies and rags.

"Hey, Ms. Clayton." Irene tugged the bandanna she wore over her dark hair from her head. Scrunching it into a ball, she shoved the scrap of dirt-streaked cloth into the pocket of her shorts. "We're all finished with the Topaz Suite. I hate that we didn't have it all ready for Kim when she came in last night. I hope you're not upset with us about that."

"Should I be?" Margaret struggled to recall her niece's exact words. Kim had mentioned a cobweb hanging in one of the corners, but she hadn't said a word about any other problems, had she?

"I sure hope not, ma'am. If we'd known she was coming, we'd have paid special attention to her rooms. Isn't that right, Eunice?" Irene shot her friend and co-worker an anxious glance.

"Yes, ma'am. We sure woulda. We've set her rooms to rights now, and we made a good start on the Jade Suite today."

As if she was batting a ping-pong ball, Irene loosed the next volley. "We'll finish it after we tidy up the downstairs tomorrow. If it's okay with you, we'll tackle the Ruby and Opal ones later this week."

"That sounds perfect." Margaret nodded her approval. "I appreciate the extra effort."

"Oh, no problem, ma'am." Irene tugged her bandanna from her pocket and used it to blot the back of her neck. "Unless you noticed something we overlooked, we'll put our supplies away and get out of your hair."

"I haven't had a chance to look around much—we haven't been back from the store that long—but I'm sure everything's fine." She paused. "You did change the linens in the occupied suites, didn't you?" It wouldn't do at all for the girls to overlook their usual duties in order to clean rooms that were currently sitting empty.

"Yes, ma'am," Eunice piped up. "We gave your apartment its usual dose of TLC, too."

"Well, I have to tell you, the house certainly smelled good when I came in this afternoon." Margaret glanced at the clock over the stove. A full three hours had passed since the women's usual quitting time. "So we'll see you tomorrow?"

"Yes, ma'am," Irene answered. She crossed the kitchen and headed down the hall to the laundry room. A minute later, Margaret heard the raspy sound of their bins sliding onto a shelf beside the washing machine. After another few seconds, their footsteps faded as the door swung shut behind them. Wanting to be sure she had the house to herself, Margaret sank onto one of the kitchen chairs.

"Mmmmm," she sighed once she sat down. It felt better than she'd imagined to take the weight off her injured ankle and, leaning back, she closed her eyes. She only intended to rest for a minute or two. Just until the girls piled into Irene's truck and left. Before she knew it, though, the sound of the beat-up old pickup truck had long since faded, and the sun had sunk considerably lower in the sky.

"Time to get moving," she told herself. As tempting as it was to remain right where she was, she forced herself to her feet. Who knew when she'd have the chance to venture out on her own again? She slowly, carefully shuffled toward the French doors that opened onto the back deck.

Though she hated to admit it, Craig's earlier comments had given her a bad case of heartburn. His suggestion that she hadn't maintained the inn as well as she should had gnawed at her through the rest of her lunch with Kim and all during their trip to the grocery store. Not even her niece's reassurances that a fresh coat of paint and a few minor repairs would set things to rights had been able to quash her fears that she'd grown too old or too complacent to take care of the property her family had left in her care. Was that why business had fallen off of late? Was it her fault? She had to know, and she didn't want anyone to sugar-coat the news for her. Which meant she had no choice—she had to see if there was any truth to Craig's accusations for herself.

Relying on her cane for balance, she stepped out onto the wooden deck. For a long moment, she didn't move away from the safety of the door while she steadied herself. She closed her eyes. Willing herself to see everything the way a first-time visitor to the inn would, she took a deep breath. When she felt ready, she opened her eyes and took a good look around.

Her heart thudded as she took in the patches

of peeling paint that marred the deck's surface. The fabric on the chair cushions had faded. Some had frayed around the edges. A wayward vine had grown between the boards in one corner of the porch. She glanced over one railing at the weed-choked flower bed and groaned.

Shading her eyes against the sun with one hand, she stared out over the wide swath of land that eventually ended at the river's edge. The parakeets she and Amy had watched the other day had stuck around. Chirping softly, they flitted among the fronds in a distant stand of palm trees. Her gaze dropped to the landscaping that lay between the deck and the tree line. Weeds grew among the clumps of palmettos and choked the paths that wound throughout the property. In several places, top-heavy Spanish bayonets had toppled over onto their sides. Why hadn't one of the gardeners removed the fallen plants, she wondered. Better yet, why hadn't someone trimmed the exotic foliage before they fell?

She swallowed. Okay, so things were a bit shabby, and the property could certainly use some attention, but nothing she'd seen came close to worthy of being called an eyesore. Were other parts of the estate in even worse condition? The temptation to abandon her impromptu tour tugged at her. She resisted it with a stern reminder that she was Margaret Clayton, owner of the Dane Crown Inn, once hailed as the jewel of Florida's Treasure Coast. If she'd failed to oversee her heritage properly, she had to know.

She edged closer to the steps that descended to a walkway of pavers that led from the main house to the cottages on either side of it. From the way Craig had described them, the out-buildings had collapsed like so many of the Spanish bayonets. She wanted, needed, to see if they had.

Her heart lurched with every step as she slowly worked her way to the ground. Gingerly, she scuffed the pavers with one shoe and took a happy breath when she felt no evidence of algae. Not only would it dull the color of the bricks, the plant created a scummy surface that could be as slippery as ice. Relieved to have one less thing to worry about, she took slow, careful steps toward the first of the three cottages on the right.

Kim had been right about the paint, she decided. Once a vibrant teal, the exteriors of the bungalows had faded to a pastel that was neither blue nor green, while the sun had nearly bleached the yellow trim white. That was bad enough, but her heart sank when she spotted boards nailed over a window on one cottage, a missing soffit on another. The tiny house at the end of the row appeared to be intact, and she blinked away a few tears. Not wanting to disturb the author who was staying there, Margaret turned around and retraced her steps to the deck.

By the time she reached the steps, the day had begun to catch up with her. She eyed the three cottages on the other side of the house. She'd intended to check them out, as well. Maybe even wander partway down one of the paths that cut through the property. Ten years ago, she wouldn't have given the matter a second thought, wouldn't have stopped to question whether or not she was up to the task. But following the accident, her stamina had plummeted. Today's outing—especially the conversation with Craig—had sapped her energy.

She was just about to call it a day and retreat inside when she spotted a long piece of metal tubing leaning against the side of the closest cottage. The downspout had probably been knocked loose by one of the mowers. Unless someone put it back in place, rain would pour out of the gutter during the next storm. Left alone long enough, the cascade of water would eventually damage the foundation of the little house.

LEIGH DUNCAN

She tsked. The repair was such a simple thing, a child could take care of it. She could, too, if she put her mind to it. Certain she had the wherewithal to manage such a small task, she set off toward the bungalow.

Thirteen

Kim

"She didn't." Amy's mouth dropped open. At the same time, her blue eyes widened.

"Oh, yes, she did." Sitting across the table in Amy's cozy kitchen, Kim watched a mix of surprise and laughter swirl across her cousin's face. She wrapped her fingers around her coffee mug. She didn't normally drink caffeine this late in the afternoon, but she needed the extra boost after her little talk with Irene and Eunice. Besides, no one brewed a better cup o' Joe than her cousin. Of course, if she roasted her own beans and owned a top-of-the-line espresso machine like the one Amy had, she could make a decent cup of coffee, too.

Easy now, she told herself as she tamped down a twinge of jealousy. She absolutely refused to be one of *those* people—envious of others and blind to their own bad choices. People like that ended up bitter and alone. So no. She absolutely would not begrudge her cousin's success. Amy had overcome some major hurdles to get where she was today. She deserved a few perks. If one of those was an impressive coffee maker, well, Kim was all for enjoying the benefits. Lifting her mug, she polished off the rest of her drink.

"So that's why she never rents out those upstairs rooms?"

"There hasn't exactly been a big demand for them." Kim debated helping herself to another cup from the carafe.

"True," Amy admitted.

"I wasn't sure whether to believe the maids when they said Aunt Margaret had been sending them home early every day, but the gardeners told the same story. Irene and Eunice say it's been years since they've been able to give the upstairs a proper cleaning."

"And the yard guys?" Amy prodded.

"Aunt Margaret told them the mowers and the weed-whackers disturb the guests' afternoon naps."

Amy clamped one hand over her mouth while mirth danced in her eyes. "Which would be true except bookings have been so low that no one cares."

"I'm pretty sure no one has stayed in Topaz since the last time I was here." Giving in to temptation, she filled her cup halfway. "You want to know what I think?"

"What?"

"I think the only nap that gets disturbed is Aunt Margaret's."

"You're probably right about that. I bet she nods off right after lunch." Amy drummed her fingers on the kitchen table. "It is a vicious circle, though. The more overgrown the grounds get, the more people will avoid staying at the inn. Fewer guests mean less need for the rooms upstairs." The kitchen fell silent for a long moment. "So what are you going to do about it?"

"Me?" The question caught her off-guard, and she nearly choked. She'd only agreed to make sure it was safe for their aunt to remain in the family home. Dealing with all the other problems wasn't her responsibility. She had her own life to get back to in Atlanta.

"Yes, you," Amy said. It was clear she was having none of Kim's protests. "You're here, aren't you?"

"I am but only for a little while." She mulled the situation over before she admitted, "I did light a fire under Irene and Eunice. I think Aunt Margaret might have been a little miffed, but someone had to do it. I'll speak with Miguel, the head gardener, too. I know they haven't been weeding and trimming along the footpaths. I nearly got a palm frond in the eye when I went to the beach yesterday. I thought I might ask him to pull together a list of all the jobs they've been putting off. Once I have it, we can decide what comes next." She pushed away from the table. "Speaking of which, I need to get back. I told Aunt Margaret I wouldn't be gone too long."

"Okay, but let's meet for dinner one night this week," Amy said, accompanying her to the door. "Just the two of us. We can drive down to Vero and eat at Waldo's."

"Oh, man. That does sound good." Kim's tummy gave a happy shimmy. A favorite of hers, the beachside bar had been around nearly as long as the Dane Crown Inn. "Do they still serve that fish dip?" Just thinking of the creamy-smooth smoked mahi made her mouth water.

"Of course."

"Then you've got yourself a date." Smoked fish dip wasn't exactly a staple in Atlanta restaurants. As long as she was here, she'd take advantage of every chance to dive into the dish, which came with finely chopped red onions and sliced jalapeños. Kim slung her bag over one shoulder. "Any night but Wednesday. That's when I'm taking Aunt Margaret to the potluck at church." She stopped for a moment to consider. Showing up empty-handed to one of those things was never a good idea. "Any idea what I should make?"

"Hmmm." Amy tapped one finger to her chin. "Not funeral potatoes—Clara Johnson always brings those. Not corn pudding—that's Mabel Torre's specialty. Vivi Borders brings fried chicken from the diner."

"What about potato salad?" Kim suggested.

"I wish." Amy gave her head a sad shake. "Olivia Carruthers already has that one covered. Every month, she brings a huge bowl of the stuff. And every month, we scrape it off people's plates straight into the trash can."

"Why?" She wasn't questioning why anyone would spoon something onto their plate when they already knew they wouldn't eat it. That's just what polite, Southern folk did. But how in the world did someone mess up a simple mix of cooked diced potatoes, chopped pickles and onion lightly coated with mayonnaise?

"Olivia believes in cooking food to death. I swear she boils the potatoes for a half an hour—it's like eating mush."

"That does sound awful." Kim gave Amy a

sheepish grin. "Your mom taught me to never overcook the potatoes."

Bring them to a boil and clamp a lid on them, Aunt Liz had coached. *Shut off the gas. Set the timer for five minutes. Drain, and then dump the potatoes into an ice bath. They'll be perfect every time. Cooked through but still firm.*

Kim had followed her aunt's directions ever since, and she'd never once received a complaint. For two long seconds, she considered showing up with her own version of the dish before she rejected the idea. The game of one-upmanship had no place at a church potluck. Whether they liked it or not, no one else would dare bring potato salad to the dinner until Olivia Carruthers died or moved into a nursing home.

What else could she bring?

"I was going to fix a vegetable lasagna for Aunt Margaret later this week. Mine's pretty good, if I do say so myself." It had taken countless attempts before she'd developed a tasty blend of carrots, bell pepper, mushrooms and zucchini that didn't turn watery. After another dozen tries, she'd perfected the balance of béchamel sauce to noodles.

"Save some for me," Amy said with a grin. "I promised to help serve dinner that night."

"Yeah? What are you bringing?"

"Oh, I don't know. A cake, maybe?"

Softly laughing, Kim shook her head. What else would a baker bring to a covered dish supper?

Twenty minutes later, Kim parked her aunt's car in the lot beside the inn. Clutching a bottle of burgundy in one hand and a bag of dinner rolls Amy had insisted on giving her in the other, she headed for the side entrance. Although it wouldn't be fully dark for a good two hours yet, the sun had dipped below the distant tree line. Above it, wide swaths of clouds reflected the last of the light in shades of pink and purple. Crickets chirped and cicadas buzzed from nearby bushes. Their noise added to the quiet symphony of the ocean.

"What the…" Kim jumped and nearly lost her grip on the wine when, midway between the car and the house, a bird swooped low over her shoulder. Her heart thumped hard as she watched a brilliantly colored parakeet glide in for a landing on the pavers up ahead. Its gray head bobbing, it cast her a single, baleful glance before it flutter-walked to the end of the stone.

Perching there, the bird probed the sand and grass with its short, curved beak.

Not wanting to startle the bird like he'd startled her, Kim stood still and watched the monk parakeet forage for food. She'd never been so close to this particular species before and was fascinated by its coloring. Various shades of bright green feathers covered its back and led to blue-tipped wings. Above a fat belly of the palest green, the bird sported a pure white throat. The parakeet's nickname came from the gray patch that draped, much like a monk's hood, across its head.

"Are you hungry, little monk?" she cooed softly when the bird had examined the ends of several pavers without finding anything to its liking.

It chirped an answer and hopped to the next stone.

Thoughtfully, she chewed on her lower lip. According to Aunt Margaret, the flock had landed in the palm trees at the edge of the property just two days before her arrival. Had the birds devoured all the berries and seeds in less than a week? She hoped not. They'd probably move to another location once they depleted their food source here. But what, exactly, did they eat? When her children were little, she'd bought them a pair of budgies. Those domesticated birds had lived on a diet of seeds and nuts, supplemented with veggies, fruits and cooked rice. Did wild birds eat the same thing? She didn't know enough about the habits of the monks to hazard a guess, but she thought she might pick up a few clues by watching the one in front of her.

Keeping her distance, she trailed the bird down the path. At the turnoff to the side door, she hesitated. She'd promised her aunt she'd return soon, and she'd already been gone longer than she'd anticipated. But if she dashed inside, even for a moment, the bird would probably take flight. Then she might never know what it liked to eat. Taking a breath, she decided to follow it for another five minutes before she went inside.

By now the bird had hopped to the fork where the path branched. One side led toward the cottages to the south side of the inn. The other circled close to the deck before snaking out to the cottages on the north. The bird hopped toward the left and, going at a much slower pace, Kim followed.

The minute the cottages came into view, Kim spotted a figure on the ground at the base of a gentle rise. She froze, unable to breathe while her stomach performed an awkward somersault. The bag of rolls fell from her limp fingers. It hit the ground with a soft splat. The plastic wrapper burst. Rolls went skittering in all directions.

"Aunt Margaret?"

The words, half whisper and half cry, flew from Kim's lips as she jolted forward, covering the ground between her and her aunt as fast as her feet would take her. Tears rolled down her cheeks by the time she reached the spot where Margaret sat, knees outstretched before her, her chin resting on her chest, her arms crossed. Blood, far too much of it, spread out in a widening stain across Margaret's white pants.

"Oh, dear Lord, please," Kim whispered. Collapsing onto the grass beside her aunt, she realized she'd managed to hold on to the wine bottle. She tossed it aside like so much dead weight while she swallowed dryly. Gently, she touched her aunt's shoulder.

Though Margaret's soft whimper sent a fresh wave of tears coursing down her cheeks, Kim banished the panic from her voice. "Aunt Margaret," she called, trying for calm concern and missing it by half a mile. "You're bleeding. Where are you hurt?"

When Margaret slowly lifted her head, Kim swore she hadn't felt such a rush of relief since the first time she'd sat in the bleachers on a Friday night and stared at a pile of football players until her son emerged from the bottom unscathed.

"My arm." Margaret's voice, normally so self-assured, rose from pale lips. "I think I've broken it." She squeezed her eyes tight. "I heard it snap."

"Oh, geez." Kim steeled herself while the coffee she'd drunk churned in her stomach. Refusing to succumb to the nausea that clawed at the back of her throat, she forced herself to slow down, ask questions, evaluate. "Is that where the blood is coming from? Or are you cut somewhere else? Let me see."

She held her breath as Margaret leaned away from the arm she cradled against her chest. Though there was no sign of blood, the older woman's forearm bent oddly between the wrist and elbow. Kim sucked air through her teeth. Continuing her search, she ran her fingers lightly over Margaret's torso and down her legs until she located a jagged cut just above one ankle. She swore softly and immediately followed it up with a grateful prayer. The blood was oozing, not pulsing. That meant, according to a first aid class she'd taken when Josh was little, no arteries had been severed. She reached for the purse she'd slung over one shoulder. "Hold on a sec." Her fingers brushed against her cell phone. She clutched it like a life preserver. "I'm calling for help."

"No, child." Margaret used her good hand to lock Kim's wrist in an iron grip. "Just get me to my feet," she said, sounding like a sullen child. "I'm all right."

"You most certainly are not all right. Your arm is broken. By the looks of it, it's a bad break." This was no simple sprain, not with that awkward bend below Margaret's elbow. She was all for supporting her aunt's independence, but this was one fight she couldn't let the woman win. "You can't fix this with an aspirin and a Band-Aid. Your leg is going to need stitches. What if you pass out? What if something else is broken? Those aren't risks I'm willing to take. I'm calling for help." She punched the numbers, and when the operator came on the line, she provided all the necessary information.

An eternity of ten minutes passed before she heard the wail of sirens in the distance. After that, things happened so quickly they passed in a blur. Almost before she knew what was happening, burly men had lifted her aunt onto a gurney, which they slid into the back of a waiting ambulance.

While the paramedics got her aunt situated, Kim hustled to the car. She followed the flashing lights and wailing siren to the hospital. On her way, she called Amy and brought her up to speed.

"Where are they taking her?"

"Indian River Memorial." The medical center in Sebastian was closer, but the facility south of them was larger and better equipped to handle Margaret's injury.

"I'll meet you in the emergency room," Amy promised once she got over her initial shock.

"There's one more thing." Kim gulped. "Someone's got to call Belle and let her know what happened."

Air whooshed softly into her earpiece. "You don't think the news would be better coming from you? She's going to have a zillion questions."

"And the first one will be, 'How did my mother get hurt on your watch?' That's one question I don't want to answer." Belle had a heart of gold. She'd literally give someone the shirt off her back. But when it came to her mom, the Queen of Pop could turn into a tigress. With claws.

"Coward," Amy accused.

Despite the seriousness of the situation, Kim managed a wry grin. "You betcha."

Fourteen

Diane

"Everything looks so pretty, Mom."

Turning away from the stove, Diane brushed a wayward strand of hair out of her face with the back of her hand. Caitlyn was right—the table did look festive with the blue, green and yellow stoneware resting atop bright red placemats. Beside each plate sat flatware decorated with hand-painted ceramic handles. Chunky purple glassware added more splashes of color, which blended well with the white flowers in low clay pots she'd chosen for centerpieces. Bowls brimming with chopped onions, diced jalapeños and two kinds of grated cheeses filled the empty gaps.

She only wished she'd been able to stick to the original plan and host the dinner party outside. She'd wanted to hang twinkle lights from the branches of the enormous oak tree in the backyard and set up the picnic table in the shady spot. But an unexpected complication at work this morning—on a Saturday, no less—had thrown her off schedule. By the time she got home, she hadn't had enough time to lug all the dishware and glasses outside and cook, too. As it was, she'd had to take a few shortcuts in order to keep her promise and host the dinner at all.

"Marty and Sarah are starving," Caitlyn declared. Laughter came from the family room, where her two best friends were watching a bloopers video from an old sitcom. She snagged a handful of tortilla chips from an earthen bowl. "Where's the salsa?"

"In the fridge. Why don't you take it and the chips in with the girls while I put the finishing touches on dinner. We'll want to eat as soon as Dad brings the corn in from the grill."

"Sure!" Caitlyn yanked open the refrigerator door and hefted the bowl of salsa. Peeling off the lid, she paused. "Hey," she said softly. "This looks weird." She dipped a chip into the spicy mix. "Did you do something different?"

Diane took a steadying breath. "I didn't make it," she admitted. She'd stayed at the office until after nine last night and simply hadn't been up to the task of chopping tomatoes, jalapeños or green and red onions when she'd finally gotten home. She'd intended to make it this morning, but she hadn't factored an emergency at work into her plans. In the end, she had to settle for store-bought salsa, and she picked up several jars of a brand that was nearly as good as her own.

"That's okay." Caitlyn shrugged. "But Dad's not going to like it," she warned.

Probably not. But then, Tim didn't like much where she was concerned these days. He hadn't wanted her to go to work today at all. Instead, he'd wanted to set a date for the cruise they'd planned to take for their anniversary last year. He hadn't been happy when she cut the conversation short to rush off to the office. And he had positively *not* been understanding when she finally came home carrying bags from the grocery store. She wished he'd at least acknowledge the tasty marinade she'd soaked the chicken in overnight. Or the flan she'd made for dessert. From scratch, thank you very much. But no. He'd focus on salsa and the canned refried beans she'd serve as a side dish. If she knew him—and after twenty-three years, she most certainly did— he'd also have something to say about pre-packaged flour tortillas. Granted, they weren't as good as the ones she made. But the homemade kind took a full day to prepare, and she just hadn't had that kind of time. Not now. In another few weeks, maybe. After she and her team met the looming tax deadline.

She caught a whiff of something burning and swung around to the stove. In the cast-iron pan on the front burner, tendrils of smoke rose from a batch of scorched chicken. Grabbing her pot holders, she jerked the pan off the heat. A quick look told her the charred pieces couldn't be salvaged. Luckily, there was plenty more still soaking in the marinade. Chastising herself for letting her mind wander instead of giving the important meal her undivided attention, she tossed the ruined chicken in the trash and started another batch. By the time the sliding glass door rattled in its track, a small mountain of perfectly prepared chicken rested in the warming tray.

Diane straightened and offered up a quick prayer for a truce in their current skirmish seconds before Tim appeared in the doorway. In his arms he carried a platter piled high with ears of corn so fresh off the grill they still sizzled. Their smoky-sweet scent wafted through the room.

"Those look beautiful," Diane said, eyeing the ears that had been roasted to a golden brown.

"Thanks." Tim sniffed the air while he cast a

critical eye over the stove and counters. "What'd you burn?"

Diane swallowed hard. She would have sworn all the spices and garlic in the marinade had masked the tiny bit of smoke. Apparently not. "Nothing much. A few pieces of chicken," she confessed. Not that there was anything unusual about it. Heating the oil in the pan to exactly the right temperature was tricky. She usually undercooked or overcooked at least one batch. "Don't worry," she said without giving her husband a chance to give her any more grief. "I made extra."

Tim only nodded and set the platter on one end of the counter. "You almost ready?" he asked.

Diane nodded as she stepped aside to give Tim a tad more space. Earlier he'd arranged bowls of spicy crema sauce, grated cotija cheese, chili powder and freshly chopped cilantro on one corner of the granite. While she set out the food buffet-style on the kitchen island, he'd work at lightning speed to douse the ears with sauce, then coat them with more cheese and toppings so his contribution to the meal was still piping hot when they all sat down at the table.

Diane took the heavy, cast-iron pan off the warming tray and carried it to a waiting trivet. She removed the lid and stood back. A cloud of spice-scented steam rose into the air. Confident that the yummy smells emanating from the kitchen would draw them, she didn't bother calling the girls. Instead, she continued ferrying dishes from the stove and refrigerator until there was just enough room left on the wide island for her husband's lone contribution to the meal.

Sure enough, the TV clicked off before she'd moved half the food onto the buffet line. A few minutes later, footsteps sounded in the hall.

As the hungry teenagers burst into the kitchen, Tim swung to face them. Grinning, he held out the platter of richly coated corn like an offering. "Ready to eat, girls?"

"Yes, Mr. Keenan," two of the girls answered in unison.

"Yes, Dad," Caitlyn added.

"Wow! This looks awesome," Marty, a petite brunette, gushed.

Tall, angular and blond, Sara complained, "I wish we ate like this at our house. My mom can't boil water."

Diane smiled at the trio of girls who'd been besties since preschool. Their appreciation for all the work that had gone into fixing the meal warmed her heart. "We don't eat like this every night," she assured them.

"You can say that again."

Tim's biting sarcasm slapped the room into utter silence.

"Tim," Diane hissed. She pinned her husband with the same stern look she'd used on Caitlyn and her brother when they were younger. The one that had stopped the children in their tracks whenever their antics went too far. The one that said she'd duct-tape her husband's mouth if she had to. No matter what was going on in their marriage, this was a special night for their daughter and her friends.

"Hmmph," Tim acknowledged the message. Without missing a beat, he smiled at his daughter and her guests. "Let's give thanks for this delicious meal." He slid the platter onto the space Diane had reserved for him and stretched his arms wide.

As she had at nearly every meal they'd ever shared together, Diane took her husband's hand. On her other side, Caitlyn squeezed her fingers tightly. Marty and Sarah had been to enough family dinners at their house that they joined them as they bowed their heads.

"Amen," Diane said at the end of the simple blessing the family had recited over meals ever since Nick had started eating solid food.

"Okay, everyone. Grab your plates from the table and help yourselves!"

Diane pushed down a mild irritation when Tim took over as if he was the one who'd spent the entire afternoon preparing the meal. She hovered, making sure her husband and the girls had everything they needed before she helped herself from the buffet. In no time at all, everyone held plates brimming with chicken tacos, refried beans, sliced tomatoes and ears of corn. Once they were seated, they doctored their own tacos from the fixings Diane had placed on the table. She tried not to notice when Tim returned his fork to his plate without eating the refried beans he'd served himself. Or when he snorted after popping a chip loaded with salsa into his mouth. Other than that, though, the meal went smoothly, and all too soon she was dishing up generous servings of flan while the girls—Marty especially—regaled them with stories about other kids at school.

At last, Sarah wiped her lips with her napkin and pushed away from the table. "Thank you, Mr. and Mrs. Keenan. That was excellent."

"Don't you want a little bit more flan?" Diane asked. She'd watched in envy as the far-too-thin girl practically licked her dessert plate clean.

"I can't. I have to fit into my dress for homecoming." Sarah patted her flat tummy.

Diane's eyebrows came together. "When is

homecoming this year?" she asked cautiously.

"Next weekend, Mom." Caitlyn traced a finger over the tablecloth without meeting her eyes.

"But we haven't even started looking for a dress!" she blurted. How was that possible? The football game and the dance that followed were the highlights of every fall season. Before Nick graduated, their house had been the gathering spot for his friends and their dates on that special night. She'd always put out a huge spread of appetizers and soft drinks for the teens, as well as for the anxious mothers and gregarious fathers who'd filled their backyard while the kids— dressed in their finest—had posed for pictures on the deck and under the oak tree. She'd assumed they'd do the same for Caitlyn. But now the all-important event was right around the corner, and this was the first she was hearing of it?

"Don't worry, Mom. I don't need a new dress. I borrowed one from Marty's older sister."

"That's right," Marty piped up. "I'm wearing one of Shelly's, too." Shelly, who'd attended Plant High three years earlier, was now a junior at the University of Florida.

"That's, um..." Stymied, Diane stared at her plate. She should argue, she told herself. She should insist on taking her daughter shopping for her first formal gown and shoes to match.

They should make a day of it, have lunch at Caitlyn's favorite restaurant, get their nails done. Only she might as well turn in her notice if she took any time off right now. And besides, it sounded like Caitlyn had it covered. Could she, should she—just this once—take the easy way out?

"Okay," she said after weighing the pros and cons. "But you and all the other kids will still come here the night of the dance, right?"

"Um." Marty's face reddened. "My parents are planning on having us at their house, Mrs. Keenan. They've been working on it for weeks. They built a fire pit in the backyard and had all the lawn furniture recovered." She gave a short laugh. "They even ordered one of those big tent things—you know, the kind with no sides?"

"A canopy?" Diane suggested.

"Yeah, one of those. In case it rains."

"It certainly sounds like they've thought of everything." She turned to Caitlyn. "And you want to go there?"

"Yeah, Mom," Caitlyn answered in that bored tone perfected by teenagers the world over. "I helped Mr. Harrison build the fire pit. It's cool."

Diane blotted her lips with her napkin. It sounded like she didn't have any say in the matter—not that she'd consider changing the plans at this late date. As much as she enjoyed hosting the Homecoming gathering, she had to admit that the thought of having one less thing on her to-do list nearly made her want to weep with joy.

"Okay then," she said, folding her napkin and placing it on the table. She nodded to Tim, who'd barely said a word throughout dinner. "Let us get the kitchen cleaned up and we'll play Rummy." Memories of teaching the girls—and their Barbie dolls—the basics of the game softened her lips into a smile.

As if someone had fired a starting pistol, Caitlyn and her friends sprang to their feet.

"No cards," her daughter announced. "We're spending the night at Marty's."

"A sleepover? No one asked me about that," Diane protested.

"Mo-o-o-m," Caitlyn said, as if she were talking to a two-year-old. "Dad said it was okay. I already packed my backpack."

"Tim?" Diane gave her husband a questioning look. It wasn't like him to go behind her back.

"I thought you wouldn't mind," Tim said. He stared out the window as if the rays of sun slanting through the oak leaves fascinated him.

Diane threw in the towel. "If your father already gave permission, I won't argue. But don't stay up too late. You have church tomorrow." Caitlyn worked in the nursery every Sunday.

"I know. I'm riding with the Harrisons."

"My mom already said it was okay," Marty volunteered.

Diane blinked. It certainly sounded like the girls had come up with a good plan.

Caitlyn stopped long enough for a quick peck on the cheek. "Thanks for dinner."

"Yes, Mrs. Keenan. Thanks for dinner. It was delish." Marty pushed her chair back under the table.

"Yeah, thanks," Sarah added.

"Would you girls like to take the rest of the flan with you?" Tim pointed to the dessert. "You might want seconds later."

"Can we?" Sarah aimed her question at Diane.

The earnest hope that flickered in the teen's eyes quashed any idea Diane had of her and Tim sharing a late-night snack of the rich custard with its luscious caramel sauce. Just as well, she told herself. Even suggesting such a thing would probably earn some kind of snide comment about her weight. After carrying her plate to the kitchen sink, she snapped a plastic lid over the dessert dish and slipped it into a carry bag.

By the time she'd handed the leftover flan to Sarah, Caitlyn had pounded down the stairs with her backpack slung over one arm. She clutched her favorite pillow to her chest, just as she'd done at her very first sleepover so many years ago. Diane walked the girls to the foyer, and before she knew it, they were heading for the car Megan had parked in the driveway.

At the last second, Caitlyn turned back to give her a quick hug. "Thanks, Mommy," she whispered. "Dinner was fan-tas-tic!" she said, emphasizing each syllable.

"Thanks, sweetie." Tears stung the corners of her eyes. She blinked to clear them while she tugged gently on her daughter's ponytail. Having her sweet girl's approval made the last few hours of hustle and bustle worth every minute.

Caitlyn's long strides ate up the yard as she hurried to join her friends. "Tell Dad thanks, too," she called over her shoulder. "Nobody fixes corn like he does. You guys have a good night."

"You, too, sweetheart. Text me when you get there."

"Aw, Mom." Caitlyn tossed her backpack onto the back seat and climbed in.

Megan started the car, and "Bad Omens" by 5 Seconds of Summer blasted out of the loudspeakers. The teenage driver jammed the car into reverse.

Diane's breath caught in her throat, but she gave herself a stern reminder that Megan was a good driver, regardless of her poor choice in music. Still, she stood on the porch and watched until the car came to a complete stop at the next intersection before turning onto a cross street. When the vehicle carrying her daughter disappeared from view, she let out a long, slow breath.

Plucking an errant weed from the raised planter that edged the front of the house, she looked longingly at the gaily striped rocking chairs beneath the porch's shady overhang. The hours she'd spent on her feet while she fixed dinner were catching up with her. Her legs ached. What she wouldn't give to sit down and simply relax for ten minutes. Or twenty.

Slowly, she shook her head. "That kitchen's not going to clean itself," she murmured.

And who knew? Maybe Tim would pitch in like he used to do before things got so tense between them. Not so long ago, they'd worked as a team. While he washed and she dried, they'd talk about the day and how Nick was doing at Virginia Tech and whether or not Caitlyn would go to college on a soccer scholarship. He'd clear the table while she stored the leftovers in reusable, plastic tubs and stacked the neatly labeled containers in the fridge.

Afterwards, they might stretch out in the TV room or, laughing like nervous teens, sneak upstairs to their bedroom, where they'd put the rare chance to have the house to themselves to good use.

Feelings that had lain dormant for too long stirred deep within her. She pitched the weed into the yard and, hoping that Tim felt the same way she did, headed into the house.

The moment she stepped into the foyer, Diane's foot rammed into the wheels of a sturdy black suitcase parked by the front door. She stumbled forward and stuck a hand out to steady herself. Her fingers brushed against plastic. She watched in growing despair as a hanging bag that had been draped over the suitcase slithered to the floor.

"What the...?" Panic clawed at her throat. "Tim?"

Something heavy dropped onto the carpeted floor overhead. Their bedroom floor, she corrected. She stared at the ceiling and blinked slowly while her mind ran through several scenarios that might result in luggage by the front door.

The annual dental conference sprang to mind. Had she overlooked the slew of reminders Tim usually sent her about it? The dates blacked out on the calendar? The endless discussions on whether he should attend a workshop on endodontics or the latest advances in adhesives? Slowly, she shook her head. The conference had been last week, and Tim had opted not to attend.

Had thieves snuck in through the open back door and stashed their loot in the roller bags for a quick getaway?

That didn't make sense. Unless would-be robbers brought their own suitcases, they'd have to search the entire house for the ones stored in the closet of an upstairs guest room. From what she'd heard, most home invasions were hasty, in-and-out affairs whose effects lasted a lifetime. So no robbers. She discarded the theory and reached for another one.

She brushed a hand through her hair. She'd run out of options. Unless Tim was gathering items to donate to Goodwill—and why would he when a donation box already sat in the garage?—she couldn't think of a single reason why her husband's luggage would be in the entryway.

Unless…

Her heart slammed against her chest. Was Tim…leaving her?

Nervous laughter bubbled inside her. She bent, retrieved the garment bag that had fallen to the floor, and neatly folded it across the suitcase. She eyed the zippered closure. Should she open it and see what lay inside? She was still considering that when she heard her husband's footsteps.

"Tim," she called, her voice as calm and reasonable as she could make it under the circumstances. "What's all this?"

In a motion far too casual to signal the end of a marriage, Tim tossed a duffle bag beside the suitcase. "It's exactly what it looks like," he said flatly. "I'm leaving."

Diane gasped. "But why?" She reeled back until her spine pressed against the wall. "Why now?" Hadn't she pulled off the dinner for Caitlyn and her friends without a hitch?

"I warned you," Tim said. He folded his arms across his chest as if those three words could explain why he was breaking her heart.

"But I did what you wanted," she protested. "I fixed a special dinner. Everything went well, didn't it?"

"You took a few hours away from the office. Big deal," he sneered. "If you think this meal lived up to your usual standards, think again. You couldn't be bothered to make the salsa, and those beans were a joke. The chicken was burnt. You may have fooled Caitlyn and her friends into thinking you did your best, but you didn't fool me."

Diane resorted to a coping mechanism her therapist had taught her use whenever her world seemed to be spiraling out of control. After inhaling for four long seconds, she held her breath while she slowly counted to seven before she pushed all the air out of her lungs. She wouldn't argue with Tim. What was the point? He was right.

"I, uh, I'm sorry." The apology was all she had to offer.

"Ever since you walked in the door, you've been rushing around like a whirling dervish, trying to get everything done."

Dervishes spun around in circles without accomplishing anything, but she caught Tim's drift. He hadn't been happy with the few shortcuts she'd taken at dinner. But no one walked out on a marriage over canned beans. She tried reasoning with him.

"Look, I know I've been crazy busy at work lately. It'll get better. I swear it will." Her middle three fingers pressed together, she held up her right hand in a Scout sign.

"When it does—if it does—call me," Tim said,

his voice flat and emotionless. "But don't bother trying to get in touch for the next couple of weeks. You won't be able to reach me until I get back."

"Where, where are you going?" she asked, breathless.

Tim shrugged. "I practically begged you to plan that trip to Cancun. When you refused, I decided to go myself. I've booked a stateroom on the Seascape out of Miami. It's a two-week cruise to all those places we talked about."

"You've got to be kidding!" Diane exclaimed. He was seriously going on a cruise without her? "But…" What could she say to stop him from walking out the door? Desperate, she seized on the best excuse she could think of. "Where will you be in the meantime?"

Tim scoffed. "That's my point exactly. I told you months ago that I was converting the back half of my office building into a small apartment."

Had he? She was sure he hadn't mentioned it to her.

"The decorator just finished with it last week. It's fully furnished, right down to carpets on the floor. Everything I need is there."

Everything but me, she protested silently. But then again, maybe Tim didn't need her in his life anymore. He'd obviously been planning to leave for some time. No one converted unused office space into living quarters unless they intended to live there. He'd bought tickets for a cruise, made sure his passport was up to date. He'd even arranged for Caitlyn to spend this awful night somewhere else. Watching him go, she refused to beg, to plead. Something told her she'd only be delaying the inevitable. Tim had made up his mind to leave, and nothing she said or did at this point would change his mind.

That didn't stop the tears that streamed down her cheeks while he loaded his bags into his car. It didn't keep her from praying that he'd change his mind once he slipped behind the wheel. It didn't stop her heart from shattering into a million pieces when he pulled out of the driveway without so much as a moment's hesitation.

She wasn't sure how long she lingered there with her head pressed against the door. It had to be a while because, by the time she forced her feet into motion, dark shadows filled the yard. A messy kitchen demanded her attention. Her briefcase, still lying on the desk in their office, contained several critical hours' worth of work. She ignored it all.

She padded through the house, locking doors

and checking windows. Green lights lit the alarm panel by the garage door. She pressed buttons until the lights turned red.

Every bone in her body ached as she mounted the stairs a few minutes later. The world pressed down on her shoulders. Her legs felt so heavy she could barely make it up the steps onto the bed, where she collapsed, still wearing the clothes she'd worn to the office that morning. Wanting nothing more than to sleep away the nightmare that had become her life, she curled on her side. But once she closed her eyes in the bed that had never felt so empty, questions played on an endless loop through her mind.

Where had things gone so terribly wrong? Was her marriage really over? How was she going to tell Caitlyn?

She must have drifted off, because it was nearly midnight when the phone woke her out of a restless sleep. Instantly, her thoughts sped to her husband and her children. Had Tim changed his mind? Had something happened to Caitlyn? Or Nicholas? Grasping her phone, she stared at the display. Her breath hiccupped when she saw her sister's number.

"Hello?" she said, her voice hoarse with tears.

"Diane, this is Amy. I'm afraid I have bad news."

She'd been so sure her day couldn't get worse. Apparently, she'd been wrong about that. She pulled herself upright. Sprawled across her bed was not where she wanted to be if the worst had happened. Afraid to hear the answer, she asked, "Aunt Margaret? How bad is it?"

"She's in the hospital. She fell this afternoon and broke her arm. It's a bad break—a compound fracture. She'll need surgery to reset the bones. They've scheduled it for first thing Monday. They'd do it earlier, but the orthopedist is out of town for the weekend. She also has a small gash on her bad leg. She lost enough blood that they're giving her a transfusion."

It was a lot to take in. "Is she in any pain?"

"They have her pretty well doped up. There's a risk with any surgery, but at her age, it's even more so. I hate to ask, but...can you come?"

Diane leaned forward until her elbows rested on her knees. A trip to Emerald Bay was a complication she certainly didn't need right now. Caitlyn didn't even know that her father had left them yet. She couldn't go anywhere until she broke that news to her daughter. Then there was the looming deadline at work. She couldn't leave before she made absolutely certain her team would finish the job on time. And to top it all off, this was homecoming week at Plant High, with all sorts of festivities that led up to the dance next Saturday. Her head spun, and she swallowed.

"Give me a day to make arrangements for Caitlyn and line things up at work. I'll be there before the surgery on Monday. It's, it's the best I can do," she finished lamely.

In the game of life, her batting average was dismal. She'd struck out with her marriage. Her job was in jeopardy, and worst of all, the news that her father had left them would destroy their daughter. But by all that was within her, she wouldn't let her aunt down, too.

Fifteen

Belle

The steady swish-swish of windshield wipers penetrated the limousine's plush leather interior, each swipe ratcheting Belle's nerves a bit tighter. The storm system that had delayed their flight out of Nashville this morning had timed its arrival in New York to coincide with her appointment at Noble Records. On the other side of the tinted glass, the pouring rain turned the city as gray and cold as her mood. People armed with umbrellas splashed through puddles on the sidewalks. The lucky ones stayed closest to the buildings and mostly avoided the plumes of spray caused by passing cars. She sent out a silent apology when her own driver inadvertently doused a group of tourists wearing "I Love NY" T-shirts who stood at the corner of Eighth and Broadway waiting for the light to change. Snugging the wide lapels of her cashmere jacket a smidge closer, she glanced at Lisa. In the captain's seat next to hers, the agent flipped from one website to another on her phone.

"Have the other rags picked up the story yet?" She didn't waste her energy hoping they'd overlook it. The news of her wretched performance in Nashville was just too juicy to pass up. Sooner or later, a picture of her in that ridiculous rhinestone getup would be featured in every gossip magazine in the country.

Lisa gave a long-suffering sigh. "Most of them. Those that haven't will run it in their evening editions. My contact at the network says Jacky Jacobs is doing a bit on it tonight."

Belle groaned. She could practically see the late-night talk show host tripping his way across the stage wearing a bad wig and dressed in an exaggerated version of the outfit she'd worn last night. Assuming she hadn't already exhausted the world's supply of rhinestones, that was.

Lisa tapped one of the earbuds she was rarely without. Listening to the incoming call, she held her cell phone in the flat of her hand. A moment passed before she cut off the caller with an abrupt, "No comment."

"Enough of that." She removed the tiny device from her ear and slipped it and her phone into the pocket of her Gucci bag.

"I'm sorry you're stuck having to deal with all this," Belle said.

"It's all part of the job, but I must say, you've never been so popular. I've fielded a dozen requests for interviews. I'm telling them all no, of course."

Careful not to smudge up her lipstick, Belle moistened her lips. "Is that the best idea? Maybe it'd be better if I told my side."

Lisa fiddled with the signature horse bit on her bag. "It's a feeding frenzy out there right now. There are sharks in the water, and they smell blood."

Anger simmered low in Belle's belly. "This is all Jason's fault. I tried to tell him that sending me to Nashville was a dumb move. Would he listen? Oh, no. If I didn't know better, I'd say he set out deliberately to sabotage my career. I have a half a mind to let him have it."

"Play nice, Belle," Lisa coached. "The way things are right now, you can't afford to burn any bridges."

"I'm not the one burning them, though, am I? Jason holds all the cards." Belle folded her arms across her chest and fought tears. She'd cut her first hit single the year she signed with Noble Records. For a little while at least, the string of top-of-the-chart singles and platinum albums that followed had made her the reigning Queen of Pop. But now that her crown had tarnished the least little bit, Jason couldn't wait to replace her. Why, he probably had a dozen singers lined up, just waiting for a chance to take her place. She sniffled. For the first time in her career, she felt powerless and out of control.

The limo turned into the parking structure beneath the record company's forty-story headquarters building.

"Ready?" Lisa asked as the car glided to a stop just beyond the private elevator that would whisk them to the top floor of the building.

"As I'll ever be," Belle said.

They rode the elevator in silence. A fresh-faced intern greeted them mere seconds after they stepped into the hushed atmosphere of the senior executive suite.

"I'm Sunny, and may I just say it's an honor to meet you, Ms. Dane, Ms. Connolly." Sunny bobbed her head but carefully averted her eyes.

Belle gave the girl a once-over. A speck of glitter clung to her cheek. Either the young woman had been playing arts and crafts with a toddler, or she'd had a gig the night before. Her money was on the latter and that the girl had taken the job at Noble in hopes of landing her own recording contract.

"It's a shame what they're doing to you, Belle. Can I call you Belle?" Without waiting for an answer, Sunny continued. "Jason asked me to show you to the conference room. He's just finishing up a phone call and will be with you very shortly."

While Belle pondered whether Sunny's "they" referred to the gossip rags or the powers that be at her own record label, the intern race-walked them past couches and chairs clustered around a rug that featured Noble's logo. Stopping, the girl gestured her into a room where four glass walls surrounded a table that could seat a dozen or more. Leather benches provided additional seating.

Still looking anywhere but straight at them, Sunny asked, "Can I get you anything? Coffee? Water? Soda?"

"Water." The pity Belle read in the intern's expression made her want to claw the girl's eyes out. She settled for giving the younger woman a hard time. "Berg, if you have it. American Summits if you don't," she said, naming two of the most expensive bottled waters in the world.

"I—I'm so sorry, Belle. We don't have either

of those." On the edge of tears, Sunny blinked rapidly.

"Don't worry." Taking pity on the girl, Lisa broke in. "Any bottled water will do."

"So what are we supposed to do—cool our heels in this fishbowl until His Majesty deigns to see us?" Belle asked once the intern had hurried off to get the requested drinks.

"Take a breath, Belle," Lisa said softly. "I know you're on edge, but let's not go off the deep end until we hear what Jason has to say, okay?"

Barely able to breathe, Belle strode to the window that overlooked the city. Lisa was right. It had been mean of her to pull that trick on the young intern, she told herself. The child hadn't deserved it. Worse, it hadn't made her feel even one tiny bit better about herself. She straightened. She was above pulling petty stunts. She was, after all, a legendary pop star.

Or she had been until one dumb move by a certain newbie executive had ruined things. But she could bounce back. She just had to get control of the narrative. She'd have Lisa demand that Noble Records issue a statement saying they were one hundred percent behind her. Then, in the space of a news cycle or two, all the hubbub would die down. After that, her life—and her career—would return to normal.

Certain she knew what needed to be done to fix the mess she was in, she spun away from the window just as Jason rounded a corner at the end of the hall. Hope blossomed in her chest when she spotted him. It faltered when she saw the line of men and women in dark suits who trailed behind him.

"Crap." The rare expression flew from Belle's lips before she could stop it. So this was what it looked like when a label and an artist parted ways, she thought as she recognized a few key members of Noble's legal team. It had never happened to her before, and she sure hadn't seen this one coming.

"Belle. Lisa." Jason nodded to each of them in turn while the members of his entourage fanned out on either side of him.

"What's this all about, Jason? I thought we were here to take a meeting," Lisa blustered. "Instead, you're ambushing us with your legal team? I don't think so. C'mon, Belle. We're leaving." The agent took two steps toward the door.

"Wait, Lisa." Belle scanned the stern-faced group while her heart sank beneath the red soles of her Louboutin Mary Janes. "Delaying isn't going to change the outcome. Am I right?" She directed the question to Jason, who nodded. "So it's come to this, has it?" she asked, unable to filter the note of disbelief from her voice. "After thirty years with Noble, after earning the label millions of dollars, you're cutting me loose without even giving me a chance?"

"I did give you a chance." Jason's words fell into the room like ice cubes in a glass. "You deliberately blew it. You were so focused on proving how right you were and how wrong I was that you sabotaged that open mic."

"I most certainly did not." She would never do that. Not ever. She had too much respect for herself as an artist, as well as those at the top of their game in country music, to pull such a stunt. She pulled herself erect, striving to use every smidge of her full five feet two inches. In stark contrast to Jason's coldness, a red-hot anger surged through her. "It's beneath you to even suggest such a thing."

His face an impassive mask, Jason swung to face Lisa. "You were there. You saw her on stage. Would you swear she did her best?"

"I wasn't though." Lisa's head swung back and forth like a ball on the end of a pendulum. "We decided I'd wait in the car in order to preserve Belle's anonymity."

Jason brushed the answer aside as if it were no more important than a stray hair on a suit jacket. His eyes locked on Belle's, he said, "I saw the video. A veteran performer like you doesn't trip and fall on her way to the mic."

"It was the boots! Another one of your brilliant ideas." No one with a whisper-soft voice rose to the top in the music industry, and Belle was no exception. Hers shook the veritable rafters. Jason had had the pricey Luccheses hand-delivered to her condo along with a note that read, "To kick off a new stage in your career." It had been a new stage all right, crudely assembled from two-by-fours. "The heel caught on one of the floorboards."

"Says you," Jason shot back.

Belle took a breath. Getting into a shouting match with the record executive was not going to end well for either of them. Deliberately calming herself, she asked, "What would I possibly have to gain by giving less than my best performance?"

"You tell me," he countered.

She had nothing and waited while the room filled with a tension as thick as the fog that rolled off the Hudson each fall.

At last, Jason jerked his head toward the door. "Leave us," he said to the team of legal beagles who'd accompanied him.

A white-haired gentleman asked, "Are you sure that's wise?"

"Probably not," Jason admitted. "But do it anyway. I want to speak with Belle alone."

Lisa positioned her Gucci purse on the table's polished surface. She made a point of pulling a chair away from the table. "I'm not going anywhere," the agent announced.

Belle gave Jason a long, steady look before she canted her head to the side. "Go on. I'll be all right."

"But…" Lisa sputtered.

"Just go. We're in a room with glass walls. We aren't going to break out the boxing gloves." Although the way she felt right now, she was pretty sure she could take the record executive down.

"Okay. But I'll be right outside those doors." The agent stalked out in a huff. True to her word, though, she went only as far as the next seating area. There she plopped down hard on a leather-covered chair.

As soon as the door closed shut behind the last of the entourage and Belle's agent, Jason sank onto one of the leather benches scattered throughout the room. Taking a long, thready breath, he softly said, "I'm not sure where we go from here, Belle."

She had the answer for that and gave it to him. "Send me into the recording studio to finish the album. By the time we lay down all the tracks, this whole Nashville thing will blow over. I'll get a couple of the guys from my band, and we'll take the new songs on the road. We'll play all those smaller venues, just like you wanted at the beginning." The scaled-down tour wouldn't turn the kind of profit she'd been hoping for, but the album would be a hit. Of that she had no doubt.

"I wish it was that simple." Jason's shoulders slumped. Wearily, he shook his head.

Watching the signs of defeat creep over one of the most powerful men in the recording industry, Belle sensed a vulnerability she hadn't expected to find in someone who'd single-handedly ruined her career. She saw further evidence of it in the stark expression he turned on her a few seconds later.

"I can't, Belle. The numbers, they just aren't working for you anymore. Pop is on its way out. Today's audience wants something different, something authentic. The guys in the home office, the money men, they wanted to cut you loose ages ago. I tried my best to keep you on." He gave a bitter chuckle. "I doubt you'll believe me, but I've always been a fan. I took this job so I could work with you. But then the orders came down to drop you. How's that for irony?"

Belle sucked in a breath and flattened one hand on the table for support.

"It was me who convinced them to let you try country. I hoped it would be a fresh start for you. You deserved that much."

Wait a second. Belle's eyes widened. Jason was on her side? "It might have worked. If—if I'd had a little more time to prepare…"

"We'll never know now, will we? That door is closed."

"Locked up tighter than a drum."

"Sealed shut with Gorilla Glue." Jason tossed out a reference to a popular adhesive.

"Couldn't open it with a pry bar."

"Not even dynamite would touch it."

"You'd—" Belle shrugged. "I got nothing." She laughed.

Smiling, Jason stretched his legs out and crossed his ankles.

He had a nice smile, Belle decided as she sank down on the bench beside him.

"Frankly, I don't know what to do next." Jason mopped his face with his hands. "Do you have any ideas?"

"Sorry. Fresh out." She was at a loss. She'd come here prepared to do battle with Jason, eager to prove him wrong. Only he was more an ally than she'd known. She'd been so focused on winning this battle, she hadn't given any thought to what came next. She only knew one thing for sure—she wouldn't be "going country" anytime soon. She could wait out a hundred news cycles, but the next time she stepped foot in a place where the barstools were made of saddles or a mechanical bull sat in one corner of the room, she'd still get booed off the stage.

"In that case…" Jason straightened. The warm smile he'd worn slipped from his face. "I think we have to part ways. At least for now."

"You're really cutting me loose?" She'd thought she was prepared for that, but it still hurt. Fighting the pain, she clenched her fists.

"Not right away, but yeah," Jason said, his voice filled with regret. "I don't see any way around it. We'll let all this Nashville business blow over first. Let's give it three months or so. Then the lawyers—yours and Noble's—can work out the details. But unless someone comes up with a new direction for you, I don't see the point of holding on to your contract. I'm sorry."

"I know you are." No one could fake the kind of sincerity she'd heard in Jason's voice. Not that it mattered. He'd dropped the axe on her career, and she'd been powerless to stop him. Not only that, but getting dropped by the record label couldn't come at a worse time. She'd been so sure the new album would relaunch her career that she'd gone out on a limb financially to hire the best songwriters and composers to work on it. But without the tour or the album to replenish her coffers, how would she survive? A tremor shot through her. She wasn't sure how much longer she could hold her emotions in check. "I appreciate all you've done to soften the blow, but, if you don't mind, I'd like to be alone for a minute."

Belle wasn't sure how she made it to the window. One minute, she was talking with Jason; the next, she was staring out over the city. Beneath a sea of umbrellas forty floors below, life went on as if nothing at all had happened. People thronged the sidewalks on their way home from work. They rushed to their favorite restaurants and bars. Cars clogged the streets, turning them into rivers of red taillights and white headlamps. She thought if the windows were open, the sounds of the city would reach her even at this height. But they weren't, so she just stood there, staring, while the pieces of her shattered career rained down around her.

At last, she blotted her damp cheeks with her fingers. Praying her mascara hadn't run, she crossed the room on unsteady legs. In the lobby, Lisa sprang from her chair.

"How'd it go?" the agent asked breathlessly.

Belle lifted her hands in a sign of surrender. "You're looking at the *former* Queen of Pop. The label's dropping me."

"Well! We'll see about that!" Her purse hanging from one arm, Lisa jammed her fists on her hips. "I'll put our lawyers on it. We'll sue them for every penny they ever made off you. When we're finished with Jason, he'll wish—"

"No," Belle said simply. Defeat washed through her. "No, let's stick a pin in that for now."

"How can you be so calm?" Lisa reeled back. "Did he give you something? A drink? A pill? You should be screaming like a banshee."

"No. Nothing." She hadn't even drunk the water Sunny brought them. "I'm devastated. Truly. Deeply," Belle admitted. "I'll probably spend all weekend in bed with a box of tissues and a pint of salted caramel ice cream. But for now, I'm just numb, I guess."

Lisa treated the room to a searching look, but there was nothing to see except chairs and couches and wide swaths of carpeted floors. "C'mon," she suggested. "Let's get you out of here."

The arm the hardened agent slipped around her waist was so totally out of character that

Belle allowed herself to be propelled forward. "One more thing," she said, following the agent's lead. "Jason's not the ogre we thought he was. In all honesty, I think he was rooting for me to succeed with the whole 'gone country' thing."

Lisa's head snapped up so fast, Belle heard the bones in the other woman's neck pop. "Are you sure he didn't just pull the wool over your eyes? Tell you what you wanted to hear so we wouldn't sue?" At the elevator bank, she punched the down button with a blood-red nail.

"Pretty sure." Belle shook her head. Jason had been far too considerate, far too caring to be anything less than sincere. "Once we were alone, he was different. There's a likeable guy beneath that starched shirt. If circumstances were different, I think we'd be friends."

"Really." Lisa drew out the word while the elevator took them to the basement. "I do have other clients at Noble, and I have to admit, Jason has treated them fairly. Maybe he's not all bad."

Their car sat at the curb of the parking garage, the motor running. The limo driver held the door while Belle, suddenly feeling every one of her fifty-two years, slid onto the leather seat.

"Let me take you out to dinner," Lisa suggested. "Or for drinks, if you'd prefer. You've had a bad day. You deserve to relax."

"Thanks, but I think I just want to go home and be alone for a while. Rain check?" she asked. She wanted nothing more than to get to the Eldorado, where she'd tell the doorman she was not to be disturbed under any circumstances. In her penthouse apartment, she'd draw the drapes, shut off her phone and the lights and climb beneath the covers of her bed.

But thinking of her phone, she rooted around in her purse for the device she'd silenced before the meeting. She found it at the bottom of the bag, as usual. After refreshing the screen, she rested her head against the seat cushion and closed her eyes. She tried unsuccessfully to ignore a sense of foreboding that spread through her when the phone buzzed insistently.

"Apparently, every reporter in town wants a comment," she mumbled as she thumbed through message after message.

"Don't bother with them," Lisa advised. "I'll have your publicity people draft a statement."

"Sounds good." Right now, posing for pictures while answering questions was the last thing she wanted to do. Her finger hovered over the Delete All key and she was just about to press it when she spotted several messages from Gretchen mixed in with the calls from reporters.

"Huh. Gretchen's been trying to reach me."

Unease rumbled through her chest. Judging by the number of missed calls and messages from her assistant, the matter was urgent. She checked her text messages and scrolled to the latest one from Gretchen.

"Your mom had an accident," she read, her breath hitching as a terrible day suddenly went from bad to worse. "She's at Indian River Memorial. She'll need surgery to reset a broken arm and stitches for a cut. Amy and Kim are with her."

Belle leaned forward and tapped on the glass divider that separated the passenger area from the front of the car. "Change of plans," she announced the instant the glass slid down. "Take me to LaGuardia."

Today might have been one of the worst days of her life, but it paled in comparison to her mother's. The woman lay in a hospital bed twelve hundred miles away. Right now, getting to her was more important than any career.

Sixteen

Diane

"Busy?"

"Yes." Diane didn't bother to look up from her computer screen. After getting the phone call about Aunt Margaret, she hadn't slept a wink. She'd finally given up and rolled out of bed at two this morning. Padding around the kitchen in her bare feet, she'd tossed the remains of last night's dinner in the garbage and scrubbed the counters and stove until they shined. With nothing else to occupy her, she'd headed for the office. Daylight had still been hours away when she'd greeted the night watchman. She'd been hard at work ever since.

"Problems?" The smooth voice carried a steely edge that didn't beg for her attention so much as it demanded it.

Diane leaned to one side and peered around her monitor, ready to give what-for to but the person who'd dared disturb her on this, her first day as a single parent.

Instant recognition made her chest seize. Jeff Thomlinson, founding partner of Ybor City Accountants, leaned against her doorjamb. His face bore a well-rested look she could only envy. A few strands of his thick white hair had fallen onto his deeply tanned forehead. He brushed them aside with fingers that, these days, held a golf club more often than they held a calculator.

"Sorry, sir. I, uh…" Heat crawled onto her cheeks as the realization sank in that she'd spoken sharply to the man who'd championed the promotion that had landed her in this very office. Her fingers slipped from the keyboard. She tucked her hands beneath the surface of the desk, where she clutched them into tight fists while she summoned an embarrassed smile. "I didn't see you standing there." Lifting one hand, she uncurled her fingers and pointed to her computer. "Just trying to wrap up a few things before I call it quits for the day."

"Oh? Knocking off early so close to the deadline? I'd think you'd be burning the midnight oil."

She would be; she wanted to be. But several

things took precedence over work. Tonight she had to tell Caitlyn that her father had moved out, that he was leaving town for a two-week cruise without either of them. And, as soon as she could, she needed to throw her own overnight bag in the car and hightail it to Emerald Bay. Diane tugged on an earlobe and realized, in her haste to get out of a house where everything reminded her of her missing husband, she'd forgotten to put on earrings. Had she even worn makeup? She shrugged. It was Sunday, after all, a day when Ybor City's dress code didn't apply.

Jeff's brown eyes darkened as he scanned the raft of paperwork strewn across her untidy desk. "You have a lot of new responsibilities on your shoulders. I've heard rumors that we're asking too much of you."

Whoa! This conversation had gone south in a hurry. It was never a good sign when the top man in the company questioned your ability to handle the job. She rushed to set him straight. Tapping the closest stack of reports, she crossed her fingers and told Jeff what he wanted to hear. "Oh, no, sir. I'm actually ahead of schedule." Or she would be, once she finished reviewing the tax returns her staff had prepared.

"Oh?" Doubt accompanied Jeff's raised eyebrow. "You look a bit harried."

She forced herself to remain calm. Okay, so she didn't look her best. But she didn't know many women who could pull off a perfect ten on the morning after their husband walked out on them. She'd tried eye drops—they weren't a match for red-rimmed eyes, the result of an all-night crying jag. Worries about the future, her aunt and Caitlyn had left bags under her eyes the size of steamer trunks. She'd readily admit that olive green wasn't her color, and the blouse she wore gave her skin a sallow tone. But she hadn't been able to look at the empty half of the closet, so she'd grabbed the first thing she'd touched without turning on the light.

"Sorry about that," she said, trying to find some humor in the situation. She didn't let Jeff's apparent concern fool her. He didn't care one whit about her personally. His only concern was the company. "I have a bad case of deadline-itis. I've already booked myself for a full day at the spa next week."

Jeff peered so closely at her, she practically felt his eyes crawl across her skin. "It's more than that, though. Isn't it? I've heard reports that you weren't yourself in this week's staff meeting."

The remark set her teeth on edge. The meeting had been on Wednesday, when she'd been late getting into the office after another round of the same old argument with Tim. She'd arrived only to discover that the server had crashed. Dealing with that fiasco and getting her team back to work had eaten up every spare moment in her schedule. With no time to prepare, she'd gone straight into the meeting. So, yeah. She hadn't exactly been at her best.

"There was a lot going on that day," she admitted. "It won't happen again."

"See that it doesn't."

There was no mistaking Jeff's words for anything but a warning. One that shifted her pulse into overdrive. A protest formed on her lips. She quickly bit it back. Having worked closely with him on numerous projects, she knew the names and birthdates of Jeff's children, his favorite brand of aftershave. More important, she knew he didn't like excuses. He demanded results, preferably good ones. The only thing he enjoyed more than a positive outcome was feeling as though he'd somehow contributed to it.

She twisted her fingers into a ball. She couldn't afford to screw up at work right now, not if Tim was serious about throwing in the towel on their marriage. Should she ask Jeff for advice? With so much at stake, she had to try.

"You're right," she admitted. "The truth is,

things at home have been a little on edge lately. I'm sure you've dealt with similar problems, and I'd really like your advice. Could we set aside some time to talk next week?" Tonight would be better, but tonight she needed to have a heart-to-heart with Caitlyn.

"Joe Smalley will be in town to discuss the Wexx contract." Jeff shot the cuffs of the long-sleeved shirt he wore over freshly pressed Dockers.

"Good luck." Landing Wexx Enterprises as a client would be quite the coup. According to an article in *Forbes* last year, their CEO shared Jeff's passion for golf. In all likelihood, the two men would spend more time out on the links than they would in the office.

"You're sure you aren't overworked?" the founder probed. "Being responsible for an entire division isn't too much for you?"

"No, the workload isn't the problem," she insisted. She had to put his doubts to rest before they festered. "I knew what was required when I accepted the promotion," she said with perfect honesty. "I was prepared for that. I just can't seem to find the right balance at home. I'm working on it, but..." She paused to take a breath before she confessed her secret. "But Tim packed his bags and left last night. He left me the not-so-pleasant job of breaking the news to our daughter. Plus, my aunt is in the hospital, which means I'll need to make a quick trip to the other side of the state."

Jeff's expression, which usually exuded calm approval, softened. His gaze swung toward the cozy seating nook in Diane's office. It lingered there only for an instant before the company founder pivoted. Frowning, he looked out over the rabbit-warren of cubicles where her entire staff was hard at work on this the final weekend before the tax deadline.

Watching him, Diane swallowed. She knew as well as he did that one of her people might interrupt them at any moment.

Jeff's bushy white eyebrows knitted. "This sounds like something we should discuss behind closed doors. Why don't you join me in my office."

The invitation was not a request. Diane gave the returns she'd been reviewing a sad pat. She'd have to trust that her junior staff had done them correctly. In that she'd have no choice. By the time she and Jeff finished their little chat, she'd need to hit the road if she was going to beat Caitlyn home to an empty house. Hustling to keep up with Jeff's long strides, she followed her boss down the hall to the largest office on

Executive Row. At his request, she shut the door behind them.

"Coffee?" Jeff crossed the plush carpet to the seating area.

"No, thanks. I've hit my caffeine limit for today." She'd practically been mainlining the stuff since she arrived this morning. With a sigh, she sank onto a club chair.

"Something stronger?"

She shook her head. Although it was five o'clock somewhere, getting sloshed was the last thing she needed to do. Not with the drive home ahead of her. Not with a difficult conversation with Caitlyn on her agenda for the evening.

Jeff sank onto one cushion of a sleek, modern couch. Leaning back, he folded his hands across his belly. "So your marriage has hit the skids. I'm not surprised."

Diane's head jerked up. She hadn't expected Jeff to hand her a tissue or offer her a shoulder to cry on. That wasn't the older man's style. But his blasé disdain for her marriage came as a bit of a shock.

"Wh-why would you say that?" she sputtered.

"Relax." Jeff's hand sliced through the air like a knife. "It's nothing personal. It's the nature of the business." Careful not to wrinkle his pants, he crossed one leg over the other. "Run your finger down a list of names in upper management. They've all been divorced a time or two." He snorted. "I learned to demand a prenup after my first wife took me to the cleaners. You and Bill Talley are the only ones still in their starter marriages. He has an excuse—he didn't tie the knot until he was forty. What's yours?"

"I…" An urge to defend her marriage, her husband, built within her. "Tim's a good man. We have a good life together. At least, we did until last night," she insisted. "We'll work through this. We have to."

"Maybe." Jeff shrugged as if the outcome was of very little consequence. "I'm just saying, it's not uncommon for people who were married in their twenties or early thirties to find they have different interests in their forties or fifties. By then, the kids are nearly grown. Faced with the prospect of an empty nest, people start looking at how they want to spend the rest of their lives." He wagged a finger back and forth between them. "You and I, we're finally reaching the pinnacles of our careers. We want to dig in and leave our mark on the world. Maybe Tim wants something else. I don't know him well enough to hazard a guess."

Diane turned Jeff's words over in her mind.

Tim had made his retirement goals clear enough. He wanted to travel, to play a round of golf at each of the top ten courses in the world, to perfect his tennis serve, to become a gourmet cook. The trouble was, he expected her to do all of those things with him. And he wanted to get started sooner, rather than later.

Jeff reined in her wandering thoughts with a polite cough. "Like I said, I won't presume to know what your husband wants out of life. But I was under the impression that helping us become the premier accounting service in the nation was your top priority."

"It was. It is," Diane rushed to reassure him. Maybe not quite as important as her family, but it was close to the top of her list. It was even more important if she would soon be facing life as a single parent.

"In that case, you need to get your act together." Jeff leaned forward. "Take the next two days off. Whatever's going on at home, deal with it. Come back to work on Wednesday, ready to set the world on fire. If you don't, the next time an opportunity to move up in the company rolls around, it'll go to someone else."

"Someone like Blake Larson, you mean." Diane's voice whispered through the office. She and Blake had been vying against each other in

their quest to reach the top of the corporate
ladder for years.

"Exactly." Jeff nodded.

Diane shuddered a breath. Over the years,
she'd witnessed Jeff deliver his stern lectures to
various employees, but this was the first time
she'd been on the receiving end. From what
she'd seen, the man had always had the best
interests of the company he founded at heart,
and he rarely pulled any punches. He hadn't this
time, either.

Signaling the end of their little tête-à-tête, her
boss stood. "So we have an agreement? You'll
take a couple of days to get your head
straightened out, and we'll see you in here on
Wednesday. Otherwise, we might lose you here
at Ybor City, and I, for one, would hate to see
that happen."

Reading between the lines, she gulped.
Apparently, the rumors about a coming layoff
were true. That certainly put a different slant on
things. Whenever a company slimmed down,
middle-level managers were the first to get their
walking papers. She and Blake had been neck-
and-neck on the ladder to success, but if she
failed to make the next rung, she wouldn't just
be stuck in her current position for the rest of her
career; she'd soon be out of a job entirely.

She couldn't let that happen. Not after all she'd sacrificed to get this far. Not if Tim was serious about ending their marriage. Her hands shook, and this time, she couldn't blame it on the caffeine.

By the time she returned to her office, a thousand different worries pressed down on her. They rounded her shoulders and stole her breath away. On the verge of a panic attack, she reached a split-second decision: She'd follow Jeff's suggestion. Tomorrow, she'd head to Emerald Bay, where she'd support her aunt and family. But tonight, tonight was all about breaking the worst news of her life to her daughter.

She'd no sooner reached that decision than her phone rang. The insistent bleating of Caitlyn's ringtone broke Diane's concentration. She took a second to reorient herself before she forced a cheery note into her voice.

"Hey, sweetie. How's it going? Did you have fun at Marty's last night? How was church?" Her questions came in a rush that she hoped would keep Caitlyn from asking her own questions. Ones Diane didn't want to answer.

Ignoring her, Caitlyn demanded, "What's going on? Where's Daddy? Why didn't either of you pick me up at church?"

Diane's stomach sank faster than a stone in a

pond. How had she forgotten her daughter? In an instant, the answer punched her in the gut. The heartbreak and confusion of Tim's leaving coupled with Jeff's unexpected warning had robbed her of all thought. Still, she could imagine how disappointed Caitlyn must have been when she didn't see either her or Tim waiting in the parking lot. Tears seeped between her closed eyelids. She scrubbed them away with her fingertips.

"I'm so sorry, sweetheart. I got caught up in something here in the office, and I completely lost track of time."

"It's okay. Mrs. Harrison gave me a ride home."

She could practically see her daughter standing at the kitchen counter, scuffing one foot against the floor as if answering took more effort than it was worth.

"Mom, where's all the leftovers from dinner last night? I'm hungry." The plaintive note in Caitlyn's voice stirred every maternal instinct Diane possessed.

"I, uh, I left it out too long, and it went bad." She absolutely refused to explain why she hadn't given the food sitting on the counters a single thought until the wee hours of the morning. Not over the phone. "I'm leaving the office right this minute. Why don't I pick up burgers and fries for us on my way home?"

"BurgerFi?" Caitlyn asked with a tiny hint of interest.

"Of course." On a day like this, only her daughter's favorite burger joint would do.

"And onion rings?"

"I'll get a double batch, and we can share." She usually avoided the horrifically fattening treat, but the last twenty-four hours had worn her self-control down to the nub. "I'm placing the order now." She brought up another screen on her phone and scrolled through the popular restaurant's menu. "I'll see you in a few."

"Wait, Mom," Caitlyn said before she had a chance to disconnect. "Where's Dad? Tomorrow is Dress For Success Day, and I want to borrow one of his shirts and a tie."

Diane rubbed her forehead, hoping to ward off a killer headache. "I'm not exactly sure. A dental emergency, maybe?" She crossed her fingers and prayed God would forgive her for lying to her daughter. "You don't want something of mine? You could wear that Michael Kors you helped me pick out at Nordstrom last year."

"No offense, Mom, but your clothes are too big for me. Besides, Marty, Sarah and I are all dressing up like our dads."

Caitlyn's soft footfalls told Diane her daughter had headed up the stairs.

"No, wait. I, uh…" The last thing she wanted was for Caitlyn to go into their closet and see all the empty hangers, but how could she stop her? "You know how your dad is about his clothes," she said at last. "Let me pick one out for you. Then if he gets mad, he'll get mad at me." It had been too dark to see anything in their closet this morning, but surely Tim had left some clothes behind. "I'll be, I'll be home in a few minutes."

"Mom, I got this."

The familiar squeak of the closet door sent ice flowing through Diane's veins. *No, no, no,* she whispered silently. This wasn't the way she wanted Caitlyn to find out that her father had left them. She wanted to be home, her arms wrapped around the teen and pulling her close when she gently broke the news. She stood, grabbed her purse and headed for the door, her phone pressed against her ear.

She made it all the way to the elevator—a full twenty seconds later—before Caitlyn's disbelieving voice asked, "Where are all Daddy's clothes?"

"I'm on my way home, honey," she said, fighting to remain calm. "I'll be there in just a few minutes." She'd break every speed limit on the books in order to reach her child.

"Daddy's gone. He…left? He left me?"

Diane thought her heart had broken when Tim walked out. She'd been wrong. The anguish in her child's voice took heartbreak to a whole new level.

"I'm sorry, honey," she soothed. "He, uh, he's just taking a little break. He'll be back. I—I know he will."

"What did you do? Why did he go?" Caitlyn's questions were darts flung at a dart board, and she was a good shot. Diane winced as each one hit its target.

Diane listened to the three beeps that signaled the end of the call. Moving as swiftly as her legs would carry her, she hurried to the garage where she'd left her car. On her way, she repeatedly punched Caitlyn's number. Her daughter refused to pick up.

She hit the gas hard enough to leave a little rubber as she turned onto Morgan Street, headed for Route 60 and the fastest way home in the heavy weekend traffic.

Seventeen

Margaret

A n irregular beeping sound came from somewhere on her left. When she pried her eyes open, the lids felt heavy, like they weighed a ton apiece. Not that there was much to see. She stared straight up at white ceiling tiles peppered with tiny holes. A vent bathed her in cold air, and she shivered beneath a thin blanket and an even thinner sheet. She struggled to sit up. Panic tugged at her when she couldn't move her arms.

Where am I? Why can't I move?

It took more effort than it should to lift her head far enough off the pillow to see her hands. Someone had taped her left arm to a board. A thin tube ran from under a bandage on the top of her hand and disappeared over a metal railing on the side of the bed. Her right arm lay across her chest, encased in something heavy and held in place by a sling.

Okay. She was in the hospital. Why? What had happened? Why did she hurt all over?

Though the move took tremendous effort, she turned her head to one side. Kim sat in an oversize chair at her bedside, her eyes closed. A book lay in her lap. From the looks of things, it had slipped from Kim's fingers when she fell asleep and now rested on one knee, ready to slide to the floor at the slightest provocation.

The sight of her niece sleeping so peacefully pushed the panic back a bit. Her breathing slowed. The monitor skipped a beat before its frantic beeping eased into a regular rhythm. She cleared her throat.

At the noise, her niece sprang to her feet. The book landed on the floor with a thunk. An instant later, Kim loomed over the side of the bed.

"Hey, Aunt Margaret," she said with a cheery voice that didn't match the concern etched deeply into her features. "You gave us quite the scare. How are you feeling?"

"Thirsty." She was so dry it felt like someone had stuffed her mouth full of cotton. Seconds later, she drank gratefully from the straw Kim slipped between her lips.

"I'm in the hospital?" she asked when questions outweighed her need to drink.

"In Vero Beach," Kim nodded. "Belle's here — she ran home to shower and change, but she'll be back in just a little bit. Diane is in the waiting room. Amy will be back soon, too. She had to check on things at the bakery. Scott stopped by last night and again this morning on his way to court."

"Everybody's here?" She let that sink in for a minute. "Am I dying?"

"No!" Kim's answer was firm and immediate. "You're going to be fine. It'll take a while for your arm to heal—you did a good job breaking it. You have a small cut on your leg and a few bumps and bruises, but other than that, you're okay. You're going to be okay."

"If I'm not dying, why are you all here?" There had to be more to the story.

"I tried to convince Belle to stay in New York, but you know your daughter—nothing would change her mind. She caught the first plane out of LaGuardia. She flew commercial, no less. In coach!" Kim laughed.

"Belle?" She managed a wry smile. "Are you sure?"

"Yes, ma'am. Diane made it here before breakfast. She's already talked to admissions and straightened out all your insurance. We called Scott out of court in case we needed his power of attorney. We didn't, but—" She paused. "I think Belle's going to want to talk to you about that," she warned. "As for Amy and me, we were already here."

Kim made it sound like no one had rushed here because she was at death's door. She guessed, maybe, it wasn't her time after all. There was just one more thing. She peered up at her niece. "What happened?"

"You don't remember?"

"It's all hazy. We had lunch, didn't we?"

"Yes, ma'am," Kim said despite the frown that tugged on her lips. "At Sweet Cakes."

"Right. We had chicken salad. Craig Morgan stopped by our table." She paused while bits and pieces of the rest of the day floated past like fluffy clouds in a clear blue sky. She'd been upset by something, but she couldn't remember what it was. She did recall going to the grocery store where Kim had bought enough food to fill the fridge and most of the pantry. Her next clear recollection was of standing on the deck out back. After that, it was all a blur. A tear rolled down her cheek.

"That's okay," Kim soothed while she blotted away the moisture. "The doctor said it's perfectly normal not to remember everything about an accident."

"I had an accident, then?" Not a stroke or a heart attack?

"You fell. We think you were trying to straighten a downspout and lost your balance. You must have put out your arms to catch yourself because your right one broke. It was…" Kim's face scrunched. "Bad. Broken in two places. They had to operate to reset them, but the orthopedist was out of town. They had to wait until this morning." Before Margaret could ask, she added, "It's Monday. You're just now waking up from surgery."

She looked down. Her arm was encased in pale pink plaster from the upper arm to the wrist. "Pink?"

"Belle chose the color." An amused smile replaced the horrified expression on Kim's face.

"It could be worse." The Henson boy had sported a lime-green cast on his arm for six weeks. In bright neon, no less. She'd often wondered if it had glowed in the dark.

On the far side of the room, the door had been left ajar. An orderly pushed a cart with a squeaky wheel down the hall. Somewhere trays rattled. The scent of antiseptic floated in the air. The smell jarred a few more memories loose.

A broken step. Peeling paint. Boarded-up windows. She groaned.

"Are you in pain? I can get the nurse." Kim reached for a button on the bed rail.

"No. I'm, I'm all right for now. I just hate that everyone disrupted their lives because of me," she said.

Kim's hand on her shoulder delivered warmth and reassurance.

"Don't give it a second thought. We're all here because we love you. We just want to make sure you get the best care."

"Speaking of that..." Her throat felt so dry and scratchy that her voice faded.

"More water?"

She nodded, unable to make a sound. When she'd had a few more sips from the straw, she cleared her throat. "What was I saying?"

Kim started to answer, but there was no need. Margaret knew perfectly well what she needed to say. "Don't be too hard on Craig."

"What's that?" Questions formed in Kim's dark eyes.

"He was right," she said on a sigh. "I haven't been keeping up with repairs and maintenance the way I should have. The inn looks shabby. Your Uncle Eric and Aunt Liz would be disappointed."

"I think you've done the best you could," Kim insisted. "The Dane Crown Inn is a big responsibility for just one person."

"I should have done a better job." Sleep tugged at her eyelids. She struggled to stay awake. "Now there's so much to do." She yawned. "I don't even know where to start." This time, when her eyes drifted shut, she didn't bother trying to open them.

The room smelled like the inside of a florist's shop the next time she surfaced from a dreamless sleep. Her eyes still felt like they were weighed down with bricks, but she slitted them open. Vases and floral arrangements crowded every inch of available counter space. A banner stretched across a wreath of red flowers someone had hung on the door. She squinted, but without her glasses, she couldn't make out the words.

Kim must have been wrong about that whole dying thing, she thought. When she tried and failed to move her arms, her suspicions were confirmed. She was lying in a coffin instead of a hospital bed. That had to be it. An odd sense of peace spread through her. It lasted until a balloon drifted into sight. She moved her head slightly and saw clusters of shiny Mylar bobbing beneath the air-conditioning vents.

No one sent balloons to a funeral home. *Okay, not dead, then.*

She opened her eyes wider. She was in the hospital, still in the same bed.

"Mama!"

"Ooof." Margaret grunted softly when someone flung themselves on top of her. Sucking in her next breath, she caught the scent of expensive perfume. *Belle?*

"Oh, Mama! I've been so worried. We all have. Are you all right? How do you feel? Are you in any pain? Can I get you anything?"

"Stand up and let me get a good look at you," she whispered. With all Belle's weight pressed against her, she struggled to catch her breath.

Belle treated her to another tight squeeze before she peeled herself away. "Mama, don't look at me. I'm a wreck. No makeup. My hair's a rat's nest." She plucked at a shirt that swam on her. "I was in such a hurry to get here, I didn't even pack. I had to borrow some clothes from Kim."

"Oh, child. You could be wearing sackcloth and ashes for all I care. You're a sight for sore eyes."

"Are you hurting, Mama? Do you need anything for the pain?"

She considered her answer. Flexing her toes, she was relieved to see movement beneath the blanket. The arm with the IV itched. In its thick cast, her other arm ached dully. An empty feeling in the pit of her stomach bordered on nausea.

"I think I'm hungry more than anything else. What time is it?" Beside a wall-mounted television, the hands of a broken clock pointed perpetually at noon and two.

"Of course you are. It's two in the afternoon, and you haven't had solid food since Saturday. Let me have the nurse bring you something to eat." Belle pushed a button on the side of the bed.

Her head swam. Somehow, she'd lost track of nearly forty-eight hours. No wonder she was hungry. She hadn't had anything to eat and only a few sips of water to drink since... Since when?

"Belle. How long have I been here? In the hospital?"

"A day and a half, Mama. Amy called me around four Saturday afternoon. Between the storm and having to change planes in Atlanta, I didn't get here till nearly midnight. By then, you were dead to the world—the doctors gave you something to make you sleep. We all took turns sitting with you until they came to get you for the surgery this morning." Belle stared down at her arm cradled in its cast. Her green eyes brimmed with unshed tears. "Mama, I'm so sorry."

"Now, now." She ached to hold her daughter's hand but couldn't move either of her own. "There wasn't a thing you or anyone else could do to prevent this. I have no one to blame but myself. It was my own foolish idea to go poking around outside." Her memories of the day before had cleared somewhat. She still didn't recollect the fall itself, but she remembered going down the steps of the deck, walking up and down the path that ran between the cottages, agreeing with Craig's assessment of the inn.

"But I should have been here. Should have…"

"Let's not play the woulda-coulda-shoulda game, Belle," she chided. "It only makes us feel bad, and it doesn't change a thing." She expelled a breath. "Now, were you going to get me something to eat?"

Belle's face broke into a smile recognized by millions. "Yes, ma'am. Let me see what's keeping your nurse. I'll be right back. Don't go anywhere."

She nodded pointedly at her broken wing. She wasn't going anywhere for the time being.

True to her word, Belle returned quickly.

"Betty—she's your nurse—she says soft foods only at first." She brandished a spoon and two plastic cups of green Jell-O. "If you keep this down you can have something more substantial for supper."

"Huh. I'm so hungry I could eat a Porterhouse and a baked potato. I guess Jell-O will have to do."

"It's nice to see you've got your sense of humor back." Belle grinned. "Betty is getting a new patient settled into a room down the hall. She said to tell you she'll be in to check on you as soon as she can."

Her daughter pressed a different button, and a motor whirred. The head of the bed rose, and she rose with it until she reached a semi-upright position.

Belle peeled a foil cover away from the cup. "In the meantime, I think it'd be best if I just fed this to you. Do you mind?"

"I don't think I have much choice." She'd tried to free her unbroken arm without much luck. It was solidly taped in place. She imagined it had been necessary to keep her from dislodging it in her sleep, but she was awake now and she wasn't about to rip the IV loose. Whatever drugs flowed through that tube, she had a strong suspicion she needed them.

Belle hovered a spoon near her mouth, and she dutifully opened it. The artificial flavors and sweeteners gave the Jell-O a slightly bitter taste, but she was too hungry to complain. "This would make a good publicity shot," she said between greedy bites. "'Queen of Pop rushes to Mom's bedside.'" She half-expected one of Belle's entourage to pop out from behind the woodwork and snap a picture of the superstar spoon-feeding her mother from a plastic cup. "Who's with you on this trip?" she asked.

"Nobody. It's just me."

That was odd. Belle had stopped traveling alone years ago after an obsessed fan had cornered her in a public bathroom and demanded an autograph. "Didn't anyone recognize you?"

"You should have seen me on the plane. On the way to the airport, I paid my driver fifty bucks for his Yankees baseball cap. I stuffed all my hair up in it and tugged the brim down low over my eyes. At the airport, I bought one of those 'I Heart NY' sweatshirts at the first kiosk I came to. Triple X. It came down past my knees. The guy at the security gate did a double take, but he was a good Joe. He didn't let on. If anybody else knew who I was, they kept their lips shut."

Something in Belle's delivery seemed off. Despite her own aches and pains and muddled thoughts, she sensed an uncharacteristic sadness in her usually upbeat daughter. "Is everything okay, Belle?" she asked.

"Me? It's you everyone is worried about. You gave us quite the scare." Her expression turning serious, Belle pulled the lid off the second cup of Jell-O. "Mama, I want you to think about something now."

"Okay," she said slowly as she braced herself for more bad news. Whatever Belle wanted, her daughter's tone said she probably wasn't going to like it.

"I want you to think about coming back to New York with me. There's plenty of room in my condo. You'd have your own room, and I have full-time help, so you'd never be alone unless you wanted to be."

"Move to New York?" Her eyebrows bunched. "Because of my arm?" She managed to lift the cast an inch. Instantly, she regretted it when pain radiated outward from her forearm.

"For now. If you like it, we could make it permanent."

Trying not to moan, she shook her head. New York was too crowded, too busy, too cold. "I've lived in Emerald Bay my entire life. My friends, my church—they're all here. I'm too old to up and move. And certainly not to New York."

"But Mama, we have to make some changes. You can't run the inn on your own anymore. Amy told me this wasn't the first time you've fallen."

"I can't believe she told you about that," she fussed. "She promised she'd keep it between the two of us."

She and her niece were going to have a little talk about keeping secrets. But not now. Now, all this talk about uprooting her life and moving to New York only made her arm hurt worse. She longed for the oblivion of sleep, just for a while. "My arm is starting to throb, sweetheart. Could you ask Betty for something for the pain? Tylenol or whatever they have."

"Of course, Mama." Instantly contrite, Belle hurried into the hall.

Margaret listened to her daughter's footsteps until they faded. With only the *beep-beep* of the monitor to keep her company, she sighed. Her daughter and the rest of her family were right, she supposed. It was time to make some changes. Much as she wanted to live life on her own terms, she was smart enough to know how lucky she'd been this time. And the time before that. And the other times that no one knew about.

Sooner or later, though, her luck would run out. Then the decision would be out of her hands. If she wanted a say in how she lived whatever time she had left on this earth, she needed to decide what she wanted while the choice was still hers to make. Much as she loved her daughter, moving to New York and living in Belle's ultra-sleek apartment wasn't an option. From the sounds of it, she couldn't remain at the inn alone, either. That left getting a small place of her own, somewhere close to her church and the grocery store. Of course, she'd probably have to move again in a few years, this time to an assisted living facility like Emerald Oaks.

She frowned. The word "facility" tasted far worse than the Jell-O. But faced with the prospect of two moves in her near future, the smart choice was to move once and get it over with. It wasn't like she'd be lonely at Emerald Oaks. Claudia Butler had moved there after she broke her hip two years ago, and she seemed to like it well enough. Grady Motes, another resident, raved about the food. She wouldn't be stuck there all the time, either. The Emerald Oaks bus brought both Claudia and Grady to church on Sundays and came back for them after the service ended. It took them on weekly shopping trips and to doctor appointments.

So no, life at Emerald Oaks wouldn't be all that bad. But before she agreed to such a major change, there was one item left on her bucket list. One thing she wanted to do. To make it happen, though, she'd need a lot of help, and she hoped, she prayed, her family would give it to her.

A few minutes later, Belle breezed back into the room accompanied by an efficient-looking young woman.

"Hey, Ms. Keenan. How are you feeling, hon?"

Above pale blue scrubs, a set of caring brown eyes peered down at her. She'd seen those eyes before and searched the nurse's face for a small port-wine stain. She found it right where she expected it to be—on the pretty brunette's forehead. "You're Betty Logan, aren't you?"

"Yes, ma'am. I was in your Sunday School class when I was just a little girl. I'm sorry as I can be about your accident. The Ladies Auxiliary has the prayer chain going for you." Betty plumped pillows and straightened bedclothes while she spoke.

"Well, you tell them all their prayers worked and I'm going to be fine." She stared up at the woman. "You aren't going to make a liar out of me, are you?"

"Oh, no, ma'am. I wouldn't think of it." Betty laughed. "The surgeon fixed you right up. You'll be in that cast for six to eight weeks, and you might need a little therapy afterwards, but in three months or so, you'll be good as new. Barring an infection, that is. We're giving you the good antibiotics to keep that from happening." Betty tapped one finger on the bandage over her IV. She pulled a stethoscope from a deep pocket and slipped it on. "Now I'm going to take a listen to your chest, and then I'll give you something for the pain. Belle said you were uncomfortable?"

Uncomfortable was an understatement. Beneath the cast, someone was beating on her arm with a hammer. Hard. She nodded.

"Your doctor left orders for pain meds, so we'll have you sorted out in no time."

Betty was right, she thought a few minutes later as the edges of her world shimmered. She wasn't sure whether the pain itself had lessened or she just didn't care about it anymore. Either way, she was still trying to figure out how to break the news of her decision to Belle when darkness slipped over her.

Eighteen

Kim

*I*ce cubes clinked gently against the sides of the four tall glasses Kim carried on a tray through the open French doors and out onto the deck. She crossed the short distance to the table where Belle, Diane and Amy had already gathered. Calendars and phones littered the surface of its glass top. Amy pushed some of the papers aside, creating room. Kim filled each of the glasses from a pitcher filled with a fruity concoction.

"Oh, that looks yummy." Ignoring the bottle of sparkling water Kim had also plunked down on the table, Belle snagged one of the tumblers. She eyed the bowl of whole wheat crackers. "No veggies?" she asked.

"There's celery in the fridge if you want to

get it." Kim doled out the rest of the drinks before she took an empty seat.

Belle shrugged aside the suggestion and reached for a handful of chips. "Stress eating," she said.

"No explanations necessary." Kim smiled. "It's been a tough couple of days for all of us." Stress or no stress, she hadn't expected Belle to break her no-carb rule for the drink, let alone the crackers. "The punch is one of Aunt Liz's specialties. I found her binder in a kitchen cupboard." The three-ring notebook was chock full of recipes the cook had followed when the inn offered full meal service for its guests.

"The cloth-covered one? With all her favorites?" Amy squealed. "I thought that was lost forever."

"It was tucked in the back, behind a row of other cookbooks. Betty Crocker. James Beard. Julia Child." Kim aimed a thumb through the door she'd left open in case her aunt called out. "Do you want it?" She tried not to let her reluctance show and thought she did a good job of it. But thumbing through the family cookbook had made her mouth water for long-forgotten dishes. She'd been planning to try some of them while she was here.

"No. You hang on to it for now. As long as I

know where it is, I'm happy." Amy nibbled on a cracker.

Diane took a sip of her drink. "Oh, I remember this. Mom and Dad used to serve it at those cocktail hours they hosted on the front porch each day."

"Adults only," Amy added.

"Aunt Liz put out snacks for the kids in the kitchen. Juice boxes and peanut butter crackers, mostly. Wait a minute." Belle turned toward Diane. "How'd you know what the adults were drinking?"

"Don't you remember?" Diane jabbed her elbow into Belle's ribs. "It was my job to clean up the porch each evening before supper. Sometimes there was a little bit of their 'special juice' left over and I'd help myself." Diane twirled her glass in her hands.

"Diane, you didn't!" Kim exclaimed. On top of its citrusy base, Aunt Liz's recipe called for two kinds of rum and a goodly helping of apricot brandy.

"It was delish. Just like this." Diane took another sip.

Amy laughed. "No wonder you were so sleepy at dinner sometimes."

"I can't believe no one caught on." Kim pictured her slightly inebriated teenage cousin.

"I can't believe she didn't share it with the rest of us." Belle gave Diane's shoulder a good-natured shove.

"Shhhh, you guys," Amy cautioned. "We don't want to wake Aunt Margaret."

Kim sent a worried look through the kitchen to the hallway that led to the first-floor family quarters. Her aunt hadn't stepped foot out of her suite since they brought her home from the hospital yesterday. "She's sleeping a lot. Do you think that's normal?"

"Her body's had quite a shock. The fall. Surgery. People her age don't bounce back as quick as they did when they were younger." Amy stared down at the handful of crackers she'd grabbed. "Is there any dip for these?"

"Sorry," Kim murmured. "I would have picked some up at the grocery store if I'd known we'd all be here."

"I'm just thankful Mama's going to be all right." Belle wiped tears from her eyes. "I know she won't move in with me—she's made that plain enough—but I want her to come to New York until her arm heals. I asked her while we were at the hospital."

"Oh, yeah? What'd she say?" Amy chewed thoughtfully on one of the chips.

"She absolutely refused."

"That's about what I would expect. Once Aunt Margaret makes up her mind about something, there's no changing it. And she's said all along she had no intention of ever leaving here." Diane stared at the distant palm trees. "Can't say I blame her. This was a wonderful place to grow up. Tampa's nice, but it's a big city. I miss living at the beach."

"So she's going to stay here, then?" Kim traced her finger around the wet ring her glass had left on the table. She swallowed. "I don't think she can manage on her own. Not now. Not with a cane *and* a broken arm."

"No." Belle shook her head in agreement. "I don't think so either. I've been thinking and praying about it." She glanced at the sky. "I haven't thought of much else, to tell you the truth. I'll be here as much as I can, but I can't be here all the time. I could hire someone full-time to stay with her or…"

Belle's gaze was so intense, Kim practically felt it when her cousin's focus shifted to her. "Or?"

"Or, if you're willing, I'd rather pay you to stay with her than to hire some stranger through a service. I know it's a lot to ask, but…"

"I'll do it." Kim didn't hesitate. She hadn't realized how much she'd missed being in

Emerald Bay until she stepped off the shuttle bus the other night. She'd known she was home again the instant she inhaled the smell of the ocean mixed with the scent of night-blooming jasmine. She couldn't think of anywhere she'd rather be or anything she'd rather do than stay right here and help the woman who'd practically raised her.

"Are you sure, Kim?" Doubt dripped from Diane's words. "What about your job? Your apartment?"

"The timing couldn't be better, actually. I've been working temp jobs, so I don't have to give notice or anything. My lease is up soon, and I was going to have to move anyway. That's the only fly in the proverbial ointment—I need to go back to Atlanta and clear out my apartment. I have about a carload to bring down—clothes, scrapbooks, personal stuff. The furniture is all cast-offs. None of it is worth saving."

"I can stay on at least for a week while you take care of things in Atlanta." Belle flattened her perfectly manicured fingers on the table.

"You can?" Surprise colored Amy's eyes. "I thought you were getting ready for a big tour or something.

"I've pushed that back a bit. The record label wanted some changes, so I'm on a break of sorts for a little while. A week, maybe two. One thing's for sure, Mama can't manage on her own till that cast comes off. That'll be what, six, eight weeks?"

Kim swallowed her own shock that Belle was not just willing to stay but able to take time away from her incredibly busy schedule. Sensing there was more to the story than her cousin was willing to share, she focused on answering Belle's question. "That's what Betty said. Aunt Margaret has a follow-up with the ortho doc in a couple of weeks. We'll know more then."

Diane cleared her throat. "I'd love to stay and lend a hand, but I've already stayed longer than I planned. I need to go back home tomorrow. It's homecoming week and the start of Caitlyn's soccer season. I promised I'd make it to the rest of her games."

"How is she? Still as sweet as ever?" Amy dusted a few grains of salt from her hands.

When they were kids, whenever Aunt Liz tried to get her youngest daughter to try something new, Diane had refused by scrunching up her nose and stomping her feet. While she didn't beat her shoes against the deck this time, her nose did twitch at Amy's questions. Why, Kim wondered. Was trouble brewing in Tampa Bay?

"She's a typical teenager, I suppose. One day,

she's my best friend. The next, I can't do anything right. We fixed dinner for her and her friends the other night. It was so good to see them all laughing and having a good time." Diane stared pointedly at the distant palm trees. "Today, not so much."

"It's hard when the chicks spread their wings and insist on flying by themselves." As one who'd had some ups and downs with her own children, Kim could empathize. "People tell me they'll come back to the nest eventually." She coughed lightly. "I'll let you know when that happens. In the meantime, you've got that new promotion to keep you busy."

Diane snorted. With a half-laugh, she added, "No matter what your job title, it's always far too demanding, and the benefits aren't at all what they're cracked up to be."

Problems with her daughter. Problems at work. What else was bothering her cousin? Feeling a little like she was picking at a scab, Kim prodded. "And Tim? What's he up to?"

"You might as well know now. You'll find out eventually." Diane seemed to fold in on herself. "We've decided—well, he decided, actually—that we need some time apart. He booked a two-week cruise to Mexico."

"Oh! You'll love it there," Belle exclaimed.

Diane grasped her cousin's wrist. There was no mistaking her hurt when she said, "His ship set sail yesterday. He, uh, he didn't exactly invite me along."

"Are you separating?" Amy's voice strained.

When Diane's upheld hands fended off any more questions, Kim scratched her head. Once they'd been as close as, well, sisters, and they'd known everything about each other, from the day Aunt Flo came to visit each month to which one of them was sweating out a C in algebra. But that had been a long time ago. They'd each changed—a lot—in the intervening years. And though they'd stayed in touch, they didn't have the same relationship they'd once had. Neither Belle nor Diane owed her or Amy the truth, the whole truth and nothing but the truth. She had to trust that they'd share more details if and when the time was right.

Belle was the first to react when something moved in the room behind them. Before Kim knew what was happening, the superstar was on her feet and dodging around the corner of the table like a linebacker on a football field. A second later, Kim heard the slow shuffle of footsteps punctuated by the irregular tap of a cane on the floor tiles. She joined the others as they all sprang into action.

Before Aunt Margaret hobbled another two feet forward, all four women had surrounded her.

"Here, Aunt Margaret, lean on me."

"Can I get you anything? Something to eat or drink?"

"Mama, you should have called. I'd have come running."

"We all would."

"We were on the back porch. Want to sit outside with us? Somebody get her sweater."

The chorus of helpful offers and suggestions drowned out the sound of birds chirping in the trees and waves rolling to shore.

"Girls! I can't hear myself think!" Aunt Margaret put an end to their chatter by thumping the floor with her cane.

Kim, like the others, clamped her mouth shut.

"Now," Margaret said when everyone quieted, "I think I would like a breath of fresh air. Diane, could you grab the afghan off the back of the couch in my room? And Kim, if you wouldn't mind, I'd love a cup of tea. Amy, be a dear and fetch me one of those rolls from breakfast, if there are any left." She extended her good arm to Belle. "You can help me outside. I'm not too proud to admit that, between this cast and my bum leg, I'm not getting around as easy as I was."

LEIGH DUNCAN

In minutes Margaret was seated, a blanket over her lap, tea and a breakfast scone on the table in front of her. One by one the rest of them took their places around her. When they were once again settled, Margaret wrapped her fingers around her mug. "This is the kind of day that makes people glad they live in Florida."

She was right, Kim acknowledged. The midafternoon sun hung in a brilliant blue sky. The temperature hovered just below 80 degrees. A gentle, onshore breeze had lowered the humidity, making it the perfect day for playing golf, taking a bike ride, or simply sitting outside and enjoying the company of family.

"I want to thank all of you for taking care of me these last couple of days. I don't know what I would have done without you." Margaret patted the cast she wore in a sling. "Anyone know how long I'll be wearing this thing? I know the doctor musta said, but that whole time in the hospital is kind of a blur."

"At least six weeks, Mama," Belle answered, "depending on how fast your bones heal. It could be as long as two months."

"Ooh!" Margaret absorbed the news like a body blow. "I didn't think it would be so long."

The ice had melted in Kim's glass. She swirled the watered-down dregs of her fruit punch and

384

polished it off while they all gave the older woman the time she needed to come to grips with the prospect of being laid up for a while.

Thirty seconds ticked by before Margaret spoke again. "I know you've all been worried about me, and I appreciate that more than you could possibly know. I couldn't ask for a better daughter, better nieces."

Kim joined the others in reassuring her aunt that they hadn't done anything more than anyone else would do under similar circumstances. She might as well have saved her breath, though.

"The way you all dropped whatever you were doing to help me, that's a rare thing these days," Margaret interrupted. "Why, when Doris Chotski had her heart attack last fall, her son didn't even visit her in the hospital."

"That's awful," Diane declared. "I hope she wrote him out of her will."

"Knowing Doris, she probably did," Margaret agreed. She broke off a small piece of her scone but only pushed it around the plate with a fork. "This accident, though. It's given me a lot to think about. I can't expect you girls to come a-running every time I stub my big toe."

"This was a little more than stubbing your toe, Mama. You had to have surgery," Belle blustered.

"Believe me. I know." Margaret lifted her cast ever so slightly. "And it's finally made me face facts. I can't run the inn anymore. I've decided to sell it and move to Emerald Oaks."

Kim sucked in a gasp. Whatever announcement she'd been expecting from her aunt, selling the property that had been in the family for three generations wasn't it. She blinked back tears as she considered what the news meant for her personally. She wouldn't be moving down from Atlanta, that was for sure. There'd be no need if Aunt Margaret was going to move to an assisted living facility.

"Are you sure that's what you want to do, Mama?" Belle reached across the table and grasped her mother's fingers. "You seemed so certain in the hospital."

"I'm sure I don't want to move to New York," Margaret insisted. "I'm just as sure it's time for me to let go of this place."

"I know Bonny Miller. She's the director at Emerald Oaks. She stops by Sweet Cakes nearly every day on her way to work," Amy put in. "She mentioned last week that she has a two-room apartment opening up at the end of the month. If you want it, we could get you in there right away."

"Wait a second," Diane cautioned. "Aunt

Margaret, you've just had major surgery. This might not be the best time to make a life-changing decision. Don't you want to think about this for a few days?"

"I'm not planning on moving tomorrow or next week." Margaret pursed her lips. "There are a couple of things I need to do first. That's where I hope you girls will come in. I could use your help."

"Of course, Mama. What is it? I'll do whatever you want."

"Don't be too hasty, Belle." Margaret slowly withdrew her fingers from her daughter's. "You don't know what I'm asking."

Belle blinked her huge eyes. "Yes, ma'am."

Margaret straightened slightly. "First, before I put the place on the market, I want to hold one last family reunion. Like we used to have before Eric died."

"A family reun—" Amy and Belle gasped in unison.

"That's a lot." Diane's shock was evident in her slow murmur.

Kim's head began to buzz. "We held those reunions at the start of every summer, just after school ended. They lasted two full weeks."

"I know, and I realize it's too much to expect of everyone. People don't take long vacations

387

like they used to. But I was thinking a week or at least a long weekend. If I'm going to let go of this place, I want one last day of yard darts and board games. One last night with all of us sitting around the campfire roasting marshmallows."

"One last fish fry," Amy added.

"One last Dane Family Talent Show," said Diane.

"Now you've got it." Aunt Margaret nodded her approval. "Is that too much to ask?"

Kim's wheels were spinning. There'd be invitations to send, food to prepare, travel arrangements to make. They'd have to give everyone adequate notice. And accommodations—where would everyone sleep?

She blinked as a new thought occurred to her. Her aunt had said she wanted two things. Was her second wish as impossible as the first one?

"You said you had two conditions, Aunt Margaret," Kim prompted gently. "What's the other one?"

Margaret's lower jaw trembled. "I don't want—no, I absolutely won't," she corrected. "I won't sell The Dane Crown Inn to some developer who wants to come in here and bulldoze the place to make way for more of those high-rise condominiums."

Looking around the table, Kim saw her own doubts and concerns reflected on her cousins' faces. Aunt Margaret was asking the impossible, but who was going to tell her? She glanced pointedly at Belle. The redhead was, after all, Margaret's daughter.

Belle's eyes narrowed, but she shouldered the burden of delivering the bad news. "Mama, I don't think we can pick and choose who buys the place."

"That's where you're wrong, honey. I talked to my friend Sharon Tatum. She's in real estate. She says the seller can set whatever terms they want as long as they're willing to wait for the right buyer to come along."

"But Mama, that could take years," Belle objected.

Margaret shifted in her chair. When she moved, the bulky cast banged into the table, and she winced. On either side of her, Belle and Amy hurried to help, but she waved them aside.

"Look," she said, her voice not unkind. "I know you've all been talking about me. And I hate that I've worried you so. But it's not easy to give up the place I've called my home most of my life. To start over at my age. I know it's time, though. All I'm asking is to hold one last get-together here and to find some nice buyers who'll want to make the inn a part of their family. If that's too much to ask, then I'll just stay put."

"But…"

"No buts, Belle." Margaret's gaze fell on her daughter. From there, she went around the table, her focus lingering on each person long enough to make them squirm. "You girls want me to move into assisted living? It's up to you to make it happen." As if delivering her ultimatum had taken every ounce of strength she possessed, she paled. "All this business has plumb tuckered me out," she announced. "I'm going back to bed."

While her mother slowly stood and awkwardly leaned on her cane, Belle sat where she was, looking for all the world like someone had punched her in the stomach. Amy's eyes had glazed over. Diane hovered on the brink of tears.

Kim forced down her own feelings and pushed away from the table. "Let me help Aunt Margaret," she offered. To the others, she added, "Don't say a word until I get back."

"I don't think that's going to be a problem," came Diane's whispered response.

As she guided her aunt into bed a few minutes later, Kim couldn't stop thinking about all the times she'd needed help and Margaret had stepped forward to offer it. When her own mother had coached her into helping her little sister up the front steps of the inn and driven off without waiting to see if anyone answered the door, it was Aunt Margaret who'd held the screen door wide and welcomed the pair of them inside. Pretending she'd been waiting for their arrival, she'd showered them with hugs and kisses. For the rest of that summer—and several summers afterwards—her aunt had never so much as hinted that raising her sister's children was anything less than perfectly normal. She and Uncle Eric had clothed them, fed them, practiced their letters and numbers with them, and taught them the value of church and chores. And after her mom had ignored a terrible cough until the cancer had spread everywhere, Aunt Margaret had welcomed her and Jen into her home permanently. From then on, her aunts and uncles had always been there for her, providing soft shoulders to cry on when she needed them and dispensing good advice whether she thought she needed it or not.

Staring down at the woman who'd drifted off within seconds after crawling into bed, Kim studied the translucent skin over her aunt's eyelids, the smile that played across her lips even in sleep, the arm in its cast propped up on pillows. Aunt Margaret had given her a second chance at life and happiness when she'd needed it most. Now, decades later, she finally had a chance to repay the debt. How could she say no?

In the kitchen, she stopped only long enough to take another pitcher from the fridge and grab a can of mixed nuts from the pantry. The murmur of low voices drifted through the doors, which stood ajar. Kim squared her shoulders and breezed onto the porch.

"I thought we could all do with another round," she said, plunking the pitcher onto the center of the table. After spilling a few nuts into the palm of her hand, she slid the can across the glass tabletop. "So what are we thinking?"

Belle's mouth worked. "I'm astounded. She's actually going to sell this place? I never thought I'd see the day. Quite frankly, I'm not quite sure how I feel about it." Her eyes swept from the porch to the cottages and the distant river as if she was trying to commit pieces of her childhood home to memory.

"She'll sell only if we agree to find the *right* kind of buyer," Diane said, making air quotes.

"And host a reunion. Don't forget that part," Kim reminded them.

"It'd be kind of fun to get everyone together again," Belle mused. "But it is a lot to ask."

"It is," Kim agreed. "But I'm in." She'd been

surprised by how easily she'd reached the decision.

"Aunt Margaret has been like a second mother to me," Amy said. "I would never have had the courage to open Sweet Cakes without her encouragement. If this is something she wants, I have to help."

"That leaves you, Diane," Belle said, pointing out the obvious.

Diane traced her finger through the condensation that had formed on her glass. "Aunt Margaret means the world to me. I couldn't have gotten through Mom's death without her. After the funeral, she called me every single day for months, just to check in, to make sure I was doing okay. She makes me want to be a better version of myself. Like Amy and Kim, I can't tell her no." She took a breath so large that her shoulders rose. "That said, between work and Caitlyn's games, I won't have a spare second until the end of soccer season in a couple of months. Till it's over, I can only be here on the weekends."

Belle grinned. "So we're in agreement? We'll get the whole family together for one last big whoop, and then we'll help Mama find the perfect buyer for this place?"

Kim looked around the table. There was a ton

of work to do if they were going to make this dream come true for Aunt Margaret. The effort was not without risks. What if they invested their aunt's money in fixing up the inn but still couldn't find a buyer? Or worse, what if Aunt Margaret changed her mind about putting it on the market at all? She swallowed. They'd cross those bridges if and when they came to them. In the meantime, the four of them would work together to plan the reunion of all reunions and get the inn in shape to host it. She waited until the others nodded before she raised her glass of punch.

"To Mama," Belle said.

The sound of clinking glasses disturbed some of the monk parakeets who were busy building nests in the palm trees. As the inn's newest residents fluttered and chirped their protests, Kim feared that, unlike the birds, she and her cousins had just taken on a bigger job than they could handle.

Thank you for reading
Treasure Coast Homecoming!

Want to know what happens next in
Emerald Bay?

Sign up for Leigh's newsletter to get
the latest news about upcoming releases,
excerpts, and more!
https://leighduncan.com/newsletter/

Books by Leigh Duncan

EMERALD BAY SERIES

Treasure Coast Homecoming
Treasure Coast Promise
Treasure Coast Christmas
Treasure Coast Revival
Treasure Coast Discovery
Treasure Coast Legacy

SUGAR SAND BEACH SERIES

The Gift at Sugar Sand Inn
The Secret at Sugar Sand Inn
The Cafe at Sugar Sand Inn
The Reunion at Sugar Sand Inn
Christmas at Sugar Sand Inn

HEART'S LANDING SERIES

A Simple Wedding
A Cottage Wedding
A Waterfront Wedding

ORANGE BLOSSOM SERIES

Butterfly Kisses
Sweet Dreams

Treasure Coast Homecoming

Hometown Heroes Series

Luke

Brett

Dan

Travis

Colt

Garrett

The Hometown Heroes Collection, A Boxed Set

Single Title Books

A Country Wedding

Journey Back to Christmas

The Growing Season

Pattern of Deceit

Rodeo Daughter

His Favorite Cowgirl

Novellas

The Billionaire's Convenient Secret

A Reason to Remember

Find all Leigh's books at:
leighduncan.com/books

Acknowledgements

Every book takes a team effort. I want to give special thanks to those who made *Treasure Coast Homecoming* possible.

Cover design
Chris Kridler at
Sky Diary Productions

Editing Services
Chris Kridler at
Sky Diary Productions

Interior formatting
Amy Atwell and Team
Author E.M.S.

About the Author

Leigh Duncan is the award-winning author of more than three dozen novels, novellas and short stories. She sold her very first novel to Harlequin American Romance and was selected as the company's lead author when Hallmark Publishing introduced its new line of romances and cozy mysteries. A National Readers' Choice Award winner and *Publisher's Weekly* National Best-Selling author, Leigh lives on Florida's East Coast where she writes heartwarming women's fiction with a dash of Southern sass. When she isn't busy writing, Leigh enjoys cooking, crocheting and spending time with family and friends.

Want to get in touch with Leigh? She loves to hear from readers and fans. Visit leighduncan.com to send her a note. Join Leigh on Facebook, and don't forget to sign up for her newsletter so you get the latest news about fun giveaways, special offers or her next book!